RIPTIDE

SUSAN HAYES

ABOUT THE BOOK

A letter from her dead mother sends Jessica Martin across the country to the wilds of the west coast in search of answers. Instead, she finds two gorgeous men who want her in their lives, and in their bed.

Rory Frazier's birthright is to lead a secret colony of mythical shifters known as selkies, but only if he and his blood brother, Evan Sinclair, can find their mate.

Fate brought them together, but uncovering the colony's dark past might just tear them apart.

**Publisher's Note – This book was previously released with the same title. It has been lightly revised and updated.

Riptide

Riptide

E-book Publication: June 2019

Published by: Black Scroll Publications Ltd.

ISBN: 978-1-988446-48-6

This one is for Corey. I miss you, little bro.
And as always, for my parents for believing in me & for Karen
for all her support.

PROLOGUE

24 Years ago

"Jessica James, at least take off your shoes before you go into the ocean!" Jess was almost to the water's edge when her mother called to her. She kicked off her shoes and headed straight into the waves, shrieking with glee as the undertow pulled the wet sand out from beneath her feet. Within seconds her parents were on either side of her. They took her hands and let her swing from them as they headed into the deeper water. Their clothes were soaked, the water far from warm, but all three of them were laughing as they played in the waves.

It was her daddy who spotted the seals first, pointing to the two gray heads that were barely visible against the green-gray water. Both seals were watching them intently, and Jess squealed in excitement and waved to them.

"Do you think they're friendly?"

"No, baby." Her mommy's voice was sad as she lifted Jess up onto her shoulders so she could see the seals better. "I don't think they're likely to be friendly at all."

"So they're not like the seals in the story then?" Her favorite bedtime story was about a pod of magical seals that would come and play with children whenever they were summoned out of the sea.

"Not like the stories I tell you. Those are about special, magical seals." Her mommy nodded to the two heads watching them intently. "Those two are just ordinary seals, and I bet their breath stinks of fish!" Her mommy punctuated her last words with a tickle to Jess's tummy and Jess shrieked with laughter, the seals forgotten.

Jess spent her days on the beach, only coming back to the cabin to eat or take the naps her mom insisted on no matter how much Jess protested. Her days were full of sunshine and fun, the seals nothing more than a distant memory. She didn't recall their visit until near the end of their vacation when once again two sleek gray heads popped up out of the water to watch her playing on the shore. She was playing tag with the incoming waves, trying not to let the water touch her feet as she streaked up and down the beach. Her parents were both up at the cabin, so Jess had to wear her life jacket. She hated the way the awkward, orange outfit rubbed at the back of her neck and made it hard to move, but her parents insisted. If she took it off, she'd be made to stay away from the beach for the rest of the day as punishment, and there was no place on earth she loved more than the beach.

When she spotted the seals, she squealed with glee and waved, calling out to them between giggles as she dashed out of range of another wave. This time the seals seemed to respond to her and swam closer to the shore. Jess stopped her game to watch them as they halted just ten short feet away from where she was standing. She'd never been so close to a seal before, and she couldn't help but wonder if their gray-and-black-spotted fur felt as sleek as it looked. She took a tentative step toward the pair, expecting them to disappear. Instead, one of them rose up out of the water and waved a flipper at her.

Just like the seals in Mommy's stories!

All the rules about Jess not going into the water alone were forgotten as she took another step, and then another. Soon the waves were up to her waist, and her life jacket made it hard to stand. Its buoyancy made her float to the top of each incoming wave. The seals were still there, just out of her reach. Jess took another step and then overbalanced as another wave rolled in and knocked her off her feet, leaving her bobbing on the surface, her feet unable to touch the bottom. Salty water was in her eyes, and she scrunched them tight, waiting for the stinging to stop. When Jess opened them again, she shrieked in surprise when she realized the two seals were right in front of her, both of them watching her with huge, dark eyes.

"Do you want to play with me?" Jess asked, reaching out a wet hand to the nearest seal. As her fingers grazed the sleek fur on its head, the seal ducked into an oncoming wave and disappeared.

"Come back!" she cried tearfully, disappointed it was gone.

Seconds later the seal returned, grabbing the thick pad of her life jacket in its jaws and tugging her further away from shore. Jess laughed at this new game and used her arms to steady herself, already feeling the undertow tugging at her feet as they moved into deeper water.

The larger of the two seals made a short, barking noise

and rose up higher in the water as if looking at something, and then it barked again, more urgently this time. It sank its teeth into the other side of Jess's life jacket and started tugging at it. The motion of both animals pulling at her sent Jess off-balance and she tumbled face-first into an oncoming wave. She came up coughing and spluttering and tried to tell the seals not to be so rough, but then another wave caught her and she was underwater again.

This time it took longer for her get her head above water, and by the time she could breathe again fear had replaced all of her earlier joy.

She wailed for her mommy, and when she heard her mother screaming her name, Jess tried to turn around and swim back to shore, but the waves were too big and she couldn't make her limbs work properly.

"Jess! I'm coming, baby!" Another wave came and Jess managed to hold her breath this time, and when she could see and hear again, she heard her mommy yelling at the seals.

"Don't you dare touch her! Leave her alone! Just leave us alone!"

Jess heard splashing behind her and then her mommy had her in her arms, dragging her away from the seals and back toward the beach. The seals fled, diving into the crest of a wave and vanishing beneath the surf. Jess watched them go, holding tight to her mommy, tears rolling down her face as she tried to give voice to her fright.

"I know, baby. Hush, it's all right. You're safe now." Jess let the words soothe her and as her fear ebbed she fell into an exhausted sleep.

Her parents never mentioned the seals again, but it was

the last year they visited the cabin in Tofino. In all the vacations they took over the years, Jess's family never went near an ocean again.

CHAPTER ONE

"Jess, are you even listening to me? Hellooo in there!" Vivian waggled her fingers in Jess's face, snapping her out of her reverie. It had been years since Jess had even thought about the cabin in Tofino, but since visiting her father earlier today, it was all she could think about.

"What? Yes, I'm listening," Jess lied, hoping Vivian would let it slide. No such luck.

"No, you weren't. You had that blank stare you get when you're off plotting with your muse somewhere and have left this plane of existence behind. I know that look. When you get it, I could probably set you on fire and you wouldn't notice." Vivian grinned. "Maybe next time I'll try it and see."

"I'm pretty sure setting your best friend on fire is against the friendship code of conduct." Jess smiled. It was impossible not to smile when Vivian did. Her friend's perpetual sense of joy was contagious.

"It's nice to see you smile. I was starting to think you

had forgotten how." Vivian wrapped an arm around Jess's shoulders and hugged her. "You doing okay?"

Jess was tired of the question. She'd heard it so many times in the months since her mother had died. There were days she wanted to cry and shake her head and scream no, she wasn't okay. She was so far from okay she wasn't even on the same planet as the concept. Instead, she would just try to smile and tell whoever was asking that she was hanging in there. She lied to everyone else, but she had never lied to Viv.

"Not even close to okay." Jess took a deep breath and then added, "I went to see Dad today."

"That couldn't have been easy, no wonder you're feeling lousy. What did he have to say?"

Jess laughed bitterly. "He's worried about me."

"*Now* he's worried? Where was he when you needed him?" Vivian's eyes narrowed and her smile faded to a sneer.

"It wasn't his fault, Vivian. As much as I would love to blame him for leaving me to cope with everything alone, he isn't…" She stopped and corrected herself. "He *wasn't* her husband anymore."

"He is still your father. He could have checked in at least once in all the months he was off sailing around the tropics with Fluffy and the wonder twins."

Jess couldn't help but snicker. "You really need to stop referring to my stepmother and her boobs as separate entities."

"No, I don't. At least not until she gets those insane implants removed. I bet she didn't even need a life jacket while they were out sailing around. Those babies are built-in buoyancy!"

Both women fell into a fit of giggles that had more than one patron of the coffee shop staring at them with raised brows. By the time Jess had her composure back, she felt much better than she had when she'd left her father's place just an hour before.

"So what did your dad want? I know you didn't just go over there to visit out of the blue."

"He had something for me," Jess said with a shrug. "It was a package and a letter from Mom."

"She gave it to *him* to give to you?"

"It's not like she had many options, Viv. She must have arranged it before she got too sick..." Jess trailed off as she caught up in bitter memories of the hellish months that followed her mother's initial diagnosis. With her health failing by the day, everything had taken on a surreal, nightmarish quality. Jess had wanted to seek alternative treatments and second opinions while her mother had just smiled and got on with what she called, "tidying up the loose ends of a life well lived."

In the end, it had just been the two of them because her father had been sailing around the Bahamas on his honeymoon, completely out of contact. It had been the hardest time of Jess's life.

"So what was in the package?" Vivian's question dragged Jess back to the present.

Jess gave her dearest friend a half smile. "I'll get to that, but there's a bit more to tell you first."

"Just because you're a crime novelist doesn't mean you're supposed to build up the suspense in your day-to-day life." Vivian stuck her tongue out at Jess and laughed. "So, spill it! What's the deal?"

Jess took a deep breath and let the words all tumble out

of her in a rush. "Mom asked Dad to give me the cabin out on the west coast, you know, the one we all used to go to when I was a kid. He's agreed to it, and he's having the paperwork drafted up to make it legal. That was what he asked me over to talk to me about. He didn't know Mom hadn't discussed it with me."

"So he's giving you the cabin? That's great!" Vivian squealed and leaned over to hug Jess again. "You are in dire need of a get-away, and the cabin would be perfect! When are you going and how long before I can come and visit?"

"Trust you to cut straight to the heart of things." Jess laughed as she tried valiantly not to spill the last few drops of her coffee. "It's tempting, but I'm not sure I should go right now. I would need to give notice at the apartment and figure out how I'm going to get everything I own from Toronto to Vancouver Island without losing my mind in the process."

"Oh, that's easy. You don't move everything. The place has been in the rental pool for years, right? So it's already furnished. You don't need to move everything across the country. All you need is a storage locker." Vivian beamed at her. "I'll help, and we'll have you packed up in no time, I think you should go, and the sooner the better."

"So even my best friend is trying to get rid of me now?" Jess teased. "What would I do without you? *If* I go, that is."

"You wouldn't be without me, not really. The wilds of Tofino have the internet, don't they? We'll Skype, and I'll come out to visit once you're settled. Tofino is a surfing town and I bet it's full of hot surfer guys. Do you really think I'm going to let you hog them all? Not a chance!"

"Well, now that you've settled my life so nicely, would you like to hear what was in the box?"

"You know I do."

"An old storybook my mom used to read to me all the time, and an animal fur," Jess said and waited for Vivian's reaction.

"What? Your mother was totally against animal cruelty. She was almost a vegetarian, for heaven's sake. Didn't she only eat tofu and seafood? Why on earth would she give you a box full of furs?"

"I'm not sure if it's a single pelt or more than one. Whatever it is, it's so brittle and aged I didn't want to touch it in case it fell apart on me. From what I could see it's a soft, pale-gray fur with dark splotches. It's really pretty, and I have no idea what I'm supposed to do with it."

Vivian's expression softened. "You haven't read the letter from your mom yet, have you?"

"No," Jess confessed. "I didn't want to cry in front of Dad." She patted her jacket pocket. "I've got it here."

"Well, if you're all right with crying in front of me and a bunch of coffee-addicted strangers, I think you should read it now." Vivian reached out for Jess's hand and squeezed it. "If you don't, it's just going to burn a hole in your pocket."

Jess blew out a short breath and pulled the envelope out of her jacket. Her mother had written Jess's name on the front in her elegant script, and Jess felt a pang just looking at it.

"Here goes nothing," she muttered and gently unsealed it, careful not to tear the paper.

My darling Jess,

By now your father will have told you that he's giving you the cabin. It was something we've been discussing since the divorce, and I know he'll do right by my memory and fulfill my last request.

I know you're hanging in there, Jess. But I also know how hurt you were by your father's actions. He's a good, decent man, and I hope one day you can forgive him. I already have.

My last request for you is one I'll hope you'll honor. I want you to go to Tofino and spend the winter in your new cabin. You gave up so much of yourself and your energy taking care of me and coping with everything, I want you to rest. You need time to heal, my little one, go to the cabin and take care of yourself for once. I've always regretted my decision to stop taking you there. I should never have done that.

There's only one other thing I want you to do for me. Your father should have given you a box along with this letter. Bring the box and its contents with you to Tofino, along with my ashes. I would like them scattered into the ocean by the cabin. As for what's in the box, I have faith you will know what to do with it when the time comes.

My greatest wish is for you to have a happy life. I will always be nearby, watching over you.

Love,

Mom

JESS'S CHEEKS were wet with tears by the time she finished the letter, and without a word she handed it to Vivian and dove into her purse to grab a handful of slightly dusty tissues. By the time Jess's eyes were dry, Vivian was tearing up and Jess just handed her one of her less sodden tissues.

"You were the one who said to read it now." Jess laughed very softly as she saw how puffy Vivian's eyes had gotten.

"Yeah, well when did you start listening to my advice? You know I'm not to be trusted." Vivian blotted her eyes and then carefully folded up the note before handing it back to Jess. "So I guess it's decided then, you're going to the cabin."

"Since everyone I know seems to think I should be there, I guess I am spending the winter on the west coast."

"Lucky you, no snow to shovel."

"Cheer up, Viv. I'm officially inviting you to visit me for the holidays. We can celebrate our first green Christmas together."

Vivian brightened immediately. "Oh that'll be so much fun! You and me and a town full of rugged outdoorsmen. I may never leave." Vivian shot Jess an encouraging grin. "And when I get there, I bet you'll have a new manuscript for me to read. I know you haven't been writing much lately."

Jess wrinkled her nose and sighed. "I'd be happy to have written anything at all by then. The words just won't come these days."

"That's because you need a change. This is all part of your destiny, you'll see." Vivian drained the last off her coffee and pushed back her chair. "Let's get started."

RORY SLAMMED both hands down on the table, making his

mother jump in her chair. "What part of this are you not understanding, Dad? You can't make me marry anyone, and it will be a cold day in Hell before I would agree to spend the rest of my life with that ice-princess you seem to want for a daughter-in-law."

"Damn it, Rory, grow up! You know the laws. You can't inherit if you don't take a selkie mate from one of the old bloodlines. Those are the rules, son. I didn't make them, but I surely will enforce them, and so will you when your time comes to lead this colony." Darius crossed his arms across his chest and glowered at his only son.

"Well, if the only way to get to lead the colony is by marrying that harpy, then you better start looking for another heir." Rory kicked back his chair and started pacing, covering the distance of the kitchen in a few long strides as he tried for the hundredth time to make his father see reason when it came to finding him a wife.

"That law was made centuries ago, when things were very different than they are now. For fuck's sake, we didn't even live on land back then!"

"Language please, Rory." His mother spoke softly, sadness filling her eyes as she watched father and son fighting yet again.

"Sorry, Mom," Rory took a deep breath and tried to rein in his anger. He knew it wasn't going to get him anywhere to rail at his father. They were too much alike for that to do any good. "Dad, I know you want to follow the old ways, and I respect that, really I do. But you have to admit, the pickings out there are pretty damned slim. There just aren't that many of us left."

"I know." Darius sighed and relaxed slightly, though

his arms stayed crossed over his chest. "We lost access to so many of the old bloodlines during my father's time."

Evan stayed silent, but Rory could see his blood-brother nodding his blond head in agreement. Evan refused to consider himself part of the family despite the bonding between the two of them, and he never spoke up during the inevitable fights that cropped up every time Rory and his father were in the same room for more than a few minutes.

"You are not your father, Darius," Emma reached out to take her husband's hand. "You've done so much for this colony and made things so much better than they were." She glanced over at Rory and he saw the reproach in her eyes. "Rory, I know this isn't easy, but there are only so many changes a leader can make before it starts to be too much for people to deal with. If we could change things for you, we would. Neither of us wants to see you or Evan unhappy."

"If you do this, I will be unhappy. We both will." Everyone at the table blinked in surprise when Evan spoke up, and Rory stopped his pacing to listen. "Rory and I just need more time to find our match, and believe me, Renee isn't the one. If Rory doesn't drown her within the first week, I will. She's an unbelievably cold-hearted bitch." Evan's gaze flicked from Rory to Emma and he added, "Sorry for cursing, but it really is the only word that describes her."

"I see," Darius mused, his tone thoughtful. "That bad, is she?"

Rory nodded, afraid to speak in case it broke the spell Evan seemed to have cast over the room. If his blood-brother had just gotten them both out of marrying Renee

Harris, Rory was going kiss his feet and then take him out for a night on the town, and to hell with the expense.

"If she's so bad not even Saint Evan can put up with her, then I suppose I won't force the issue." Darius pointed a finger at Rory and Evan. "*But* the two of you need to find someone to bond with, and soon." Darius glanced at his wife and gave her a wink and a grin that made him look years younger. "We are hoping to have a few years with our grandchildren, if you ever get around to giving us any."

Rory let out a sigh of relief and mustered a smile for his parents. "Thank you."

"Just get on with it son, you're thirty-one years old. If you sew any more wild oats, you'll be a farmer instead of a fisherman."

Evan snorted with laughter and Rory actually felt his ears get hot as even his mother burst into gales of laughter. "All right, I'll get on with it. But for the record, Evan's two years older than I am and I am damned sure he's sewn enough oats to start a cereal company already."

"Nonsense, our Evan is the sweetest boy I know." Emma beamed at her son's companion before looking back at Rory. "You're the wicked one, Rory Frazier. Just like your father."

As Rory and Evan headed out to their truck a few minutes later, Rory shot his best friend and blood-brother a dirty look.

"Evan's the sweetest boy I know." He mimicked his mother's gushing tone and rolled his eyes. "How the hell do you do that? You drink like a fish and have more notches on your bedpost than one man should legally be allowed to have. I've had to bail you out of the drunk-tank so often I should get frequent flyer miles, and she thinks *you're* the good one!"

"Easy." Evan brushed his sandy blond bangs out of his eyes and chuckled as he climbed into the passenger side of the truck. "I smile and you're always frowning. I stay quiet and listen while you always have to be heard. Oh yes, and I don't curse in front of your mother."

"Smart ass," Rory grumbled as he started the truck and backed onto the gravel road connecting all the residences sprawled around their collective home.

"If you're done insulting me, I'm still waiting for my thank you for saving us from the misery of being married to that bitch from the Haida Gwaii colony."

Rory grinned over at his best friend. "I'm going to do more than say thank you. Tomorrow night you and I are going to drive into town and celebrate our freedom, however fleeting it may be."

"Breakers?" Evan grimaced. "I don't think that's a good idea. Trish is still mad at me."

"Serves you right, too. Tucker warned you about hitting on his staff, but you just couldn't keep your hands to yourself." Rory laughed as he pulled into their driveway and shut off the motor. "You earned that beer shower. But no, I didn't mean Breakers. You and I are going to drive over to Nanaimo and enjoy ourselves. My treat."

"Holy shit, you're spending real money on me? You really are happy your dad agreed to forget about marrying Renee." Evan hopped out and headed for the house the two of them shared. "I'm holding you to the celebration idea, but honestly I did it for my sanity, not just yours. She'd barely give me the time of day. I'm fine with sharing, but I have no plans on being celibate for the next sixty years!"

"And I would rather be celibate than face a lifetime of sharing a bed with a woman who could give frostbite to a penguin." Rory followed Evan inside and went to the fridge to grab them both a beer.

"So how long do you think we have to find a compatible mate?" Evan asked as he cracked open the bottle and flung himself into the nearest piece of furniture.

"Not long. We better start praying for a miracle."

"And you better learn to start smiling, or you're going to scare them all off," Evan teased and took a drink.

"I do just fine with the ladies, thank you very much."

"Oh sure, and every one of them was human and short-term only. We're selkies, we've been seducing human women for centuries, they're easy. I'm talking about wooing a selkie mate."

"It can't be that difficult. If my father managed it, anyone can."

Evan burst out laughing. "You really should ask your mom about it one day. It's a fascinating story. She made your dad and Torin work their asses off before she agreed to marry them."

"What? I never heard the story. How the hell do you know it and I don't?" Rory stretched out on the couch and downed his beer, shooting daggers at Evan the whole time.

"See? This is why she thinks I'm a sweetheart. I actually listen to her. You should try it sometime. It may make the difference between us getting married to a compatible mate and us spending the rest of our lives with the likes of Renee." Evan shuddered.

"I'll abdicate first," Rory vowed.

"Let's hope it doesn't come to that. I'm supposed to be the bonded blood-brother of the next colony leader. I have great plans to live a life of luxury while you run things."

"Nice to know you've got ambitions of your own," Rory muttered.

Evan just grinned. "Drink your beer. You need to get your liver primed for what we're going to do to it tomorrow night."

CHAPTER TWO

JESS STEPPED out of the terminal and immediately regretted not packing an umbrella. Everything was shrouded in fog and it was raining. By the time Jess found her car her hair was plastered to her skin and she knew she was going to look like a drowned rat when she met with the realtor to get the keys to her new home. *A drowned rat with purple streaks in her hair. What the hell was I thinking letting Vivian near my hair after we'd been into the tequila!*

She started the car and then fiddled with the seat adjustments until she could comfortably reach the pedals. "In my next life, I want to be a long-legged redhead," she muttered and then laughed. With her luck she'd wind up reincarnated as an Irish Setter.

The fog got thicker as she drove through the heavily forested area to her new home. She was straining to see the road at all when a darker shape appeared out of the mist and she had to hit the brakes and swerve onto the shoulder of the road to avoid a collision.

"Holy shit!" Jess swore as the shape came close

enough for her to recognize what it was. "Oh my god, there's a deer in the middle of the road," Jess muttered, suddenly aware she was a long way from downtown Toronto.

Amazement slowly faded to irritation as Jess realized her unscheduled wildlife encounter was going to make her late. She was supposed to meet Nadine, the realtor, at the cabin at four o'clock, and time was growing short. Uncertain how one got a deer to move along, she flashed her high beams a few times. Nothing. *Shit.* Feeling foolish, Jess rolled her window down halfway, getting wet all over again as she leaned out and yelled at the deer. "Hey Bambi, move it! Go on, shoo!"

The deer startled at the noise and went bounding off the road and out of sight. "And so begins Jess's grand country adventure."

She made it to the cabin only a few minutes late, and was relieved to see she'd beaten the realtor. Leaving her things in the car, Jess got out and made a dash for the porch, trying to dodge the heavier raindrops that were starting to come down.

The place looked familiar and yet different at the same time, and Jess's head was flooded with memories as she walked around the wraparound porch. The old, heavy driftwood picnic table still sat in the middle of the small back lawn, but beyond it was a gazebo perched on the small, mist-shrouded headland that was part of the property.

"Is that a hot tub?" Jess wondered aloud as she managed to spot what looked like a vinyl cover jutting just above the gazebo walls despite the fact it was nearly dark now.

"Yes, it is. Sorry to interrupt your exploration. I'm Nadine."

Jess spun around and was met by a sight she knew would have to make it into one of her books, if only she could find the words. Nadine was wearing a lime green and hot-pink poncho that looked like it had been handwoven. She was wearing a pair of bright pink duck boots and Jess could have sworn the woman's pink lipstick had been selected because it was an exact match to the rest of her ensemble.

"Hi Nadine, it's nice to meet you." Jess managed to avoid giggling as she offered the woman her hand in greeting.

"Your father kept the place very well maintained, and I think you'll find it's been vastly improved since you were here as a child. I understand it's been more than twenty years since your family last used the place. There's a gas fireplace, a modern kitchen, and of course, the hot tub and storm watching gazebo." Nadine took Jess's arm and led her around to the front of the house again. "Do you want me to give you the tour? Or would you like to settle in and relax? The keys are on the table, and I put a casserole in the fridge last night, so you have dinner all ready for you. I didn't think you'd feel like going grocery shopping after travelling all day. Oh, and I baked you some brownies for dessert. I hope you like chocolate!"

Jess blinked at Nadine in shock. "You made me dinner and brownies?"

"Why, of course, dear. I just hated the idea of you having to drag yourself out to the store again tonight. Goodness, do you even know where the store is? There are shops in Tofino of course, but if you need a carton of milk or an ice cream fix one night, then Jo-Jo's is just up the road to your left about a kilometer or so."

"That's so nice of you, thank you so much!" Jess felt a little overwhelmed by Nadine's kindness and she caught herself tearing up. Her mother would have liked Nadine. They were both good-hearted women.

"Well, I've been taking care of this place for nearly a decade now, and even though I never met your parents, we certainly talked on the phone enough I considered them friends. Now I know you've had a tough time of it, so if you need anything, you just call me, all right? I've kids of my own and I know I'd want someone to be looking after my girls if they were a long way from home." Nadine patted Jess's arm. "I've left a list of contact numbers by the phone, the one at the top is mine. My husband, George, is the local handyman, and he's been the one looking after things here and seeing to the hot tub. If you like, we can just keep doing that for you."

"Oh, yes, please!" Jess sniffled and suddenly found herself engulfed in a wet, wooly hug. "We're a bit different out here on the west coast, dear, but you'll find we take care of our own, and since you're going to be living here for the next while, you're part of the family."

Nadine hugged her again and then released her so quickly Jess nearly stumbled over backward. "Now, get your things and get in out of this weather. Umbrellas are by the door, and next time you're in town, you find yourself a proper raincoat or you'll catch your death of cold."

With that, Nadine was off, striding through the puddles toward a bright-green Volkswagen camper van older than Jess. As it wheezed to life Jess made a dash for her car and had her luggage on the porch before Nadine had made it to the end of the driveway. With an asthmatic honk of her horn, she turned onto the road and vanished out of sight.

"Now that was the oddest welcome I've ever had." Jess laughed to herself as she dragged her bags inside. The moment she crossed the threshold, she felt like she was coming home. It didn't matter that the harvest gold appliances of her memory had been replaced with gleaming chrome, or that the fireplace had been converted to gas, this was still the place she remembered from her childhood. Jess dropped her things and ran to the living room's bay windows, the ones overlooking the ocean. The view was exactly the same, and in her mind's eye she could see her parents and the girl she had been wading through the waves, all three of them holding hands and laughing.

There were tears in her eyes as she turned away from the view, but for the first time, the sadness didn't feel like it would crush her beneath its weight. "You were right, Mom," she whispered into the air as she hugged her arms to her chest and then went to unpack. Before anything else, she needed a hot shower and some quality time with her hair dryer.

She grabbed her suitcase and went to what had once been her room, then stopped and put it in the master bedroom instead. With her bag of toiletries and a towel in hand, she headed down the short hall to the bathroom. Jess still wasn't sure how she felt about taking her parent's old room, but all thoughts stopped dead at the sight greeting her. Instead of the faded, powder-blue vinyl bathtub surround and matching toilet she remembered, the entire room was done in soft creams and glass. The tub had been replaced with a walk-in shower, the entire bottom paved with dark gray river rock that matched the marble tiling.

"Holy hell, that's some remodeling job." She shed her travel-creased clothes and turned on the shower, nearly cheering in delight as she realized the showerhead was one of the new rainfall types, positioned so it hovered overhead. A second, more standard shower head with a detachable handle was set in the wall as well. She turned on the water and let it run as hot as she could stand before stepping under the gentle cascade.

She groaned and rolled her shoulders, easing the tension that had built up in them over the last frantic days of packing and getting herself ready to leave. The cold that had seeped into her bones since her arrival was banished by the hot water, and she felt some of the fatigue and worry being washed away.

"I could get used to this," she sighed. "And once Vivian sees it, she's going to want to move in with me."

After her shower Jess felt more like herself, and as she put the kettle on she made a mental note to find out where in town she could find a decent espresso machine. If she was serious about getting back to her writing, then she was going to need the proper fuel. On her way back to the fireplace Jess grabbed her phone and hit speed dial, only to be surprised when the call didn't go through.

"Right, she's long distance now." Jess had switched her phone plan to reflect her change in location, one of the hundred details she would have never remembered if Vivian hadn't been there every step of the way.

She dialed in the number manually and smiled the instant she heard Vivian's voice on the other end.

"Hey stranger! How's the new place? Met any cute guys yet?"

"Hey yourself. Things are good here, but I miss you already."

"I miss you too. So, are you settling in all right? Is it like you remembered it?"

"I'm settling in just fine. The realtor actually made me a casserole and left it in the fridge, and she baked me brownies, too. It's not quite the same as I remember it, they have had some serious renovations done in the last few years, but yeah, it feels familiar." Jess curled up in one of the overstuffed chairs near the fireplace and looked around her. "It feels good here. You were right to encourage me to get out of Toronto."

"You timed it well, too. We're supposed to get the first blizzard of the winter hitting sometime tomorrow."

"No snow here, but it hasn't stopped raining since I landed."

"There's a reason they call it the wet coast, you know."

"Thanks for the warning." Jess laughed. "And yet you let me leave without reminding me to take an umbrella, or a proper rain jacket."

"You're right, I have completely failed you as a friend. When I get out there in a few weeks feel free to punish me by making me sit in the hot tub for hours on end while consuming copious numbers of Irish coffees."

"You got yourself a deal."

"Hey, Jess?" Vivian's voice got softer.

"What is it?"

"I really do miss you."

"I really miss you, too, Viv, but you'll be here soon. And I promise to have scouted out all the best places to meet the local men by the time you get here."

"You're the best."

"Right back at you." Jess hugged her knees to her chest and swallowed past the lump in her throat. "I'll Skype with you tomorrow, once I've got the laptop set up."

"It's a date. Toodles, Gator."

"Later, Poodle."

Jess pressed the disconnect button on her phone, but she didn't put it down. She knew she should call her dad and let him know she had arrived safely, but things had been strained between them since he'd left her mother for another woman. It wasn't an easy thing to forgive, but she was trying. It didn't help that Jess suspected her mother's illness was brought on at least in part by the stress of the divorce. The day her dad had moved out, some of the light had gone from her mother's eyes, and every day after she seemed to fade a little bit more. Jess wanted to hate him, but it wasn't in her heart to hate anyone, especially not her dad. *Even if he did go and marry his secretary. His much younger, silicone-enhanced, secretary.*

Jess still couldn't believe he'd embraced the stereotype so completely. The only thing her father hadn't done was buy a sports car or a Harley Davidson motorcycle.

"Thank you for small mercies," she muttered to herself and set down the phone as the kettle started to whistle. She'd make herself a cup of hot chocolate and then decide if she was going to call or not. Even with the time difference, he'd still be up for another hour or so.

On her way to the kitchen her eyes fell on the strange wood and metal box her mother had asked her to bring with her. It was sitting by the front stairs where Jess had left it. The thing was *heavy*! Her laptop was still packed and her e-reader needed recharging before she could use it again, but Jess recalled the book her mother used to read to her was tucked in with the odd fur. It would give her something to read while she relaxed before bed.

She settled back into the chair a few minutes later with a hot chocolate in one hand and the book in her other and started reading the storybook her mother had left for her. She'd remembered it from her childhood, a collection of stories about a group of men and women called selkies. They were magical beings who could transform from human to seal and back again. It had been her favorite growing up, but now Jess realized her mother had been lifting small sections out of a much larger story.

"Well, that's certainly not something that should be in a children's book," she muttered to herself after one particularly adult passage told of lonely fishermen's wives, their husbands off at sea, crying into the ocean to summon a virile selkie lover to keep them company.

Jess looked at the cover again, and then at the inside flap and discovered the book was much older than it looked. It had been old when her mother had read it to her, more than twenty years ago. *Why would she read this to me? It's not even written for kids.*

Jess had always just called it her "seal people" book, but now she realized it was a collection of legends and tales, and all of them were about selkies. She flipped through the book randomly, skimming bits and pieces as she tried to reconcile the stories she remembered her mother telling her with what she was reading. There were dog-eared pages that Jess realized marked the passages her mother would read aloud to her, and as she let her tired mind drift she could almost hear her mom's voice, soft and comforting, reading along beside her. It made Jess's heart ache with loneliness and loss.

"I miss you, Mom," she whispered and touched the page she was reading with a loving caress. "I'm not sure why you wanted me to have this book, but I'll read it, I promise."

Jess smothered a yawn and closed the book, hugging it close to her chest. "Just not now. Right now I need to start figuring out how to turn this from a rental cabin into a place I can call home."

CHAPTER THREE

OVER THE NEXT few days Jess reclaimed the cabin. She set up a writing area near the bay window so she could stare out at the view when she needed a break, and there was now a gleaming espresso maker sitting on the kitchen counter. Brand new raingear hung by the door, and she'd stocked the fridge and cupboards with every single one of her favorite foods.

As she had settled in, her eyes kept sliding to the carefully wrapped case she had placed near the living room window. Inside the case was the urn holding her mother's ashes. Every time Jess passed the case she looked outside, unable to shake the feeling her mother was waiting for her to fulfill her last request.

Jess split her time between settling into the cabin, writing, and reading more of the book her mother had left for her. The more she read, the more she wondered why it had been so important to her mother that she have it. The stories were from Scotland and the Orknie Islands mostly, both places Jess knew her mother, Mara, had never been.

Mara had always wanted to go to Scotland, but there was never enough money, or the timing was wrong.

"And now you'll never get to go there," Jess sighed. "Though I suppose when I scatter your ashes, some of them might make it there eventually. Not much a vacation, Mom, but I'm afraid it's the best I can do."

She sipped her coffee and went back to her reading. The story she was engrossed in was one that appeared more than once in the book. While the selkie men were off chasing lonely human females, the selkie women were often at risk of being captured and taken as wives by human men. When in human form a selkie left their fur pelt behind, usually well hidden. If a human man managed to find and take possession of a selkie's pelt then the selkie was forced to stay on land in human form and obey the one who possessed their pelt. They could only return to the sea if they were freed or could steal their fur back from the ones who had taken it.

And Vivian wonders why I have trouble trusting men, Jess thought. *Wait until she sees this, I think we've found the answer. I was read some seriously dark stuff as a kid! What the hell was my mother thinking?*

Jess had been there nearly a week when the weather finally broke. Despite the winter temperatures, she grabbed her coffee and padded out onto the back porch in her slippers to take in the morning. The sun was fighting to burn through the layer of marine cloud shrouding the sky, but the rain had stopped and the world was brighter than it had been since her arrival. The sea was choppy, and gray-green waves crested and crashed onto the rocks with enough force to throw up a curtain of spray every third or fourth wave. Her gaze swept along the small stretch of sandy beach that curved in behind the headland. Tucked away from the worst of the ocean's pounding, the waves here were milder, surging up the sand to break gently and then flow back into the ocean.

Above the high water line stunted trees clung to the sandy soil, their trunks growing at odd angles and their branches twisted by the constant wind. It was a far cry from the concrete and steel of Toronto, but there was something about this place that called to Jess's soul. Her mother had been right to send her out here.

"I just wish you were here to share it with me, Mom," Jess murmured. She stayed out on the deck until the chill bite of the wind finally drove her back indoors, and she laughed at herself for standing outside in her pajamas.

Feeling restless, Jess dressed quickly and headed back outside. She hadn't had a chance to explore yet, and she was dying to get out for a walk before the weather forced her indoors again. Her writing may be going well, thanks to the enforced solitude, but Jess was feeling the first twinges of cabin fever.

In the short time she'd been inside, the weather had already started to shift, and Jess could see a fresh band of dark clouds hurtling toward shore, darkening the skies as it rolled in.

Jess headed down to the gazebo, her booted footfalls echoing loudly on the wooden walkway built from the deck all the way down to the hot tub and its enclosure. She'd only been down here once since her arrival. The hot tub was the height of luxury, but she'd quickly learned that any benefit of a heated soak was lost racing pell-mell back up to the cabin in the freezing rain.

"Next spring I'm going to see about getting the

walkway covered," she mused to herself and then nearly tripped over her own feet as she realized what she'd said. Spring? She hadn't really been here long enough to decide if she was going to stay, had she? Looking around her, the scent of the ocean in her nose and the wind tugging her hair free of its braid a few strands at a time, Jess realized she might just have been here long enough to know she wasn't going to leave. This felt like home.

Smiling to herself, she walked around the gazebo and headed out onto the headland, picking her way carefully over the rocks once she left the security of the walkway. The waves were coming in hard enough to throw spray, and she could feel the salty mist clinging to her face and hair as she made her way further down. When Jess got down close enough that the air was full of spray and the waves crashing around her were loud enough to drown out every other thought in her head, she stopped and found a relatively flat spot to stand and watch. The wind whipped around her and the breakers crashed against the rocks as heavy foam surged and swirled between the jagged gaps. A glance at the beach told her the tide was on its way out, the high tide mark at least a foot further inland from where the waves currently ended.

The wind threw up a wall of spray as another wave hit, and Jess laughed as she wiped the salt and water from her face. If the spray was reaching this high, it was clearly time to go. She had no interest in getting any wetter than she already was.

As she turned to go the sun vanished behind the oncoming clouds, and Jess shivered as the last bit of warmth was drained out of the day. She made it a single step back up the rocks before the wave hit her.

Jess's world vanished in an instant, replaced with a roaring in her ears and an icy blackness that blotted out all of her senses. Cold pierced her down to the marrow of her bones and she opened her mouth to scream, and it filled with more of the icy water. Panic rapidly escalated to terror as she tumbled and thrashed in the alien darkness. She struck out blindly, half clawing, half swimming as she fought to move against the suddenly terrible weight of her own clothes. Her lungs were burning by the time she managed to get her head above water, and she had just enough time to cough once before a wave crashed over her head. Frantic, Jess kicked herself back up to the surface and gasped in a lungful of air, treading water as best she could. *What the hell just happened?*

She couldn't see over the waves surging around her, and when she stretched out her legs she couldn't find the bottom, either. She was in serious trouble.

Fighting to keep her head above water, Jess managed to wriggle out of her boots one at a time and immediately her kicks grew stronger, lifting her a little higher in the water. Strange instincts kicked in and she had a sudden urge to dive beneath the water, away from the froth and chop to where the water was peaceful. Jess shook her head to rid herself of the odd thought. If she dove down into the water, she sure as hell wasn't going to come back up again.

Waves surged over her head time and again, and soon she was choking on seawater. The cold burned at her limbs, and as she struggled to get her jacket and sweater unzipped she couldn't seem to make her fingers work. Every time she managed to grasp the tab of her zipper a wave would hit her and she'd be left flailing and fighting to breathe past the raw, rasping cough as her lungs rejected the water she'd inhaled.

The waves around her were growing bigger, but they were no longer breaking over her head and she managed to ride to the top of some of them. That was when she realized how bad her situation really was. She was caught in a current of some kind and she was being drawn out to sea with no way to get back. The rocks she'd been standing on were already more than a hundred meters away, and the cold was making her weaker by the minute.

So much for the majesty of the ocean, she thought to herself in a flash of bitter humor. Her teeth chattered so hard she could hear them clattering, and her hands were now so numb she gave up trying to shed her sodden clothing. As another wave closed over her head, she was filled with a sense of dread darker and colder than the sea around her. If someone didn't find her soon, she was going to die.

"DIDN'T Nadine say something about that rental cabin having a new owner?" Evan nodded to the log cabin that was tucked into the woods beyond the headland that separated the colony's land from their nearest neighbor.

"Yeah, the guy who owned it gave it to his daughter, I think. Why?" Rory glanced up from the deck where he was kneeling beside the open hatch that covered the inboard motor.

"Because I think that's her standing out on the rocks." Evan swiped his bangs out of his eyes and pointed. "At least I think that's a she, it's hard to tell with the bulky jacket."

Rory got to his feet and stood just as a large wave rolled the boat far to starboard and he had to brace his legs to stay upright as they dropped into the trough behind it. As he turned to look at the shore he heard Evan swear and gun the motor.

"Easy with the throttle, we're still breaking that engine in!" Rory barked and then swore as he realized what had Evan worried. "Shit! She's going to get nailed by that wave!"

"And we're too far out to stop it," Evan was leaning into the wheel as if willing the boat to go faster, but they both knew that if he pushed the engine right now, they could damage it.

Both of them watched as the figure on the rocks turned her back to the ocean just as the wave that had sent their boat rocking broke over the headland in a surge of water and foam. As the water retreated they both swore in unison when the figure in the blue jacket was nowhere to be seen.

"Fuck!"

"You can't get in close enough to get to her, if you try we'll end up on the rocks for sure!" Rory was already toeing off his shoes and tugging his jeans off as Evan tried to get them in close enough to spot the missing woman.

"Once we spot her, I'll get you as close as I can, but then you're going to have to swim for it." He glanced back at Rory, a grim smile on his face. "Let's hope she's not afraid of wild animals."

"If she is, she's going to drown." Rory kicked his jeans

off and yanked off his jacket and shirt, the winter wind instantly cutting through him like an icy dagger.

"Found her! Port side!" Evan cranked the wheel and the boat cut hard to the left. "She's caught in a riptide by the looks of things, and being pulled out by the current. At least you'll be swimming with it once you get to her. I'll get in as close as I can."

Rory spotted a flash of blue in the water and uttered a groan. She was still more than fifty meters from the boat, and in water this cold, she'd already be suffering the first stages of hypothermia. It was going to be close.

He summoned the change as he dove over the gunwale, gritting his teeth against the cold that burned his skin for a brief moment before the transformation finished. Thick fur covered bare skin as he claimed his true form, and by the time he broke the surface a few feet from the boat, he was completely comfortable. Rory drove himself upward with a thrust of his tail, trying to spot the woman he knew was somewhere beyond the waves. *She went under and hasn't come up yet.* Evan's voice sounded in his mind.

Rory didn't waste time replying. He dove back under the water and swam as hard as he could in the direction they'd last seen her. In this form he could hold his breath for ages, and his senses were more acute underwater. He dove deep enough to escape the churning chaos of the waves and almost immediately picked out her scent and the sound of her panicked coughing. *At least she's still breathing.*

The roar of the boat's engine faded as Rory swam toward the strangely enticing scent of the woman he needed to find. He put the enticing part on hold and focused on finding her, relief coursed through him when he spotted her treading water at the far range of his vision. He started swimming hard toward where she struggled, but another wave pushed her under before he could reach her. He covered the last few feet as quickly as he could and situated himself under her outstretched arm, using his momentum to drag her up to the surface with him.

She clung to him weakly, too disoriented from the cold and exhaustion to do more than gasp for breath.

"Seals again?" she finally spoke, her teeth chattering and her voice hoarse from coughing.

With no idea what she was talking about and no way to speak to her even if he did, Rory grabbed a mouthful of her sodden jacket and started tugging her toward the boat. He managed to keep her head above the surface when the next wave rolled beneath them, and she uttered a sob of relief as she spotted Evan steering the *Storm Lord* straight for them, right in the path of the current so the tide was doing the bulk of the work of carrying them to the boat.

Her clothes made her almost impossibly heavy to pull along, and she was too far gone with cold to manage more than a weak kick of her legs as she struggled to stay above water.

Rory let go of her jacket to nudge her sharply with his nose, trying to rouse her from her stupor. She groaned, and this time when he grabbed ahold and pulled she managed to kick a little harder and paddle with her arms.

As they got nearer Evan killed the engine and let the boat drift toward them to avoid injuring them when they swam for the stern. By the time Rory got her to the swim platform at the back of the boat, they were both exhausted. Evan was already leaning over and he grabbed the nearly unconscious woman by the arm and hauled her bodily up into the boat. As she vanished into the craft, Rory swam himself onto the platform and transformed, hanging onto the pitching grid as the icy water washed over his very naked ass.

"Jesus that's cold!"

"Who was that?" the woman asked, her speech slurred.

Rory ducked back down just in time for another wave to drench him from the waist down. The last thing they needed was for her to do the math and figure out her rescue party had lost a seal and gained another human. Not that she'd likely remember any of this after what she'd been through, but secrecy was paramount to the safety of Rory's family and the whole colony.

"Come on, sweetheart, let's get you inside the cabin where it's warmer."

"Y-yes puh-puh-please."

Rory waited until the deck was quiet before he hopped back onboard and wrapped himself in the thermal blanket Evan had left for him. From inside the cabin he could hear Evan calmly chatting to their unexpected guest, and he felt an urgent need to get dressed and join them. Ever since Rory had detected her scent in the water he'd been feeling odd, and now the idea of her being out of his sight had him fighting to get his jeans back on over still-wet skin. He needed to get in there and see for himself that she was going to be okay. He didn't even bother with shoes, and his shirt was still in his hand as he started to head for the cabin. He made it halfway there before he stopped dead and swore as Evan's voice sounded in his head again.

"You need to drive the boat. I'll take care of her."

No matter how much he wanted to join them, there

was no way he could. Someone had to stay and get them back to a safe harbor, or they were all going to be swimming again.

"Bastard." He sent the blistering thought back to Evan before turning his attention to the wheel. He dragged his sweater back over his wet hair one-handed and started the engine, swinging the *Storm Lord* around in a wide turn so that they were heading back to the colony's private dock.

He glanced down into the cabin and bit back a growl as he realized Evan had taken their passenger past the kitchenette and into the cramped space that passed as onboard sleeping quarters. His fingers tightened on the wheel and he found himself increasing the speed of the engines, despite the risk of damage. *What the hell is wrong with me?*

CHAPTER FOUR

EVAN TOOK one look at the woman's pale face and knew she was in shock. Worse still, her lips were almost blue with cold and her teeth chattered so hard she could barely speak. She leaned against him as the boat pitched and rolled, and he found himself wrapping his arms around her as he bundled her in layers of blankets and bedding. He heard Rory curse at the cold and knew he'd reverted back to human form, but only a small part of Evan was thinking about his blood-brother. Most of his thoughts were taken up by the curvy bundle of shivering woman currently clinging to him. A bolt of pure lust thrummed through him as he caught a hint of her scent beneath the smell of wet wool and seawater.

He drew her tighter against him and then turned them both, pointing the way to the cabin as he distracted her from the fact there was a naked man cursing and crouched out of sight on the swim platform. Evan got her into the narrow galley and was about to sit her down at the table when Rory's mental snarl of frustration hit him.

So he was grumpy about driving the boat, was he? Then Evan was going to give him something to be grumpy about.

He half walked and half carried the shivering blonde down to the sleeping area and helped her get seated at the edge of the bed. Then he crouched down in front of her and unwrapped the blankets from around her shoulders with gentle hands.

"My name's Evan Sinclair and you're aboard our boat, the *Storm Lord*. Want to tell me your name, sweetheart?"

"J-J-Jessica," she stammered and tried to smile. "But every-y-one c-calls muh-me J-Jess."

"We saw that wave hit you and drag you into the water, Jess. This time of year, rogue waves happen. You were lucky we were around to pull you out."

"W-was going to die." Tears welled up in Jess's ice-blue eyes and she shivered again.

"Not today you're not." Evan felt a wave of protectiveness wash over him as he brushed a strand of pale-blonde hair off her cheek. "You're safe now, Jess. We'll get you home. But first I need to get you warmed up. Will you let me take off your wet clothes?"

Jess's eyes widened but then she nodded and reached up to try to grasp the zipper of her jacket. When she couldn't wrap her fingers around the metal tab she looked into Evan's eyes and nearly melted his heart as she tearfully asked, "Help me?"

"I got this." He winked at her, trying to make her feel at ease as he unzipped her jacket and peeled it off her, tossing it onto the floor of the small cabin where it landed with a squelch. "How did you manage to stay afloat at all wearing this?" He grabbed the sopping weight of her woolen sweater and shook his head in amazement. "It must have been a bitch to swim in."

"Nearly imp-possible." Jess nodded and he was pleased to notice her speech wasn't quite as slurred now.

Suddenly her eyes widened and she grabbed his wrist with both hands, locking onto it with a death grip. "There was a seal out there, wasn't there?" Her hands were like ice where they clung to him. "I didn't im-magine it, did I?"

"A seal?" Evan's thoughts raced as he tried to come up with an answer that wouldn't out his entire colony's secret while not denying everything and making Jess question her sanity. "Yeah, there's a whole colony of them living in Kismet Cove. That's where we're going, by the way. It's where we live and we have a private dock there."

"I saw…" Jess trailed off and frowned. "I thought there was a seal helping me."

"Really?" Evan quirked a brow at her and smiled. "Well, who knows, maybe there was one, I was too busy steering the boat to notice." He got her sweater off of her and tossed the entire soggy mess onto the floor on top of her jacket. Beneath she was wearing a light T-shirt, and he skinned it over her head before she could even think to argue.

Without thinking his gaze fell to her tits and all the blood left his brain to flood his cock. *Hello, curves!*

He managed to force himself to look up before she caught him staring, but the image of her ample breasts spilling over the lacy cups of her bra was still burned into his retinas.

It was only when she shivered and wrapped her arms around her bare stomach that he remembered she was still freezing cold and half drowned.. He lifted the thermal blanket back up around her shoulders. *Get your shit together*.

"Do you think you can stand up? If you can, I'll get these jeans off of you and then we'll wrap you up good and tight until we get to shore."

Jess nodded slightly and stood, nearly falling forward as she tried to cope with her lingering exhaustion and the rolling of the boat. "I don't usually l-let guys get this far on the first da-date."

"I promise I'll behave." He winked at her again and prayed to whatever gods were listening she didn't notice the rock-hard evidence of his interest tucked behind the fly of his jeans. Evan moved as quickly as he could, one hand wrapped around her hip to steady her as he undid her pants, trying to focus on helping her and not the fact that his mouth was at the perfect height to…No. I am not going there, he told himself again and glanced up to see the faintest hint of pink on her cheeks. Realizing she was blushing, he gave her a lopsided grin and let go of her pants to grab her hands. "Hold onto my shoulders and I will have this done before you know it. Then you can curl up and get warm again."

"Okay." She placed her hands like he told her and hung on as he wrestled the wet denim down and off of her. He caught an eyeful of black lace and satin underwear and had to bite back a groan. It was an act of pure will to tear his gaze away from her lace-framed pussy and tip his head up to smile at her.

"All right, back into bed with you. Uh, I mean…shit. You know I didn't mean that the way it came out, right?"

She managed to grin as she sat back down and moved into the middle of the bed. "I know."

As another bout of shivering hit her. Evan realized she was going to need more than blankets to get her body temperature back up. "Without sounding like I'm hitting on you yet again..." He stripped off his shirt and gave her a sheepish grin. "You need a heat source, and well, I'm it."

"Skin to skin cont-t-tact," she agreed, and he was grateful she understood he wasn't a lecherous creep.

"Exactly. So move over a bit, sweetheart."

Jess scooted further into the middle of the bed and Evan lay down beside her before piling every bit of spare bedding he could reach over the top of her shivering body. He moved closer and drew her into his arms, wincing as her icy skin made contact with his chest. Her ample curves pressed into him and that delicate, enticing scent was back in his nose as she cuddled up to him and wrapped her arm around his waist.

"Better?" he asked.

"Yes," Jess gave a contented sigh that sent another surge of blood straight to his dick. Evan was stiffer than he'd ever been in his life, and he shifted his hips back and away from her before she inadvertently snuggled up to his hard-on.

"Pervert." Rory's mocking voice filled his head, but Evan could sense there was tension behind the joke. Tension and...jealousy? What the hell? In all the years since Evan had been Rory's friend and later his blood-brother, the two of them had never been jealous of each other. They shared everything, including the women in their lives, and until now there had never been a problem.

Evan glanced down at the woman that was more or less wrapped around him, and he gave in to the urge to stroke the silken strands of hair that fell over her face. It was so light it looked almost platinum blonde, and he grinned as he noticed the purple streaks in it for the first time. It seemed their little mermaid had a sense of whimsy. Without even thinking about it he stroked down her back until he found the bound end of her braided hair and undid the elastic. He started undoing the strands with his fingers, and was halfway up the length before he realized what he was doing.

I'm just being practical. It'll never dry in that braid. He tried to rationalize his actions and then snorted in derision at himself. He wasn't sure what was going on, but he'd never had the urge to play with a woman's hair before. He was usually too busy trying to get them out of their clothes.

The engine noise shifted to a low grumble and Evan realized they must be nearing the dock. He didn't bother to get up and help. Both of them were able to run the boat single-handed when required, and right now Jess needed him more than Rory did.

He felt the bump as they touched the dock, and the boat rocked as Rory shut off the engine and made the short jump to the wharf to tie them up.

The movement was enough to make the woman in Evan's arms stir and lift her head, her pale eyes blinking sleepily as she looked around. "What was that?"

"Just Rory's heavy-handed driving, sweetheart. Nothing to worry about." Evan grinned up at her before drawing her back down into his arms. "He's tying us up right now. You're safe and sound."

"M-kay." Jess's eyes were already closing again as she settled back onto the bed. Unable to resist any longer, Evan cupped her cheek, his thumb tracing the plump pout of her lower lip. He'd never had a woman trust him so completely, and it worried him. Was she like this with everyone? If so, she was going to get hurt, or likely had been already. The thought of someone hurting Jess made him grit his teeth, and he held her tighter as the need to protect her coursed through him.

Holy shit. Evan tensed as he finally figured out what was going on with him and Rory. He made a mental list and ticked off the symptoms one at a time. Protectiveness, check. Possessive feelings, check. Powerful attraction, check and double-fucking-check. He blew out a breath as the truth hit him like a punch to the gut. The woman he and Rory had fished out of the ocean was a potential mate. The only trouble was, true mates were never human, and he'd never heard of a selkie damned near drowning. Something wasn't adding up.

JESS KNEW there was a reason she should open her eyes, but for the life of her she couldn't figure out what it was. It was easier just to drift in the comforting warmth surrounding her like a cocoon than to puzzle out what was wrong. She was warm, and Evan had said she was safe… Jess's brain slammed on the brakes and then reviewed her last thought and a second later she was sitting up in bed, her arms crossed over her nearly naked chest as she stared down at the blond god looking up at her in alarm.

"What—" was all he got out of his mouth before she started screaming.

"Where am I and why am I naked? And who the hell are you?"

Jess grabbed the blankets still wrapped around her and scrambled backward until she hit a wall.

"Just calm down for a minute, Jess. I'm Evan, remember?"

"No! I mean…maybe?" She realized he was only half dressed and panic washed over her again. "Where are your clothes? And where the hell are mine?"

She heard footsteps coming at a dead run and the next thing she knew another man burst into the room. Jess squealed in fright and tried to stand up, slamming her head on the low ceiling. Stars burst behind her eyelids and she dropped back down to the bed with a cry of fear and pain.

"What the fuck did you do to her, Evan?" the new arrival bellowed.

"Nothing! Now will you shut up? You're scaring her."

"I'm scaring her? Really? I was up top when she started screaming."

"Shut. Up. Rory," Evan snarled and Jess could hear him moving on the bed. "Jess, sweetheart, it's okay. You got taken out by a wave and we pulled you out of the water. Your clothes are right over there, but they're soaking wet. Do you remember any of this yet?"

Jess opened her eyes slowly and found herself staring straight into the face of a dark angel. His black hair fell to his shoulders, and his eyes were the color of onyx. She could tell he hadn't bothered to shave in a day or so, and the dark stubble added to the surreal sense of danger the man projected. Even stooped over to fit inside the strangely configured room. He looked absolutely huge and more than a little intimidating.

"Hi, Jess. I'm Rory." The dark-haired man gave her a

slow smile and she felt her insides turn to molten mush. That smile transformed his face and softened the impact of his powerful presence.

"Uh, hi." She tugged the blankets tighter around her and glanced over to Evan again. He was like sunshine after the storm when she compared him to Rory. He had sandy blond hair and a friendly smile she recognized from the tumble of terrible memories crammed inside her head. "You're the one who pulled me out of the water," she said to Evan and he nodded, still watching her with concern gleaming in his sky-blue eyes.

"That's right. Rory was there, too, but he was dealing with the boat, so I was the one who took you down here and got you warmed up."

More memories came back and Jess blushed as she remembered being undressed and then burrowing into Evan's arms.

Evan grinned and she found herself dazzled by his smile. "Oh yeah, it's all coming back to you now, isn't it?" he chuckled. "Now that we've established the fact that no one here's an ax murderer, why don't you lie back down and finish getting warmed up while I check to make sure you didn't give yourself a concussion."

"I'll do it," Rory offered and the two men exchanged a look Jess didn't quite catch the meaning of. It must have meant something, though, because Evan grinned and nodded before flopping back down on the mattress and patting the spot beside him.

"I'll leave the first aid to Rory's gentle touch, then. Come here, sweetheart. You're nowhere near recovered yet. You need to rest."

A fragment of another conversation popped into Jess's

head and she grinned at Evan as she carefully made her way back to his side. "I thought you said he was heavy-handed?"

Rory growled and Evan groaned with laughter. "Oh sure. You didn't remember getting rescued, but you managed to remember me insulting his driving? You're going to be a world of trouble for us, I can already tell."

Jess was intensely aware of Rory as he moved around behind her, and she felt a shimmer of heat dance over her skin as he gently stroked her hair and explored her scalp around where she'd bumped it.

"You gave yourself a nice goose-egg, but I don't see any blood."

"So I'll live?" She tried to keep her tone light, but she could hear the tremor in her voice. She hoped they'd think it was from the cold and not because of the effect the two of them were having on her.

Rory's hands stroked over her wet hair and came to rest on her shoulders as he leaned down so his mouth was beside her ear. "You'll live, but only if you stop wandering out on the rocks during storm season. Promise me you won't do that again."

His breath was warm as it fanned over her skin and Jess had to focus hard to form a coherent response.

"I didn't know it was dangerous."

Rory's hands tightened around her shoulders and his voice rumbled like distant thunder. "Promise me, Jess. I don't want you taking that kind of risk again."

Annoyance burned off some of the warm fuzzies she'd been feeling and Jess spun her head to snarl at him, forgetting he was only a few inches away. "I don't have to promise you anything!"

"Uh oh, wrong thing to say, sweetheart." Evan chuckled somewhere to her left, but Jess barely heard him. She was staring into Rory's dark-chocolate eyes, his mouth hovering a finger's breadth away from hers.

"Yes, you do," Rory told her.

"Like hell I do! I'm grateful for both of you for rescuing me, but whatever it is that you think is going on here, it's not. So, get your hands off me and I'll be on my way!"

"No," Rory growled and then he was kissing her, his mouth hard and hot as he slanted his lips over hers. The stubble on his cheeks rasped against the sensitive skin of her face and that friction blended into the heat that flowed from him where his lips touched hers.

As quickly as he had taken her, he retreated again, and Jess found herself following his mouth as he pulled away. She knew she should have been angry, or scared, but instead she couldn't feel anything past the driving need to feel his lips on hers again. This time she kissed him and she heard one of the men groan. She wasn't sure which it was, and she didn't care. Jess turned on the bed so she was facing Rory and speared her fingers into the dark waves of his hair, tugging him closer to her as she explored his mouth with hers.

Rory tasted dark and smoky, like autumn leaves and bonfires. She ran her tongue along the seam of his lips and he opened his mouth with a groan that inflamed all her senses. His hands circled her hips and hauled her up against the solid wall of his body.

Again Jess's brain tried to send up a warning flare, reminding her that this was a stranger she was so recklessly kissing, but she ignored everything but the need to touch and be touched. Their tongues tangled and a flame sparked in Jess's womb, sending a flood of liquid heat gushing between her thighs and soaking her pussy.

Another groan, and this time she knew it was Evan that was giving voice to his arousal because he was behind her a heartbeat later, the bare skin of his chest pressing up against her back as he swept her hair aside and blew a puff of air across her ear before sucking on her earlobe. For one perfect moment the three of them were in harmony, but then Jess's brain screamed in denial at what was happening and tore her out of her reverie.

She broke off the kiss with Rory and let her hands fall from his hair as she found herself sandwiched between two of the hottest men she'd ever met, wearing nothing but her underwear. *How the hell did this happen?*

"Jess?" Evan's voice was a soft caress that flowed over her rattled nerves. "You okay, sweetheart?"

Her answering laughter had a brittle edge to it that even Jess could hear. "No, I'm not even close to okay. I damn near drowned a while ago, and now I think I'm hallucinating."

"What makes you think you're seeing things?" Rory asked, his voice still a husky with desire. He stroked his thumb down her cheek and she felt her pulse race at that simple contact.

"There's no way this can really be happening. I don't— I've never even dreamed of doing this."

"Doing what?" Evan purred and brushed several delicate kisses from her ear to the top of her shoulder.

"This! You, me, him! This isn't happening! It can't be, because I would never do something like this." Jess took a deep breath and struggled to make sense of what was going on.

"Sweetheart, I promise you, this is as real as it gets." Evan chuckled near her ear as Rory tucked a finger under her chin and lifted her head so she was looking in his eyes.

"You're not the only one wondering what the hell is going on, but believe me, it is happening." Rory gave her a smile and kissed her. It was a sweet, soft kiss that was nothing like the passionate possession she'd experienced from him only minutes before.

Jess shivered with cold and confusion and both men reached around to hold her, nearly crushing her between them. She idly noticed they didn't seem bothered by the fact they were holding each other as well as her, and then she shut down that line of thinking before she ended up jumping one of them again. *Or both of them.*

"Uh, guys? We're docked, right? So you can take me back to my cabin now."

"Not yet," Evan murmured as he nuzzled her neck. "You need to rest a bit more first, and Rory needs to find you something to wear."

"Rory isn't going anywhere, thank you." The big man arched a brow over Jess's shoulder to glower at Evan.

Evan ignored Rory and kept talking to Jess as if the other man hadn't said a word. "You're shivering again, Jess. Get back under the covers and let us take care of you. I promise, nothing is going to happen without your permission, okay?"

Something deep inside her whispered that she should do as they wanted. That she could trust them. She wanted to, so badly, but she needed help to make the leap.

"Promise me. Both of you promise me you won't hurt me."

"Hurt you?" Rory sounded horrified at the idea. "Never, baby. I would never hurt you, I promise."

"Me, too," Evan stated solemnly. "Now will you please lie down and rest some more? You're not ready to be up and around yet."

Jess smiled tiredly as she nodded and let the two men guide her back down to the mattress. They had her lie down on her side and then settled down on either side of her, cradling her between them like a pair of warm, muscular bookends. She closed her eyes as they covered themselves with the blankets again, her cheek resting on Evan's chest and Rory's big body curved around hers. She'd never felt so protected in her life, and when Evan's arm wrapped around her shoulders and Rory's hand settled on her hip, she didn't do anything but sigh in contentment and let herself drift deeper into sleep.

When she had recovered from her near-death experience she'd have to decide what she was going to do about the fact she was attracted to two men at once, but for now her instincts were insisting she could trust them, and she was simply too tired to do anything else.

CHAPTER FIVE

RORY COULD TELL the second that Jess fell asleep, because her body finally relaxed completely and her breathing slowed and deepened. Evan cleared his throat very quietly and Rory finally met his blood-brother's gaze and asked, "Do you know what the fuck is going on?"

Evan nodded once and then tapped his temple.

Great, Evan wanted to do this telepathically. Rory sighed inwardly. He tended to keep his mental shields up at all times, and not even Evan was allowed past them for more than a few sentences, usually when one or both of them were in seal form and all other communication was impossible. All selkies could relay their thoughts when in seal form, but only blood-bonded selkies could read each other's thoughts and emotions when human. Still, Rory had learned early that as the future leader of the colony, it was important that no one be able to get into his head or influence his decisions.

Rory opened the link to Evan, and the strength of the thoughts coming at him so strong he winced. *"Ease up, dude. You're giving me a headache."* He sent the thought back to Evan.

"Sorry, it's a bit hard to be calm at the moment."

"Is the naked woman in bed between us distracting you?" Rory added a mental snicker to his message.

"She's not just any woman, Rory. Can't you feel it?"

"I'm feeling something, sure. But I have no idea what the fuck it is."

Evan's next thought came with a surge of emotion so strong it made Rory's breath catch. *"She's a true mate, brother. For us."*

"No." Rory's first reaction was denial. She couldn't be. True mates were rare these days, and they were *always* selkies, no exceptions.

"Yes," Evan argued back along the link between them. *"How else do you explain what's going on? She feels it, too, and she doesn't understand it any more than we do. Less I think."*

"She can't be. She's human!"

"Human or not, I think she is. Try imagining letting her get up out of this bed and walk away from us so we never see her again."

Rory did, and the idea of letting her go had him seeing red. His arm tightened around her and he knew there was no chance in hell he'd ever let her out of his sight, never mind out of his life.

"Yeah, I feel the same way. So, I'd say we found ourselves a mate."

Rory's mind was reeling. They'd found her. After years of looking, they had finally found the woman destined to complete their lives, and she was human. *Fuck. Dad isn't going to like this.*

Evan picked up on his stray thoughts. *"I know. The*

prince has to marry a selkie from one of the old bloodlines. But not even your father can't make you marry someone else if you've found a true mate."

Evan's blue eyes met Rory's as they stared at each other across the sleeping form of their very human mate. "If he tries to do that to us, you know what will happen."

"That's only a legend."

"True mates are only supposed to be a legend, too, and apparently we've got one sleeping between us right now."

They both glanced down at Jess and Rory could feel Evan's feelings were the mirror to his own. Neither of them was willing to give her up, but to keep her they were going to have to break with traditions that went back to ancient times.

"The things in life truly worth having are worth fighting for," Rory said the words out loud and their exhausted mate stirred and then settled back down with a sleepy sigh that pumped all the blood in his body straight to his cock. As Evan chuckled Rory realized that the telepathic bond between them was still in place, and his blood-brother had felt his response to Jess's sigh.

Rory severed the link, but as he stared down at Jess he couldn't help but wonder what life would be like if she agreed to stay with them. Mated trios often formed intimate bonds, even when one of the group was human. He had always kept Evan out of his head as much as he could, but if Jess was theirs, then those days may well be coming to an end. Rory had kept part of himself a secret, and he wasn't sure how Evan would feel after he knew the truth about the darkness in Rory's soul. Finding Jess might be the answer to their prayers, but she could also destroy what they already had. He hoped like hell that she was strong enough to deal with all the changes that were coming, and then he amended that thought. He hoped they were *all* strong enough to cope with the changes her arrival heralded.

～

JESS WOKE up and found herself cradled between her rescuers. They were still, but the moment she moved she felt both tense and she realized they were awake.

"Hi," she whispered, feeling shy despite the fact she had already traded toe-curling kisses with one of them and the other had actually undressed her not very long ago.

"Hey, sweetheart, welcome back." Evan's sky-blue eyes gleamed with warmth as he lifted his head enough to smile down at her. "Feeling better?"

"Well, at least this time she didn't wake up and start screaming." Rory rumbled from behind her and she blushed at that memory.

"Sorry about that, but, well…can you blame me?"

Rory laughed and his voice flowed over her like melted chocolate, dark and sweet.

"Not really. I'm still glad you seem calmer this time." He feathered a kiss to her bare shoulder. "And warmer. I swear you were halfway to being an icicle by the time I got you back to the bo—" He stopped talking for a second. "I mean by the time we got you into the boat."

Jess frowned as she tried to remember the details of her rescue, but it all seemed like one big blur of cold and fear and waves. "I don't really remember much after the wave hit me. I just remember thinking that I was going to die, and then Evan was pulling me up into the boat." Another fragment of memory popped into her head. "And there was a seal, there, too." She rolled onto her back and glanced at Rory. "Did you see a seal?"

"A seal?" He got an odd look on his face and then nodded. "Now you mention it, I think there was a seal out there. They're pretty common around here."

"Is it common for seals to grab people and pull them around, too?" she asked.

"What? No. Seals don't do that. They're playful sometimes with divers, but they're not aggressive." Rory shook his head. "And I didn't see a seal pulling you around."

"Well, it did." Jess folded her arms over her chest. "And that's not the first time it's happened, either."

The two men looked at each other and then down at her with such intense expressions that Jess wondered if she'd said something wrong.

"What do you mean, it's happened before?" Evan asked, his usually gentle voice rife with tension. "When? Where?"

"Here, when I was a little girl."

"You're from *here*?" Rory interjected.

"Well, no, but my cabin has been in the family a couple of generations. We used to come here for summer vacations when I was a girl. We stopped coming when I was six or seven. The last year we came was the year I saw the seals. I remember thinking they wanted to play with me. They were pulling on my life jacket like the seal today was doing. It's strange that I didn't remember that until recently. I never remembered why we stopped coming out here. I guess my parents got a little freaked out. And here I am twenty-odd years later, and my first time in the water there's another seal. Weird, huh?"

"I'd say so." Evan grinned. "Maybe it's your perfume?"

"Ha-ha." She stuck out her tongue at him, only realizing her error when she saw the flare of lust in his blue eyes.

"If you stick that out at me again I'm going to put it to good use, sweetheart. As I see it, you still owe me a kiss. Right now Rory's one up on me."

Arousal collided with panic somewhere in the vicinity of Jess's chest and suddenly it was very hard to breathe. She managed to choke a single word past the iron bands squeezing her lungs up through a throat gone completely dry in a matter of seconds. "What?"

Evan's lower lip stuck out in an overly dramatic pout. "You've kissed him twice."

"Please tell me you're kidding." Rory clapped a playful slap up the side of Evan's head. "Don't you even think of keeping score, Ev, or I swear I'll dropkick you off the back of this boat the next time we're out in deep water."

Jess hugged her arms tighter across her chest, her gaze bouncing from one to the other and back again.

"So you two…" She trailed off and tried again. "I mean the three of us—hell, I have no idea what I'm even trying to say here!"

"I think that in this case, the word you're looking for is yes." Evan waggled his brows at her. "I'm sure hoping that's what you're going to say, anyway."

"Oh, very smooth." Rory leaned down and pressed a soft kiss to the corner of her mouth and she felt his tongue briefly dance over her skin. He kept his lips just brushing hers as he continued talking. "Evan and I have been best friends since I was ten years old. He's a part of my life, and I'm part of his. We share everything."

"Everything…as in…*everything*?" Jess stressed the last word, her heart beating faster at the erotic images that invaded her mind as she considered what Rory meant.

"Absolutely everything, baby."

Evan chimed from her other side as he brushed back her hair to kiss her temple. "Not everything. I have my own toothbrush."

Jess giggled. She hadn't meant to, but the ridiculousness of the entire situation simply made it impossible to do anything else. Giggles turned to laughter, and she found herself reduced to chortles and snorts until her cheeks were hot and there were tears streaming down her face. Still sniggering, she reached up a hand to each of them and patted their stunned faces. "You should see your expressions!" She fell into a fit of giggles.

"I think she's lost it." Rory looked slightly panic-stricken as he stared at Jess. "Maybe she hit her head harder than I thought?"

"You'll have to excuse him." Evan finally joined in the laughter, leaning down to cut off her giggles with a kiss that seared her all the way through to her bones. "He's always too damned serious. I really hope you can help me fix that."

Jess was too surprised by the kiss to react at first, and by the time she got over her shock, her body had very definitely overridden her mind. At least that was what she told herself as she found herself burying her fingers in Evan's sandy hair, her tongue dueling with his.

"Holy shit, that's hot." Rory swore and reached out a

hand to cup her breast. "So I guess this means you don't have a concussion?"

Jess giggled again and Evan lifted his head to glower at Rory. "You are ruining this moment for me, bro."

Jess managed to gather her scattered wits and scooted out from underneath Evan until she could sit up. "I think we need to get me back to my cabin before we have any more conversations about seals, or sharing, or well, anything! I can't seem to think straight when I'm around the two of you, and half of us aren't wearing much in the way of clothing."

"Fair enough." Rory released her breast and Evan sat up, giving her an eyeful of sculpted male flesh that distracted her to the point she forgot what she was going to say next.

As Evan moved away from her and retrieved his shirt from the floor her synapses started firing again. "Guys? I'm going to need something to wear, please."

Rory sighed. "You really don't need clothes. We could bundle you up in the blankets and then I'll carry you to the truck. That way when we get to your place we can pop you straight into the shower to get cleaned up."

Jess turned and looked at him, doing her best to hide her smirk. "Nice try. But when we get to my place you two are going to let me out and I'm going to go home, *alone*."

Just then her stomach growled and Jess ducked her head to hide her blush of embarrassment.

"New plan," Rory announced. "We're taking you back to our place first and feeding you. Then we'll take you home."

"I'm fine."

"No, you're hungry." He quirked a brow at her and

gave her a sardonic smile. "Or are you going to argue with me about that, too?"

"I can eat at home. The two of you have done more than enough for me already." Jess took a quick breath and then looked up at Rory. "In fact, I would like to invite you to dinner tomorrow night. Both of you. I'll cook you a 'thank you for not letting me drown' meal."

"Can you cook?" Evan asked her, grinning.

"I promise you'll leave full and satisfied," Jess answered and then winced inwardly as she realized the sexual undertone to her words.

Rory rose up off the bed, stooping to avoid hitting his head on the ceiling. "Then we are most definitely coming to dinner tomorrow. However that doesn't mean you're not coming home with us right now to get something to eat. I know I'm starving, and Evan's delicate constitution can't go long without food or he whines, so we're eating. I'd really like for you to join us."

Jess clutched at the blankets and tried to decide what she wanted to say. She was hungry, and she did want to spend time with the two of them. But it was all so much to take in. They were too much. She needed time alone to think about what they'd said, and what they'd offered her. Though she still wasn't entirely sure what it was they'd been suggesting.

Before she could come up with an answer Evan dropped back down onto the bed. "Hey, sweetheart, it's all right. You've had a rough day and I swear we'll be complete gentlemen." He glanced up at Rory. "Isn't that right, Rory? And don't think I'm going to forget about that delicate constitution crack either. You're going to regret that."

Rory just laughed and then reached up and skinned his sweater over his head, baring a chest that made Jess's eyes widen in appreciation. He was broader than Evan, and where Evan's chest was sculpted muscle, Rory was a solid wall of muscle and dark hair.

"Put this on while we go see if we can't find you something to wear on your bottom half." He tossed her the sweater and ducked out the doorway.

Evan made to follow him and then stopped in the doorway and looked back at Jess. "We'll be back in a second with more of your wardrobe, sweetheart. Rory's right, you need to be taken care of for today." Evan's eyes softened. "Please let us."

She gave him a faint nod and his answering smile warmed her to the tips of her toes. He left her alone then, and she pulled on Rory's sweater. It was still warm from his body and she found herself surrounded by his scent as she rolled up the overlong sleeves. When she stood up she laughed as she realized that it came to nearly mid-thigh, and no matter how many times she tried to adjust it, the whole thing kept shifting to one side or another, baring her shoulders. Jess was still fighting with it when Evan reappeared at the door, a pair of heavy wool socks in one hand and a rain jacket in the other.

"The only pants we could find on board were in the rag bin, and believe me you did not want those touching your skin. So I'm afraid that we're going to complete this stunning fisherman ensemble look you have going on with a pair of ugly gray socks and a jacket to keep the rain off." He offered her the items as his eyes raked over her body from top to bottom. "That sweater has never looked so good. I think Rory should let you keep it."

Jess laughed and shook her head. "I'm going to look like a complete ragamuffin. If we run into a single soul, I'm never going to forgive either of you!"

"Right, I'll tell Rory to cancel the parade through town, then." Evan winked. "Get dressed and come on up when you're ready. We'll have to make a run for it. The weather went to absolute hell while we were all taking our naps."

He scooped her wet things off of the floor and vanished back through the door. "And hurry up, Jess. I am starving!"

She tugged on the socks, happy to have something to cover her bare feet, which were already chilled from standing on the thinly carpeted floor. With the rain jacket in hand, she made her way back into the galley, and then stopped, stunned as she realized the low roar she was hearing was the sound of rain hitting the roof overhead. The noise had been muffled down in the fore-cabin, but now it was obvious that they were in the middle of yet another storm. She put on the jacket and listened to her two rescuers banter. They both had their backs to her and were bent over an open compartment at the back of the boat, completely oblivious to the rain that was coming down in sheets.

"If that offer for food is still available, I'm ready to take you up on it," she called out to them. Both men turned around immediately, and Rory's deep-brown eyes widened as he stared at her bare legs and then slowly perused the rest of her.

"I take it back, Evan. You're right, she does look better in it than I do."

"Told you so."

"You both need to have your eyes checked," Jess said,

deflecting the compliment. She wasn't exactly comfortable showing so much of herself. She knew her body was far from perfect, and she usually worked hard to dress to her strengths. Bare legs and a baggy sweater weren't going to help highlight her assets, and she really hoped she could find something else to wear soon.

"Just give us a second here, baby. We need to put this new engine to bed and then we'll be heading home." Rory turned back to the compartment and tugged a cover back into place over the top of it. He was wearing a rain jacket, but he'd left the hood down and his dark hair was streaming with water. Jess could see he wasn't wearing anything under the jacket, either, and she wondered how he was managing to stay warm. A gust of wind blew the rain nearly sideways and she heard him cursing under his breath. Apparently he wasn't warm after all.

"If you don't get out of this weather soon, we're going to be treating *you* for hypothermia next," she scolded him.

Evan snickered, "I think we finally met your match, Rory. She doesn't seem to be the least bit intimidated by your dark and glowering persona."

"Don't you get cocky, Evan. You're the one standing there watching him get drenched. I thought you two were supposed to be looking out for each other." Jess tipped her head to one side. "Or do you share your colds, too?"

"If you're so worried about my catching cold, why don't you help keep me warm?" Rory covered the short distance in a few quick strides and before Jess could take more than a single step backward she found herself swept up into his powerful arms. "There, now you can keep me safe from the elements while Evan runs up to the truck and gets it started."

"Fine, fine. You can carry her to the truck, but I've got dibs on carrying her into the house!" Evan shot back and leaped neatly up onto the gunwale and then onto the dock. He tugged his hood forward with one hand and made a dash for the ramp leading to the shore, leaving Jess and Rory alone.

"You two certainly bicker like you were family," Jess observed as she wrapped her arms around Rory's neck and held on as he stepped up onto the side of the boat and jumped to the dock. His muscles flexed as he cradled her to his chest as they landed, and then he was heading up the dock. He reached up and tucked her head under his chin, sheltering her from some of the rain and wind. The only parts of her really exposed were her bare legs, and she knew by the time she got back inside, she was going to need another pair of socks and a towel.

"We're like brothers. It's been that way for so many years I can't imagine my life without him."

"I understand. My best friend and I are like sisters. Leaving her back in Toronto was the hardest part about moving here." She paused and then added. "But maybe we're not as close as you and Evan. We most certainly do not share *everything*."

Rory laughed as he carried her through a small, gravel lot and past a handful of buildings. "I'll admit it's a bit unconventional. I promise once we get you inside, you can ask any questions you want."

"I'm not even sure where to begin," Jess said and shivered as a gust of icy wind howled past them.

"How about we start with hot chocolates and double marshmallows?"

Jess groaned in agreement, suddenly starving. "That sounds perfect."

As he carried up to the passenger side door of a massive black pickup truck, Rory quietly said, "You can trust us, Jess. We would never let anything happen to you. I promise."

Then he was bundling her into the warm interior, and she found herself hauled into his lap, his arms closing around her as he settled his big body into the seat.

Evan smiled at them both and dropped the truck into gear. "Let's go home."

CHAPTER SIX

JESS WOKE up the next morning and for a minute she couldn't figure out why she felt like she'd been hit by a truck. Her entire body ached, and getting out of bed was a slow-motion affair. "Nearly drowning comes with a hangover, too? Come on universe, gimme a break here," she groaned and tried to stretch out the worst of the stiffness, but quickly gave it up in favor of a long, hot shower.

By the time she'd showered, taken a couple of ibuprofen and downed half a cup of coffee Jess was feeling more herself, though she was still moving slower than she would have liked. She had big plans for dinner, but before she tackled that she wanted to sit down and get all her memories of yesterday down on paper. It was part therapy and part research. If she ever decided to nearly drown one of her characters, she would have firsthand experience to draw from, but only if she made notes while it was still fresh in her mind.

Jess settled down in front of her laptop and began

typing. As her fingers flew over the keys she found herself reliving every second of terror and pain she'd experienced the day before. She hadn't meant to document the entire encounter, only the experience up until she was rescued, but as details came to her she continued to type, entering it all into a file and saving it.

There were still some gaps in her recollection, but now she *knew* that she had seen a seal, and it had pulled her toward the boat! She remembered Evan helping her on board, but nowhere in her memories could she recall seeing Rory. He had to have been there. She'd heard him cursing about the cold. His voice was too distinctive to have been anyone else. Maybe the rest of it would come back to her in time, but at least she'd preserved this much.

It had been a very surreal day, and looking back at everything, Jess couldn't decide if what had happened between Rory, Evan, and herself was the product of stress, a real connection, or temporary insanity. "At least I hope it's temporary," Jess muttered to herself. "I have to be crazy, don't I? To even consider dating two men at once is definitely not normal."

She pushed back from the desk and was about to get up when an idea struck her. There was one person who would never turn down a chance to tell her she was crazy. She needed to talk to Viv.

Before Jess could second-guess herself, she turned on the laptop once again and called up her e-mail program and attached the document she'd just finished typing. She addressed it and tapped out a brief message, explaining to Viv that she needed to read the attachment and then please call her back. As her cursor hovered over the send button she nearly chickened out, but then she clicked and sent the e-mail on its way.

"She's going to think I'm making this up." Jess stared at the monitor for another few seconds and then stood up, stretching her back yet again before heading to the kitchen. She needed to get started planning dinner, and if yesterday was any indication, she was going to need to make a massive amount of food. Those guys could eat!

When they had arrived at the guys' place yesterday, Rory had tucked her into a massive couch and ordered her not to move, and she'd enjoyed watching the two of them banter and sidestep each other as they had conjured up a simple meal of tomato soup and a mountain of grilled ham and cheese sandwiches. Not just any cheese either, but a blend of brie and Monterey Jack that had melted into a mound of black forest ham. It had tasted even better than it looked, and she'd eaten two of the crispy, golden creations along with a bowl of creamy tomato soup. The two of them had managed to polish off the rest of the platter between them and chase it down with the promised hot chocolate with masses of marshmallows.

Thinking of their meal, Jess headed for the kitchen and started pulling out all the ingredients for homemade hot chocolate, and she grinned to herself as she added a bottle of peppermint schnapps to the ingredients on the counter.

"In for a penny, in for a pound," she told herself with a grin. She was still trying to decide between roasted chicken or a casserole for dinner when her phone rang, and the opening notes of Pam Tillis's *Mi Vida Loca* blasted from the phone's speaker. Viv must have gotten her e-mail.

Jess managed to get in a brief hello before her best friend cut her off with a squeal. "Oh my god, Jess! You've not even been there a week yet and you've managed to find two hotties? And you kissed them both! I don't know whether to be proud or jealous!"

"Did you forget about the bit where I nearly drowned?" Jess asked with a laugh.

"Close only counts in horseshoes and hand grenades. You didn't drown, for which I am grateful. But more importantly you did meet two cuties! They are cute, right? Please tell me they are cute or I'm going to have to take back that bit about being proud of you."

"Yes, they're cute. Actually, I think they are way better than cute, but it's possible that hypothermia and near-death trauma have affected my judgment."

"Names. I need last names. And then details. All of them!"

"Rory Frazier and uh, Evan Sinclair. Viv, what are you doing?" Jess asked.

"My Google-fu is strong. I'm—holy shit!"

"What? What is it?"

"I found your guys' website. You lucky, lucky bitch. They are not cute. They are smoking hot!"

"They have a website?"

She heard Vivian groan. "Grasshopper, you have much to learn. Lucky for you I am better at this dating thing than you are. They run an eco-tour company out of Tofino. They have a website, and pictures, and...ooh, hello, I have their phone number! Shall I call them and get the scoop directly from the horse's mouth?"

"Don't you dare!"

Vivian laughed. "Okay, okay. No phone calls to the owners and operators of Hotties Incorporated."

"That cannot be the name of their company."

"You got me. It's Pacifica Tours. It could be Hotties Incorporated, though. Have you seen these guys?"

"Yes, I've seen them. Shirtless, in fact."

"Bitch. Don't remind me. It's really hard to be supportive when I'm suffering from terminal jealousy."

"There's nothing to be jealous of, Viv. At least I'm not sure there is."

Vivian sighed. "I knew it. You're listening to that little voice in the back of your head again, aren't you? How many times have I told you not to listen to Negative Nelly? They kissed you, *and* snuggled with you, and told you they are best friends who share everything. Heavy stress on the word everything. That's the greenest light I have ever heard of. If you don't go for it, I will fly down there and kick you in the ass until you do, or I'll see if they want to trade in a blonde for a redhead."

"They're smoking hot and amazingly nice guys, can you blame me for questioning my sanity?"

"Of course I'm questioning your sanity, because I know what you're not saying. What you're thinking is that they are smoking hot guys and you think you're an overweight cream puff. You're a bestselling author, a beautiful woman, and have so much to offer, but you keep forgetting all of that and fixate on the fact you are not a size two. They kissed you, remember? Which means they are already attracted to you. Get over it, girl, and get onto the good stuff already!"

"What would I do without you?" Jess asked, laughing past the lump in her throat at her friend's honest assessment.

"Well, for one thing, you'd probably be considering cancelling dinner tonight and locking yourself in that log cabin until I got there and dragged you out into the world again." Vivian's voice softened. "You deserve to be happy. If they make you smile, then I think you should go for it."

"But, Viv…two? How does that even work!"

Vivian cackled and then said, "If you're lucky, you'll be finding out for yourself soon. In the meantime I'll send you a few book titles you need to go buy from Amazon. Call it research."

"Oh god."

"You had lunch with them yesterday, didn't you guys talk?"

"We did, but it was more getting to know each other stuff. Where did we grow up, school, interests, you know, the safe stuff."

"Did you tell them what you do for a living, Jess?"

Jess wrinkled her nose and glowered at the phone before answering. "I said I'm a freelance writer."

"So you lied."

"I panicked."

"What is the point of being a bestselling author if you never tell anyone?"

"It's…complicated."

"I know, but only because you let it be. No one is going to be disappointed to discover you're not one of the characters in your books, Jess."

"I know. And you're right, I'll tell them tonight."

"So you are still making them dinner? Good! By the time they've tasted your cooking they'll be more than halfway in love with you. What are you making?"

"I can't decide between chicken or a casserole."

"You have got to do your beer chicken thing. It is

delicious, and what man can resist a girl who knows how to cook with beer?"

Both of them laughed at that and Jess felt some of her worry and doubt fade away.

"Okay, chicken it is. Which means I need to head into town and grab some beer and a few other things for tonight."

"Do yourself a favor, buy whipped cream." Viv snickered. "And some condoms. Just in case."

"I cannot believe you even suggested that!"

"Trust me, once they realize you're a hottie who can cook, you're going to need them."

Jess felt her cheeks heat and realized she was grinning at the idea. "You know, I hope you're right. Okay, I'll do it."

Vivian crowed victoriously, "That's my girl! And tomorrow morning I want details. Graphic—no. I want *pornographic* details."

"Maybe."

"No maybes, I think this is kismet. It's time for some good things to come your way."

"Kismet, huh?" Jess smiled. "That's the name of their home. Kismet Cove."

"You see! I'm brilliant. Have fun tonight, and remember, if in doubt, do it!"

"I love you, Viv. I can't wait for you to come and visit."

"Love you, too, and when I get out there I expect you to have organized up at least a few guys for me."

"It's a deal."

"Toodles, Gator."

"Later, Poodle."

They exchanged their traditional good-byes and Jess

hung up the phone, feeling far more confident. She grabbed a piece of scrap paper and started making a list of things she was going to need at the store. The first thing she wrote down was whipped cream.

~

"DID YOU SLEEP?" Evan asked as he gave Rory a bleary-eyed smile from over the top of a mug of black coffee.

Rory shook his head in the negative and headed straight for the coffee maker. "Not much. You?"

"Same as you. The few times I did get to sleep all I accomplished was to dream about her."

Rory laughed. "Yeah, tell me about it. This morning's shower is going to be a cold one or I'm not going to survive until dinner tonight."

"Think of all the money we're going to save on hot water if she makes us work for this." Evan snickered and then winced. "Gods, I hope she doesn't make us wait too long. I'm not sure I can take it."

"What if she decides she doesn't want us at all?" Rory poured himself a coffee and dumped two spoonfuls of sugar into it, then added a third. "We're not exactly offering her a normal dating life. She's human, Ev. She might decide to bolt like a scalded cat, and I wouldn't blame her."

"Selkies aren't the only ones who have polyamorous relationships. Humans do it, too. It's not like we've cornered the market here."

"Polyam—what now?" Rory quirked a brow at Evan as he tossed a couple of slices of bread into the toaster. "You been reading the thesaurus in the bathroom again?"

"Polyamorous. More than two people in a relationship. You really need to read something other than those crime thrillers of yours. There are all sorts of interesting words you probably don't even know exist."

"I know the ones I need to know." Rory ticked off the fingers on one hand as he spoke. "Smartass, hull check, today, and oh yeah, *dive gear*."

Evan groaned. "You don't seriously intend to make me do an underwater check on the hull today? Have you looked outside? It's miserable out there!"

"Hey, I did say you could scuba dive instead of transforming. At least that saves you getting naked out there in the elements, like I did yesterday rescuing our reluctant mermaid." Rory's head filled with memories of how Jess had tasted when he'd kissed her. Her lips had tasted of the sea, but beyond that she'd had a delicate sweetness that he knew was entirely her own. He really wanted to taste her again. He realized he'd gone silent as he'd been distracted by thoughts of Jess's lush curves and sweet mouth and picked up his previous train of thought. "Do you think that it's possible she feels what we are? I mean, I know some humans develop a link to their selkie mates, but that usually takes time and a full bonding."

Evan shrugged, his blue eyes full of uncertainty, which was rare. "I don't know. She acts human, but there's something about her…"

"You mean the way she smells? God, the first time I scented her it was like a punch in the gut."

"You, too?" Evan looked surprised. "That's a true mate reaction, but those are never human. At least I don't think they are." He sighed and scrubbed a hand over his unshaven jaw. "I need to do some research, and then talk to your mom."

Rory shook his head. "If you tell Mom, she'll have to tell Dad, and then all hell is going to break loose. We can't risk it. I don't want Dad to know a thing until after we've already made up our minds."

"We can't tell Jess what we are without your dad's permission, and I for one am not going to let her agree to a permanent arrangement without telling her she's hooking up with a couple of mythical creatures who can turn into seals."

Rory nodded. "Fair enough. But let's see if she's even willing to date us before we get to the bit about being shapeshifters." He drank down more of his coffee and then asked, "Do you think it's possible she's got selkie blood? Maybe that's what's causing this reaction. She could she have just enough to cause this reaction but not enough to transform?"

"Are we even sure she can't shapeshift?"

"You saw her yesterday, Ev. Five more minutes in that water and she'd have been dead. If she could have transformed, she would have, even it was purely out of instinct. She didn't, so I think we have to assume she's not one of us."

"Yeah, I suppose. When I'm done with the hull check, though, I'm going to see if I can't find out something about where she comes from, just in case. That cabin is right beside our land, and it's been in her family for a long time. I think we should cover all our bases."

"Anything that makes it easier to convince my father to accept her would be welcome. I'm tired of fighting."

Evan laughed at him. "Bullshit. You and your dad are

going to be going at it hammer and tongs until the day he passes. You're too much alike for it to be any other way."

"Don't insult me like that. You may be older, but I'm still bigger than you and can whip your ass."

"What color is the sky in your world? Is it pretty there? Because a fantasyland is the *only* place you can kick my ass, my prince." Evan scrambled back from the table with a chuckle as Rory nearly choked on his coffee.

"Do not fucking call me that! Ever! God I hate that title."

Evan grinned. "That's why I love using it. I'm going to go grab my dive gear and do the hull. See you down at the dock in a bit?"

"Yep. As soon as I finish my breakfast."

"I can't wait to see what Jess is making us for dinner. Do you think she can cook?"

Rory's heart beat a little in his chest at the thought of the evening to come. "I don't care if she can cook. I can't wait to see her."

"I know the feeling. Hey, if we get a move on, we can drive into town and find a nice present for her tonight," Even suggested.

"Good idea. But what do you get for the woman you're hoping will sleep with you and your best friend on a first date?"

"Booze. Definitely booze. And flowers can't hurt, either."

Rory nodded. "I'll get the booze. You're the one in touch with his feminine side so you can pick the flowers."

"Bite me."

"I'd rather bite Jess."

"You and me both."

CHAPTER SEVEN

SINCE SHE'D TALKED to Vivian, Jess had been in an exuberant mood. It had been months since she'd felt the urge to cook, and she was enjoying the opportunity to say thank you to her two rescuers. She'd tucked most of the beer into the fridge, leaving out a can to use as the basting liquid for her roasted chicken. She tried not to grin as she tucked a spray bottle of whipped cream into the fridge door, along with a squeezable container of chocolate sauce. "It's for the hot chocolate, that's all." She told herself, but there was a flutter in her stomach and a tingle in her pussy that made it clear at least part of her was hoping it would be for something much more interesting.

Within two hours she had the chicken roasting along with a medley of winter vegetables. The potatoes were all ready to be boiled and mashed, and she'd set out everything she'd need for cooking up their hot chocolate cocktails. So far, so good. With no time to make dessert, she'd dropped by the local bakery and grabbed an assortment of éclairs, tarts, and other pastries. Hopefully she'd gotten at least one thing they'd enjoy.

Jess glanced out the window and realized that time was getting away from her. She still needed to shower and change, and the guys were going to be arriving in less than an hour. She dashed down the hallway, stripping off her apron and then her clothing as she went. The guys had seen her at her worst, and tonight she was hoping to prove to them that she didn't always look like a drowned rat.

Jess took longer in the shower than she'd planned, but she knew it had been worth it. She'd indulged herself from head to toe, and every part of her felt silky smooth and softened by the tangerine and vanilla body lotion she'd rubbed into every bit of her she could reach. There hadn't been much time to do anything with her hair, so she'd settled for a simple blow dry and left it loose, falling down her back in a straight, shimmering curtain of silvery blonde. Jess held no illusions about her appearance or her faults, but her hair had always been one of her few vanities, and as she gave it one last stroke of the brush, she knew that at least her hair looked good.

She didn't usually do much with her makeup, so she settled for a bit of eyeliner and a silver-blue shadow that she'd been told would enhance her eyes. A bit of lipstick, a touch of powder, and she was done.

She'd been tempted to dress up, but then she reminded herself it was only supposed to be a thank you dinner. So instead she'd picked out one of her favorite silk tops and worn a pair of black jeans with a smattering of sequins and silver embroidery running down the calves. The dark-blue fabric flowed down over her hips and helped to hide some of her abundant curves.

"That's as good as it gets," she told her reflection in the mirror and smiled. "But it sure beats drowned-rat chic."

Jess headed back to the kitchen and got the potatoes cooking, humming to herself mindlessly as she flitted about, checking on everything and literally zipping around the kitchen in a happy frenzy. She'd forgotten how much she enjoyed cooking for other people. Her last boyfriend had been a picky eater, and no matter what she'd served him he'd always managed to find fault. Eventually she'd given up, and they'd always gone to the few restaurants he enjoyed. It was only in retrospect that Jess realized she hadn't even liked half of the restaurants they'd gone to, but she'd let herself be guilted into it to appease Richard.

"No wonder Viv is always on my case to stand up for myself. How did I not see this before?" Jess groaned and poured herself a glass of wine, determined not to listen to the voice that Viv had long ago named Negative Nelly. She wasn't going to doubt herself or let her insecurities get in the way.

She heard the rumble of an engine and the crunch of gravel beneath truck wheels and she knew that her guests had arrived. Suddenly Jess's stomach exploded with butterflies and her heart slammed so hard against her ribs she was certain they'd be able to hear it racing from the other side of the door. Her hands were shaking as she quickly rinsed and dried them and then hurried across the cabin to peek out the window. Rory was stepping down out of the truck and as her gaze slid over him she felt her stomach do a complete somersault. He was even better looking than she'd remembered. He was wearing dark pants that tapered in to fit his waist, and his dress shirt was a crisp white that almost glowed in contrast to his black leather jacket.

Evan came around to join Rory and she caught herself sighing as her clit started to throb. They were both gorgeous. Taller than Rory by a small measure, Evan was dressed almost identically, save that his dress shirt was a deep blue, and his leather jacket was gray. They were both carrying something, but she couldn't make out the details without staring and she didn't want them to catch her spying on them through the window.

"You are thirty years old, so stop thinking like a sixteen-year-old girl on her first date and breathe!" She gave herself a little mental shake and stepped back from the window just as their footsteps sounded on the front porch. She ran her hands down her outfit and squeaked in bemused horror as she realized she'd never put on shoes.

"Too late now, at least I have toe polish on," she muttered and went to answer the door as they knocked.

EVAN HAD CAUGHT her peeking out at them, and it had taken more determination than he cared to admit not to wave at her as she had watched them with hunger in her pale-blue eyes. He'd been worried that she'd changed her mind about them in the twenty-four hours they'd been apart, but one look at her beautiful face had reassured him. She was still interested, and he was fairly sure she was more than interested, if he'd read the heat in her expression correctly. *Thank god.*

Evan held the flowers he'd bought for her behind his back, waiting behind Rory as they waited for the door to open. When it did, Evan forgot to breathe. Light, warmth and the tantalizing aromas of the coming meal flowed out the door and surrounded them, every element adding to the sense of welcome he felt. Jess was standing in the doorway, her deliciously curvy body silhouetted by the lights inside the cabin. Her hair was glowing like a halo, and she was wearing an outfit that made his dick twitch in approval. Beside him Rory groaned under his breath and Evan caught the direction of his blood-brother's gaze, which was straight down at Jess's feet. *Holy hell, her feet were bare.*

Both of them had a thing for a woman's feet, and neither of them had time yesterday to pay proper attention to Jess's. Tonight, though, they were going to have trouble looking anywhere else. She had pretty feet, and her toes were painted a shade of purple Evan was certain matched the vibrant streaks in her hair. Evan's cock was hardening fast and he knew he was in for a long, torturous night.

"Hi." She greeted them both with a shy smile and hovered at the threshold for few seconds before stepping out onto the porch and reaching up to hug Rory. Her blonde head barely came to the middle of his chest and as Rory's arms closed around her shoulders Evan had to bite back a bark of laughter at the lustful expression on his blood-brother's face. At least he wasn't going to be alone in his suffering tonight.

Still wrapped in Rory's arms, Jess turned her head and smiled at Evan, and his blood heated further as he caught her scent. He smiled back at her and caught the feral gleam in Rory's eye and knew both of them had reacted to her as strongly as the day before. There was no doubting it anymore. Human or not, she was their true mate.

Rory released her and she moved into Evan's arms with another of her sweet, shy smiles.

"You look amazing, sweetheart."

Rory startled as if only just realizing he hadn't said anything yet. "You really do, baby," he drawled and grinned as she burrowed into Evan's embrace. "So amazing I forgot how to talk."

"You're both sweet to say so, but it's only because yesterday you didn't see me at my best. Frozen and soggy is never a good look, unless you're a mermaid, or maybe a seal." She threw her arms around Evan and hugged him, and her cheeks flushed a bright pink as she rested her head on his chest for a sweet second. His arms were around her and he drew her even tighter against him, forgetting the flowers he carried as he buried his head in her hair and inhaled.

"Whatever perfume you're wearing right now, I like it," he whispered into the silken strands and lifted his head with reluctance.

Jess shifted in his arms, leaning back just enough she could look up at him. "It's only body lotion, nothing special. It's more likely you're smelling dinner. Why don't you two come inside and get settled? The food is almost ready, but we have time for a drink first if you'd like."

"Drinks sound good," Rory said and finally produced the bottle he'd been carrying. "We brought you something. We didn't know what you were making for dinner, so we split the difference and got a blush sparkling wine.

"Oh!" She looked so pleased with the gift Evan wished they'd brought more, just to see her smile like that again. "You two didn't need to bring anything. This was supposed to be a thank you dinner!"

Evan let go of her and presented her with the flowers. "We wanted to bring you something, sweetheart."

"Oh! Oh my goodness, you got me roses!" Jess squealed and took the coral- and apricot-shaded blooms out of his hand and lifted them to her face to inhale their fragrance. "They're beautiful! You are both so sweet."

A timer went off somewhere inside the cabin and Jess glanced up. "Right, everyone inside and I'll get dinner out of the oven. I hope you like roast chicken!"

"We love it," Evan said and then hung back, letting Rory go in ahead of him so he could take a moment to adjust his slacks to accommodate the hard-on he was currently sporting. He was no stranger to sex, and he loved women in all their various shapes and sizes, but his reaction to a simple hug from Jess was more intense than anything he'd ever experienced before. *If you get this hard from a hug, what's it going to be like when we're both inside her, making her come?*

The thought came out of nowhere and he had to bite back a groan at the erotic images that accompanied it. He was still in a daze when he heard Rory's mocking laughter in the back of his mind and he knew he'd been projecting his thoughts.

"Right there with ya," Rory's mental voice confessed.

They were so screwed.

"Please leave your jackets on the chair and I'll hang them up in a second. I need to get this out of the oven!" Jess called out as she placed her roses carefully on a countertop and bent over to check on their dinner, inadvertently presenting both of them with a stunning view of her heart-shaped ass.

"You need some help in there?" Evan asked,

shrugging out of his jacket and passing it to Rory on his way by. "Wow, nice kitchen," he exclaimed as he came closer and realized that every appliance was modern and nearly new, right down to the espresso maker on the counter.

"My dad ordered a bunch of renovations a few years back. He said it was to increase the rental income on the house." Jess lifted a roasting pan full of vegetables out of the oven and set it down on a silicone pad, then leaned back down to retrieve what Evan assumed was the chicken. He couldn't see anything other than the way her jeans were hugging her curves as she struggled to lift their dinner out of the oven. He stepped up behind her and reached around to help her steady the tray, trying to keep his mind on dinner and not on the fact her ass was now rubbing up against the erection he'd been hoping to hide from her.

Well, too late to stop that horse from leaving the stable at a gallop.

He watched the blush climb up her neck as she realized he was wrapped around her, and Evan was tempted to brush a kiss over the heated skin below her ear.

"I got it, sweetheart." He finally looked at their dinner and burst out laughing. "Whatever the hell it is. I hate to ask, but why is our entree sitting up and looking like it's about to take a walk?"

"It's beer-can chicken." Jess laughed as they managed to maneuver themselves over to the counter and set the tray down on another pad.

Rory came over to join them, staring at their dinner in some amusement.

"Does that bird have a beer can up his…" He trailed off

and leaned over. "You've got a dark streak in you, sweet Jess."

She burst out laughing. "It's not like I did that to it while it was alive! And the beer bastes the chicken from the inside out. You'll see, it's amazing."

"Wait, so there's beer in that can?" Evan asked. "You cooked us a beer for dinner? I think I'm in love."

"Beer, garlic, and some of the dry rub I coated the chicken with."

Rory grinned at Evan over Jess's head. "She can cook. We're saved."

"You seemed to manage yesterday's lunch just fine," she pointed out, looking slightly puzzled.

Evan barked with laughter. "I'm afraid that's as good as Rory's cooking gets. Though he can manage a pretty mean omelet, too. He was pulling out all the stops in hopes of impressing you."

Jess smiled at them and then left the circle of Evan's arms to see to the potatoes. "Well, it worked, because I was impressed. Now I am hoping to impress the two of you with a proper thank you meal. Everything here needs just a few minutes. Shall I get us some wine glasses and we can open that bottle you gave me? Oh, and I need to get the roses in water before they wilt."

Jess started moving around the kitchen like a hummingbird, flitting here and there with what he could clearly see was nervousness. Taking the bull by the horns, he stepped into her path as she turned to hand him several wine glasses. She squawked with surprise and started to step backward, but Evan moved with her across the floor until she bumped up against the cabinets.

"Sweetheart, relax." He took the glasses and set them

down on the nearest countertop. He grazed his knuckles down her cheek and marveled at how soft her skin was.

"I'm not used to having anyone else in the kitchen, that's all."

"Liar," Evan used his arms to cage her in as he stepped in close enough their bodies were connected from thigh to chest. "You're feeling exactly the same thing we are, aren't you?"

"I—what?" She blinked up at him, confusion and desire at war in the depths of her crystalline eyes.

Unable to resist, Evan dipped his head and feathered a delicate kiss over her trembling lips. She tensed and lifted her hands to his chest, but instead of pushing him away, her fingers curled into his shirt and held on.

"So what happened to our plan to go slow and easy?" Rory asked dryly from somewhere behind him.

Evan grinned down at Jess's flushed face and stood up slowly, happy to note she didn't move her hands from his chest. "Change of tactics."

"You two had a plan?" Jess asked as her curious gaze darted between them.

"Not so much a plan, really. More a fervent hope you'd still be interested in getting to know us better," Evan explained.

"Well, I think the answer to that is…" Jess flashed them both a grin and reached for a wine glass. "More booze. I am not ready to discuss this, at least not while completely sober."

"Fair enough." Evan stepped back and gave her enough room to move again, immediately missing her soft warmth.

"What can I do to help?"

"You could start by getting out of my way, blondie."

"Blondie?" Evan reached out to tweak a purple-streaked lock of hair. "What does that make you then, Barney?"

"Barney?" Rory asked, confused. "Why do you think she looks like one of the Flintstones?"

"Not Barney Rubble, Barney the Dinosaur. Big, purple, slightly creepy?" Evan shook his head. "You have to forgive him, sweetheart. He lives in his own world, and they don't have much pop culture there apparently."

"If you want dinner, you better not call me Barney." Jess laughed and slipped past Evan to hand Rory the bottle of wine. "Could you please open that for me, Rory?"

"The streaks were my best friend's idea. Coming here was supposed to be a fresh start, and she figured this was a good way to mark the occasion." She touched the strands and nibbled on her lower lip. "Do you think it's too much?"

"Just the streaks?" Rory asked as he effortlessly popped the cork from the bottle and came around to the other side of the counter to pour their drinks.

"Afraid so. The old lady hair is all me. It runs in the family." Jess ducked her head, avoiding looking at either of them as she left the kitchen to scoop their jackets off the back of a chair and hung them up beside the door.

Evan glanced at Rory and let his concern for Jess flow along the connection between them. Rory nodded his understanding and Evan hung back as his blood-brother set down the wine bottle and crossed the room to where Jess was taking far longer than she needed to hang up their coats.

"Baby, you shouldn't put yourself down like that."

Rory folded her into his arms, drawing their woman back against his chest.

"That's sweet of you to say," Jess murmured and started to move away from him, only to have Rory tighten his hold.

"Don't you dare say 'but' and then argue with me. You're beautiful. You have two men standing right here who are very much in agreement on that topic, so you're already outvoted."

That sweet blush crept up Jess's cheeks again and Evan felt his cock swell in response. He couldn't wait to teach Jess how lovely he and Rory thought she was.

Rory dropped a kiss to the crown of Jess's hair and told her, "You've got gorgeous hair. It's like moonlight dancing on the ocean."

Evan's jaw nearly dropped to the floor. *Moonlight on the ocean?* He wanted to interrupt and ask Rory who he was and what he'd done with the real Rory Frazier. Still, if Rory could keep up the charm, maybe they would have a shot at convincing Jess they were serious about wanting her in their lives.

CHAPTER EIGHT

JESS SAT in her chair and watched in appreciation as the two men cleared the table. She'd tried to do it herself, but they'd each laid a gentle hand on her shoulders and guided her back to her chair.

"You cook, we clear," they'd said at almost the same time, and she'd been too busy laughing to try to argue. The wine had been excellent, and she could still feel the slight buzz she'd picked up after her third glass. They'd tucked into the meal with relish, and she suspected she was glowing from all the compliments that had accompanied the meal.

Or it could be I'm glowing because I am having dinner with two of the hottest men I've ever seen, and both of them have made it very clear they want to date me. Together.

Evan went to put the cling-wrapped leftovers into the fridge and she watched his face light up as he spotted desert.

"You got lemon tarts from Sandy's Bakery? Score! I get

dibs." He pulled out the tray and nearly ran back to the table with Rory close behind him.

"How can you possibly still be hungry?" she asked them both as Rory reappeared at the table, too, already reaching for one of the éclairs.

"You two hang on a second and I'll grab us some plates. Oh! I was going to make us some peppermint schnapps hot-chocolates, too, if you two think you'll have room?"

She grinned at the instant reaction she got from the two of them as they both looked up from their dessert selections to nod enthusiastically.

"We'll have room," Rory declared.

"Want a hand?" Evan offered as Jess got to her feet.

"You've done more than you should have already, considering you're my guests. You sit down and relax. I've got this."

Jess brought a few plates to the table and then made quick work of combining all the ingredients and setting it on the stove to heat. She set three mugs onto the top of the espresso machine to heat, and she was retrieving the whipped cream from the fridge when she sensed another presence in the kitchen.

"When you said you were making hot chocolate, I thought you meant hot water and a packet of instant mix. What are you doing in here, sweetheart?"

"I'm making you two a proper hot chocolate for dessert. It won't take long." She shooed Evan out of the kitchen with her hands. When one of them came close to her she found it hard to think of anything past their broad shoulders and the way their hands felt when they stroked along her…She stopped that train of thought before she forgot what she was doing in the kitchen at all.

Evan didn't move, instead he folded his arms across his broad chest and crossed one leg over the other as he leaned back against the countertop. "Rory? You need to see this. She's got whipped cream."

"It's for the drinks!" Jess heard the scrape of a chair being moved back and then they were both in her kitchen, one of them on each side of the entranceway.

"I think we can wait a bit for the drinks," Rory said and glanced at Evan before nodding toward where she was standing. "Ev, turn off the stove."

There was something new in Rory's voice, a sense of command that she'd never heard from him before. Jess's stomach fluttered and her pussy clenched as Rory turned his dark-chocolate eyes to her.

"Jess, come here." Rory pointed to a spot directly in front of him and she froze, torn between some strange desire to obey him and her fear of what might happen if she did.

Evan reached past her and turned off the element and moved the saucepan away from the heat, completely ignoring her.

"I said, come here." Rory's gaze locked onto hers and Jess felt her pulse quicken as a shiver danced down her spine. She took a single step in his direction and was immediately rewarded with a faint smile that softened his fierce expression.

"I'm not going to hurt you, baby. I just want you to do as I say."

"He's bossy that way. You'll get used to it," Evan

whispered behind her. He was close enough she could feel the warmth of his body, but he was not quite touching her.

Jess took the final three steps to the spot right in front of Rory, the bottle of whipped cream still in her hand. He took it from her and set it aside before cupping her chin in his hand and coaxing her head up so she was looking in his eyes.

"Dinner was amazing, and Evan and I are going to enjoy the pastries and the hot chocolate later, but for right now I know there's only one thing I really want for dessert."

The callused tip of Rory's thumb traced the outline of her lips as he stared into her eyes. He wanted her, she could see it. His expression, the heat in his eyes, everything was sending her a very clear message. He wanted her.

Jess nodded, the barest tip of her head, but it was signal enough for Rory. His mouth was a searing brand as he claimed her, his fingers spearing into her hair as he drew her up onto her toes. A low growl rumbled up from the depths of his chest and Jess felt the vibration traveling from his body to hers. Jess reached up and wrapped her hands around the back of his neck. She was still standing on her tiptoes and their bodies were fused together from thigh to chest. Her heart was hammering against her ribs and her senses were scrambled. His tongue traced the seam of her lips and she parted them, inviting him into the warm depths of her mouth so she could savor his smoky taste again.

Evan came up behind her, his powerful body pressing up against hers, pushing her into Rory so that she was caught in a vise made of muscle and heat. Evan's hands traced down the inside of her arms, stroking her through the silky fabric of her top and sending waves of goosebumps chasing along her skin. Evan slid his hands between her body and Rory's, palming her breasts and squeezing them as he rocked the hard shaft of his cock against the small of her back. Each press of Evan's body against her back arched Jess into Rory, and she could feel the long, thick evidence of Rory's arousal pressing into her stomach.

Need sizzled through Jess and she moaned, the sensation of being sandwiched between two hot, hard bodies almost more than she could bear. When she moaned Rory took their kiss deeper, teasing and tasting every corner of her mouth as if he were a man savoring his last meal.

Evan nuzzled his face into her hair, his mouth sucking and nibbling at the soft skin of her neck. The sensory onslaught sent a flood of liquid flowing from Jess's pussy and she shifted her body so that Rory's thigh slid between hers. Mindless with need, she rubbed her aching clit against his leg, arching her hips in time to the slow, sensual thrusts of Evan's hips against her back.

This time both men growled in stereo, and the deep vibration of their response was the most erotic thing Jess had ever experienced. When Evan's fingers pinched her nipples, her knees turned to water and she would have fallen if not for the steady solid support of their bodies holding her up, keeping her trapped between them.

Rory sensed what had happened and lifted his head, breaking their kiss to smile down at her with heat sparkling in his deep brown eyes.

"Even better than those lemon tarts, right, Evan?"

"Hell yes. No comparison." Evan nipped her neck lightly and lifted his head as well. "She tastes as sweet as I remember."

Rory gently untangled his fingers from Jess's hair and lowered his arms to his sides. The two men were looking at each other, and Jess could have sworn they were having some sort of conversation, despite the fact that neither of them said a word. That strange feeling she'd been left out of something got stronger when Evan released her and stepped back, leaving her clinging to Rory. The moment Evan was gone she felt colder, and she knew it was more than his body heat she was missing. When the three of them had been together, she had felt complete in a way she'd never imagined possible.

"Come on, baby. We're not done with you yet," Rory said, a sexy smile tugging at his lips.

He leaned down and scooped her into his arms, carrying her out of the kitchen as she looked around wild-eyed.

"But dessert!" She gestured back to the kitchen and then again to the table as he carried her right past it and over to the couch in the living room.

"I told you, we'll get to that part of dessert later." Rory settled his big body onto the couch and settled her crosswise in his lap so that her back was against the armrest and her feet rested on the cushions. It didn't take long for Evan to join them, flicking the fireplace switch with one elbow on his way in. He claimed the spot beside Rory, and Jess had to pull her feet in as he sat down.

Her eyes widened and she realized he hadn't come empty-handed, but Rory had his arm wrapped around her waist and she knew there was no point in struggling. Not that she really wanted to. Evan had brought in a washcloth and a towel he'd clearly snagged out of the kitchen, along with the whipped cream canister and the bottle of chocolate sauce she'd used to make the hot chocolate.

"Now I'm going to have dessert," Evan told her and her body hummed with anticipation. He gathered her feet up and lifted them into his lap, and Jess felt Rory's arm tighten around her as Evan began slowly washing her feet. The cloth was warm and wet and Evan took his time, especially with her toes.

"This polish matches the roses we bought you." He stroked a fingertip over one polished toenail and then along the top of her foot to her ankle. "I think it's my favorite color for you."

"I like it, too," Jess whispered, her voice barely more than a whisper.

Rory gently brushed back her hair from her neck and started nibbling his way from her shoulder up to her ear. "Don't be nervous, baby. If this gets to be too much, just say so."

"This is all a bit surreal."

Evan kept up his ministrations as he glanced over at her and winked. "What, you've never had two guys cuddle up on the couch with you before?"

She laughed. "Whatever is going on here, it's definitely more than us cuddling."

"That's up to you, sweetheart." Evan finished washing one foot and dried it just as carefully before moving onto her other one. "I know what Rory and I want, but you're the one calling the shots."

Warmth blossomed deep in Jess's heart and spread

outward, lightening her spirit and easing away the last of her worries. "I thought you said Rory was the bossy one?"

"I am." Rory growled into her neck and then nipped at her earlobe. "But that doesn't mean I'm going to force you to do something you don't want to do."

Jess leaned back and closed her eyes, reveling in the luxury of having two men's complete attention. "I trust you," she told them and was rewarded with a low, approving growl from Rory.

"Good."

She felt Rory's hand move to cup her breast and her nipple instantly tightened to a diamond-hard nub. Callused fingers stroked and teased at her areola, sending tingles and flashes of pleasure through her body and making her clit throb. Evan finished washing her foot and she sighed softly as he began to massage the arch even as he was drying the last of the moisture off her skin. Evan worked the tight muscles of her feet firmly, lifting her foot higher as he worked his knuckles into the arch. Jess groaned in appreciation and then gasped as Evan's tongue swirled over the top of her big toe. Her eyes flew open and she found herself staring into Evan's bright blue gaze as he slowly lifted her foot higher and sucked her toe into his mouth completely.

"Do you like that, baby?" Rory murmured by her ear. Jess tried to speak but all that came out of her mouth was a low, breathy moan.

"I think she likes that, Ev. Better do it again to be sure."

Evan ran the tip of his tongue around her toes again and this time Rory timed his caress of her nipple to coincide with the subtle bob of Evan's head. The resulting flood of pleasure nearly sent Jess rocketing to orgasm then and there, and she cried out in shock and amazement.

Evan brushed a kiss to her toes before lifting his head and setting her foot down so she could feel the hard ridge of his cock straining beneath the fly of his trousers. "Fuck me, that is so sexy. Sweetheart if you are going to go off like that just from us touching you fully clothed, then I cannot wait to see what happens when we get you naked."

Jess managed a crooked smile as she struggled to catch her breath. "Honestly? Me either," she confessed. Both men groaned and Rory gently caught her chin, turning her head so he could kiss her deeply.

While she was distracted, Evan picked up her foot again, and she squealed in surprise as something cold and sticky was suddenly drizzled over her toes.

Rory broke their kiss to glare at Evan. "Damn it, a little warning next time!"

"Sorry." Evan didn't look the slightest bit sorry as he added another squirt of chocolate sauce to the top of Jess's foot and then leaned his head down to lick it off with slow, careful swipes of his tongue.

"You're going to get chocolate on your shirt," Jess observed.

Evan ignored her and Rory just chuckled. "If he does, would you be all right with him taking it off?"

Jess swallowed and then nodded. "Yes."

"You hear that, Ev?"

Evan deliberately ran his finger through a swirl of chocolate and then drew a line down the pocket of his shirt with the sticky syrup. "Oops. Guess you were right, sweetheart."

"That's cheating!" she protested and was about to say

more when Rory cut her off with a kiss that melted her brain and turned her insides to mush.

Rory's tongue swept into Jess's mouth and twined with hers. His kiss was almost brutally intense, pushing her body to react in kind. Flames of passion flared deep inside her and she twisted her upper body around so she could face him, allowing her to deepen the kiss as she reached up and slid her hands into the dark mane of Rory's hair. As she tugged it he groaned and she felt a shudder run through him. She tugged at his hair again, harder this time and his cock twitched against her hip in response.

"You're playing with fire, doing that to him." Evan's voice sounded like it was a long way off and Jess cracked one eye open to peek at him.

Evan had stripped off his shirt and was watching Jess and Rory, a look of pure lust gleaming in his eyes as he slowly stroked his fingers over Jess's foot. As Evan met her gaze he lifted her foot to his mouth again and started devouring the chocolate sauce still stuck to her skin. Jess moaned into Rory's open mouth and her world spun out of kilter yet again as a hand slid under her top to play with her breasts. Her mind was so hazy it took her a moment to figure out it was Rory touching her, teasing her nipples with strong, rough fingers.

Jess wondered what it would be like to have both of them making love to her at once, two handsome men working together to give her so much pleasure that she'd lose track of who was doing what to her body. The thought added yet another layer of arousal to what she was already experiencing, as she lay with her body cradled in the laps of her two men. Jess froze as she realized that was how she felt about them, Rory and

Evan were *her* men. *How the hell did that happen so quickly?*

They both sensed her tension and stopped what they were doing to look at her, and Jess felt her heart twist as she felt herself the focus of so much tender concern.

"What's wrong, sweetheart?" Evan asked as he settled her feet into his lap and wrapped his warm hands around her ankles.

"Do you want us to stop?" Rory stroked her cheek, his dark eyes staring into hers.

"No." Jess hesitated for a moment and then let the truth burble out of her mouth. "No, I don't want you to stop. I realized something, that's all. You and Evan, you're mine. At least I think of you that way. I know that sounds strange, but I do."

She blushed so deeply it felt like her cheeks had been scalded and even the tips of ears were tingling.

"We are," Rory said simply, his voice low and husky.

Evan nodded his agreement. "We've been yours since we pulled you out of the water, sweetheart. And you belong to us." His fingers tightened around Jess's ankles as Rory's free arm reached around her stomach to pull her tighter into his lap.

"Ours," Rory growled.

Evan snickered. "Dude, try using words with more than one syllable. She's going to think you've gone caveman on her."

Jess laughed and leaned back into Rory's arms, enjoying the moment. "If he starts grunting and dragging me back to his cave, you have to promise to help me, Evan. Otherwise, I think it's sort of cute."

"I am not *cute!*" Rory grumbled, sounding almost

petulant. "Ev's the cute, delicate one. Please don't mix us up, baby."

"I think you're both cute." Jess moved her foot slightly, running her toes along the length of Evan's erection. "Cute, sexy, wonderful...do you want me to go on or are you appeased for now?"

"You forgot handsome," Evan teased her.

"You're right, I did. But I'm not hearing a whole lot of compliments coming back this way, so I think I'm keeping that one to myself for now." Jess couldn't believe the things coming out of her mouth. She'd never been like this with any of her boyfriends, not even Brad, and they'd lived together for a time. There was something about these two men that made her feel sexy and a little wild, and she wanted to feel like this more often.

"Have we been skimping on the compliments, Rory?" Evan asked with a grin.

"Maybe. But my mother always taught me it was rude to talk with my mouth full, so I suspect that's been the problem." Rory nuzzled her ear. "You're gorgeous, and tasty, and sweet, and possibly the best cook I've ever met. Just don't tell my mom I said so."

"You're also, sexy, sweet, and have the prettiest feet, sweetheart."

"That's better," Jess beamed and blushed and felt her heart swell with happiness.

"Now, I think that maybe you two should let me up so we can have those hot chocolates. If we're really going to try this, then I have a few questions."

"Ev, you make the hot chocolate. I'm not ready to let her up yet."

Evan shook his head at Rory. "Not a chance. I'm very comfy right here myself."

"I think I can give you both some incentive to let me up." Jess took a quick breath and blurted out her idea before she could think twice about it. "You let me up, and we can all go down to the hot tub to drink and talk. Deal?"

Both of them went completely still, and she had to laugh when she saw the look of hopeful lust on both their faces.

"You have a hot tub?" Evan found his voice first. "Where? And why aren't we already in it?"

"It's outside, under the gazebo. You're telling me you guys have been driving past that headland all this time and didn't realize there was a hot tub in there? It's *huge*! How did you miss it?"

"When we're on the water, we're not looking at the shore, baby. I've seen the gazebo, but I never realized there was a tub out there." Rory dipped his head to whisper in her ear. "Evan and I didn't bring swimsuits."

Jess's pussy clenched and her stomach did a complete roll at the thought of getting into the water with these two naked. "Then I guess I better not put one on either, just to be fair."

The next thing Jess knew, she was on her feet and being half carried back to the kitchen by a laughing Evan, with Rory only a few steps behind. "So make that hot chocolate already! We'll pack up some of these desserts to nibble on. What are you waiting for?"

CHAPTER NINE

JESS WENT FIRST, carrying a small tray of pastries and trying not to think about what she was about to do. Not that it was easy to pretend everything was normal when she was wearing her bathrobe, rubber boots, and nothing else at all. The guys were walking behind her, and they were laughing with every step they took. They'd started the moment she'd slipped her bare feet into her boots and they hadn't stopped yet.

"I had no idea that rain boots were sexy, did you, Rory?"

"I don't think they are, unless they have little pink ducks on the side. Then I think they are smoking hot."

"My hiking boots sank to the bottom of the ocean yesterday, and I didn't pack slippers! And I thought the ducks were cute." Jess tossed a glance back over her shoulder and stuck her tongue out at the two men following her. "The way it rains out here, I'm amazed you haven't all gone permanently pruned."

Evan had insisted on carrying the tray with their

drinks, and Rory had an armload of towels so they could dry off before making the walk back to the house. All three of them stopped as Jess stepped into the shelter of the gazebo and set down the tray on one of the narrow benches that lined the wall. She flipped on the power and smiled as the soft glow of a hundred or more fairy lights lit up the area without making it too bright to see the ocean outside.

"Very nice," Evan set down his tray and turned his attention to the cover on the hot tub. "Give me a hand here, Rory. Cute as that outfit is on our girl, I'm betting she's getting pretty chilly."

He dropped his load in a pile on the bench and went to help Evan lift the cover, leaving Jess staring out at the darkness as she absently refolded the towels, stacking them neatly. When she was done she fished a scrunchie out of the pocket of her robe and twisted her hair up into a knot so it wouldn't get wet. Behind her she could hear the two men lift the cover and set it on end so that it provided a sort of shelf where they could rest their drinks and the desserts she'd brought down.

Almost on cue, the voice of her self-doubt started whispering in the back her mind. *What are you doing out here? When you take off that robe there is no way they are going to want you. Don't you think you should at least turn out the lights?* Jess squeezed her eyes shut and wrapped her arms around herself, holding tight as the barrage of negativity continued inside her head. She was almost ready to bolt for the house when a pair of strong arms encircled her and drew her back against a warm, bare chest. A faint whiff of citrus tickled her nose and she knew who held her. *Evan.*

"You've gone quiet, sweetheart. Everything all right?"

"Just thinking too much."

"I know the solution to that." He brushed a kiss to her cheek and slid a chilled hand inside her robe to palm her breast. "Let us distract you."

"You're sure?" Jess hated sounding so uncertain, but she knew she needed to hear them say it again.

"We've never been more sure of anything in our lives," Rory spoke as he moved, coming around to face her as he stepped in close enough they were touching chest to chest.

"My sexy bookends." She smiled up at him, loving the way it felt when they both held her like this. When they were like this, it was impossible to have doubts.

"I like the sound of that," Evan nuzzled her hair and removed his hand from inside her robe, letting it fall to the knotted belt at her waist. "Do you want us to promise not to peek so you can get in without feeling embarrassed? I know you're feeling shy, and that's all right."

Jess wrapped one arm around Rory's waist and reached down to squeeze Evan's hand at the same time. "Thank you for understanding."

Rory looked at her, puzzled. "Baby, you're beautiful. Why don't you want us to see you?"

"Soon, okay? But not yet," Jess promised. "You two are drop-dead gorgeous, it's going to take me a little while to get used to the idea that you want to be with me."

"One day you're going to give me the name of the guy who convinced you that you're not beautiful, and I'm going to go and kick his ass," Evan muttered darkly.

"No, *we're* going to go and kick his ass. And then thank him for being stupid enough to let you go so we could get our chance." Rory leaned down and kissed her gently and then stepped back again, making a show of turning out toward the water, his eyes firmly locked on the moon as it played peek-a-boo with the clouds.

"You two are too good to be true, thank you."

Evan kissed her cheek and then stepped over beside Rory, leaving her privacy to undress and get into the hot tub.

The moment Jess undid her robe the chill of the night air bit into her skin and she almost scampered over to the tub, dropping her robe in a hasty tangle and kicking off her boots as she stepped up and into the water.

"Hot!" she yelped as the temperature of the water reminded her that she'd let her bare legs go nearly numb with cold. It was a painful few seconds as she waited for her body to adjust, but finally she was up to her neck in the water, watching the steam rise from the surface as she settled back into one of the seats with a contented sigh. Instead of telling them it was all right to turn around, Jess took the time to truly look at the two men who had made such an impact on her life. Both of them were tall, but Evan stood an inch or two higher than Rory, while Rory was broader across the chest and shoulders, bulkier whereas Evan was sculpted, his body a little leaner. Jess knew Evan had to be feeling the cold as he stood there shirtless, but he showed no sign of it. Feeling a little guilty for having kept them both waiting, she crossed her arms over her chest and called out to them.

"You can turn around now."

Both of them turned and she was greeted to two nearly identical expressions of eager desire as they both moved toward her at the same time. Evan had the advantage of already being shirtless, and Jess realized he'd already managed to toe off his shoes while they'd been waiting for her to get into the water. As a result, Evan was well ahead of Rory and he didn't hesitate to shed his pants and boxer briefs, giving Jess an eyeful of glorious and very aroused male flesh as he hopped into the water and hauled her into his lap. Evan was sex personified, and he was all hers.

"You snooze, you lose," he mocked Rory and then lifted a dripping hand out of the water to point to the control panel. "Last one in has to stop and turn on the jets."

Rory grumbled, still unbuttoning his shirt. "So that's why you didn't bother getting dressed before coming outside."

"I was planning ahead," Evan gloated and then gave Jess a hot, sultry kiss, his muscular arms pinning her against the hard planes of his body so she didn't float away from him. "I wanted to steal her away from you for a few minutes."

As the jets roared to life Evan groaned and settled his back firmly against one of the nozzles. "I've died and gone to heaven. Good food, good company, a hot tub by the ocean, and an angel in my arms."

Jess couldn't argue, not when she was pretty sure Evan was right, that this *was* heaven. Evan held her close and she could feel every inch of his gorgeous body, including the rock-hard length of his cock that brushed up against her ass with every small move she made.

She ran a wet hand down his chest, enjoying the chance to explore. He didn't have much chest hair, but what he did have was the same tawny blond as the hair on his head. Come summertime, she imagined it would turn a sun-kissed gold, and part of her hoped she would still be here to see it.

Beside them Rory was still undressing, and she looked up from Evan's chest to drink in Rory's body. His chest was as broad as she'd remembered, and her fingers already itched to stroke through the dark hair that dusted across his pectoral muscles and then formed a treasure trail that led her eyes downward. Rory caught her staring and his hands froze on his zipper as he gave her a feral grin that made her squirm in Evan's lap as she squeezed her thighs together.

"You've got her all hot and bothered, bro." Evan slid a hand down her tummy until his fingertips rested at the crest of her mound. He dropped his voice to a whisper. "Do you like what you see, Jess?"

Blushing wildly, Jess nodded.

"Say it," Rory instructed her in a commanding tone. "I want to hear you say it."

Jess opened her mouth but no words came out. She didn't know what to say, or how to say it. This was a whole new world for her and she was certain she was going to screw it up.

"They're only words, sweetheart." Ethan insinuated his finger the tiniest bit lower, parting her labia before he stopped moving again. "If you say it, Rory will let me reward you."

Jess quivered and her gaze flew up to meet Rory's.

"Tell me what you're thinking, baby. Evan won't move his hand until you do."

Jess tried to buck her hips against Evan's fingers, but he moved with her and laughed. "Now she's cheating!"

"Jessica James, don't you *dare* move until you tell me what you're thinking!" Rory's tone brooked no argument and Jess was stunned by the authority he poured into every word.

"I think you're both gorgeous, and I really wish you'd hurry up and get undressed and get in here with us," she babbled her answer and then added. "And no one has called me by my full name since I got too big to be spanked!"

Rory's nostrils flared as he leaned forward, his hands still on the fly of his trousers. "Believe me, baby, you're not too big to be spanked."

Jess's jaw dropped open and she stared up at Rory in shock. He couldn't possibly have meant that...could he? Before she could ask Rory nodded to Evan and Evan's fingers dove into her pussy, rubbing hard against her clit.

Jess moaned, her hips writhing against the pleasurable pressure. Rory finally moved his hands, undoing his pants and sliding them down his hips. Jess realized he wasn't wearing any underwear, and her entire pussy clenched, her inner walls suddenly aching with the need to be filled. Rory's cock rose up almost to his navel, the tip already engorged and gleaming with pre-cum.

Evan's clever fingers were making it hard for her to think, but she managed to reach for Rory with trembling fingers, and he took her hand as he finished kicking off his clothing and stepped up and into the tub.

"Is she as responsive as I think she is?" he asked Evan.

"Better."

"Then I think we should let her come before we start discussing how this is all going to work. A demonstration might help make things clearer."

Jess whimpered as Evan kept stroking her clit, up and down in a slow, leisurely rhythm.

"Would you like that, Jess?" Rory asked, his tone dark and commanding. "And don't you dare just nod. I want to hear you say it."

"Yes, please."

"Oh god, she said please," Evan groaned and flicked her clit harder.

"Now that's sexy." Rory lowered himself into the water until only his head and neck were visible and Jess realized he was kneeling on the floor of the tub. "You got to taste her cute little toes, Ev. So I'm going to be the first to taste her pussy."

"What?" The word flew out of her mouth before she'd thought of anything else to say.

"Trust me, we've got this." Rory reached out and snagged her ankles in his hands, drawing her feet up to his shoulders. "You got her, Ev? We don't want her getting a dunking or I think she's going to have a few things to say to us."

Evan's fingers left her pussy and she bit back a mewl of frustration at the loss of contact. Evan reached up around her ribcage and then crossed his arms near the wrist so he had her in a firm hold, his hands eagerly cupping her breasts. "Got her," he told Rory and brushed a kiss to the side of her mouth. "You may want to hold onto something, sweetheart."

"Why would I—oh!" Jess exclaimed as Rory lifted her legs over his shoulders and moved toward her until her hips were clear of the water and her pussy was a scant few centimeters from his mouth.

"That's why." Evan chuckled and pinched her nipples between his fingertips as Rory's hands came over her thighs and parted her labia. Without another word Rory lowered his head and let his tongue swipe along the entire length of her pussy and Jess cried out at the pleasure of it.

She clutched at Evan's wrists, bracing herself against the sensual onslaught that Rory's mouth and tongue were unleashing on her clit.

Rory plunged a long, thick finger into her channel and groaned. "She's so tight." The words came out muffled, but Evan clearly understood because his arms tightened around Jess and he kissed her hard.

Jess's body was a sponge, soaking up every glorious touch and sensation. Hands and mouths stroked and sucked until she was quivering and panting, suspended on the precipice of an orgasm. Evan lifted his head and stared into her eyes, his own gone a stormy blue-gray in his passion.

"I want to watch you come. I want to see your beautiful face when it happens." He pinched her nipples harder than before. "Come for us, Jess."

His words triggered her release and her body shattered into a thousand pieces, each one of them vibrating with the force of her orgasm. Jess's heels drummed against Rory's back as she arched hard against his mouth, and she could feel the rumbling vibration of his groan as he drew her clit into his mouth and focused all of his attention on the sensitive pearl.

Evan carefully kept her head above the water as she bucked and thrashed, so lost in her pleasure she could do nothing but trust in the two men holding her. Rory's tongue lashing extended her release, demanding nothing less than her complete surrender. Only when the last of her shuddering cries finally quieted did their touches gentle, soothing her instead of arousing. As Rory submerged his shoulders and freed her legs to drift, Jess could barely find the strength to sit up and lift her head from Evan's chest.

She was passed from Evan to Rory and she didn't have the energy to do anything more than curl into his arms and lay her head on his shoulder.

Rory held her wrapped in his strong arms, but she could also feel Evan's hand resting lightly on her hip as if he wasn't ready to let go of her completely.

"That was..." Evan trailed off, a note of awe in his voice.

"Indescribable," Jess whispered.

"Just the beginning," Rory added and hugged her closer. "If you're still interested, that is."

"I thought you said he didn't have a sense of humor?" Jess glanced at Evan and then back at Rory with a shy smile. "I wanted you both before this. Now? Now I want to know how this is going to work."

"Ev, grab us those drinks, will you?" Rory nodded to the tray and the three of them rearranged themselves so that Jess was sitting in Rory's lap, her legs entwined with Evan's to serve as a sort of anchor. As they all sipped their hot chocolate, both men paused and then downed a healthy measure of the contents before they stopped again.

"So that's what it's supposed to taste like." Evan grinned. "I'm never going back to powdered pouches of crap again."

"It tastes like a chocolate candy cane. What's in this?" Rory asked and scooped a finger's worth of half-melted whipped cream out of the mug and offered it to Jess. She sucked the cream and his finger into her mouth, swirling the tip of her tongue over him slowly, savoring him and his offering.

"I'm pretty sure she can't answer your question if you've got your finger in her mouth," Evan pointed out, his expression one of complete enthrallment.

She released Rory with a laugh and shrugged. "It's nothing special - milk, chocolate sauce, a pinch of cinnamon, and a dollop of peppermint schnapps." Jess licked her lips playfully. "And of course, whipped cream."

She felt Rory's cock pulse to life beneath her, and a fresh surge of arousal coursed through her in response. She'd never come so hard in her life, and now she was eager to go again. Her men had quite the effect on her, and she was quickly learning to love it.

She took a drink and tried to organize her thoughts, but she quickly realized there was only one way to ask what she wanted to know.

"So how does this work? Am I dating one of you and sleeping with you both? Dating both of you? Is this all going to be a secret?"

"You're dating both of us," Rory and Evan said in unison and she had to laugh at the possessive tone they were both using.

"Well, that's pretty clear." She grinned at them both. "And it's really cute the way you guys answered that together."

"She's calling us cute again," Evan grumbled.

"I noticed. We'll punish her for that later."

"Don't you dare bring up spanking me again. That is never, ever going to happen." Jess glowered playfully at Rory. "Forget it."

"Oh, sweetheart. It's rarely in your best interests to tell Rory something is *never* happening. He tends to take it as a challenge. Though in this case, I'm really going to enjoy watching how this unfolds. If I'm lucky, it'll turn out to be my new favorite fantasy."

Rory cleared his throat. "Do you want this to be a secret? The three of us?"

Jess sensed there was a lot riding on this answer, and she looked from Rory, to Evan and back again as she considered her answer. Both men were watching her with carefully blank expressions, but she could read the glimmer of hope that showed in both their eyes, peeking out from behind the masks they wore.

"I don't like secrets. I don't like lying, either. But I'm not the one who lives here full-time and has friends and family and jobs at stake. So if you want me to keep this a secret, I will."

"What do you mean you don't live here full time?" Rory's arms tightened around her and she felt Evan's hand return to her thigh.

"You said your father gave you the cabin, so we assumed you were going to be living here from now on." Evan's voice had an edge to it now, and when she looked at him there was a look of pure determination on his handsome face.

"Well, I'm staying for the winter, absolutely. I have to finish my book and this is the perfect place to do it. After that...I'm not sure. I like it here, but I haven't made up my mind yet."

"Stay," Evan asked her. "We just found you, Jess. Please don't say you're going to leave. We don't want to keep you a secret. We want to have you in our lives. I know this is all a bit fast, but believe me, this is not some sexual adventure we're on here. We want *you*. In our lives, in our bed, and in our house as soon as we can get you there."

All the blood drained from Jess's face and she suddenly felt light-headed. This couldn't be happening. Not like this, not so quickly.

"I think you're scaring her, Ev. Dial it back a bit before she decides were crazy."

"She can't leave us." Evan shook his head and looked over her shoulder to Rory. "You know that."

"But she doesn't know it, not yet." Rory pressed a kiss to Jess's cheek and then lowered his voice to a stage whisper. "You see what I mean? I told you, he's the delicate one, and a drama queen."

"Bite me," Evan snarked, but some of the intensity faded from his expression.

"That is never going to happen. The only one in this hot tub I'm planning on biting is Jess."

Jess took in a slow, cleansing breath and then let it out again before she started speaking. "So you two want to date me openly. No secrets?"

"Tofino isn't like Toronto, Jess. We're a lot more laid-back out here. We wouldn't be the only unconventional relationship in town, not by a long shot." Rory glanced at Evan and the two seemed to have another of their silent conversations. When it was done, Evan was the one who spoke next.

"My parents are in a polyamorous family group, so are Rory's. Many of the families that live in Kismet Bay have a two man, one woman ratio. It's the way we live."

"Really?" Jess was caught between relief and curiosity. Relief that if there were others already living this way, it wouldn't be necessary to hide it so much. And she was really curious to know how this could work in the long-term. "So if I stayed, we could live like that?"

"Could and would, baby. Evan and I have always known we'd live that way, if we could find the right woman to share our lives with."

"So you two..." Jess blushed and waved to the two of them. "You two aren't, um, *with* each other, right?"

"Did she just ask if we're banging each other?" Evan asked, spluttering and choking on the hot chocolate he'd been drinking as she'd asked her question.

"Hell no, we are not with each other that way!" Rory declared with a great deal of volume. "He's like a brother to me. I love him, but I'm not in love with him and I never will be. We're not bisexual, we only like women. Specifically we like one woman, you."

"Okay." Jess managed to keep most of the laughter out of her voice. Not all, but most. "So, do you guys have separate bedrooms?"

"She's getting down to the technical stuff now, so does that mean you're going to be with us?" Evan asked, looking hopeful.

"I'm seriously considering it, but I have a few more questions. And then there's something I need to tell both of you."

"I'm glad you're considering it, because if you do say no, I should warn you that we're not giving up that easily. It would be easier on all of us if you just give in now." Rory nuzzled her ear. "I'm not letting you go, baby. And to answer your question, yes, we have separate bedrooms. Our house was built for people with our lifestyle. It has two regular bedrooms and one large master suite with a bed big enough for three. Sometimes it will be all of us together, sometimes just one of us, and whenever you need time for yourself, that will be your bedroom and private space. We don't come in unless invited. At least that's how it works with my parents."

"You're talking like I'm moving in with you," she pointed out.

"I've seen your bed. We're not all going to fit that well," Evan observed with a laugh.

"I'm not ready for that, not yet. Bad enough I'm naked with both of you and have no intention of letting you go home tonight. But moving in when we've known each other barely more than a day? That might be moving a little fast."

Rory nodded. "We'll get you a key anyway, but you're right. This must be feeling a little fast for you."

"And it doesn't for you? Neither of you?" she asked, surprised by their instant denials.

"Nope."

"Not really," Rory told her. "But we've wanted this our whole adult lives."

"How many others have there been?" Jess asked, her mind suddenly filled with images of her men with other women, loving them, sharing them the way they were now sharing her.

It was Evan who answered. "If you're asking if we've ever shared a woman in bed before, then the answer is yes. But it wasn't all that often, and we've never taken a woman back to our house for sex. If you are there with us, you'll be the first and only woman we've ever brought home."

"Okay," Jess said simply and reached under the water to squeeze Evan's hand as she wrapped her free arm around Rory's neck. "This is insane, but I'd be crazier to say no and never give this a chance."

Both men whooped with pleasure and first Rory and then Evan kissed her until she was breathless. She finally managed to get them to stop long enough for her to get her breath back.

"Before you guys celebrate my lapse of sanity, there's one more thing you need to know."

Both of them looked at her, concern on their faces.

"What is it?"

"I didn't tell you the whole truth about what I do for a living."

"You're not a freelance writer?" Evan looked confused. "Why would you lie about that?"

"You lied?" Rory's voice was a low, unhappy snarl. "I don't like liars."

Jess twisted around to look at Rory and quailed at his dark expression. His eyes had narrowed and his lips were drawn down in a thin line.

Evan reached out to lay a hand on his arm. "Rory, stop it. You're scaring her! C'mere, sweetheart." Evan drew her out of Rory's arm and cradled her against his chest, and Jess burrowed against him.

"Chill out, bro, or you're going to ruin everything." Evan's hands stroked up and down her back, soothing her. "He didn't mean to scare you, Jess."

Jess nodded, but she didn't want to look at Rory. There was darkness in him she'd not seen until that moment, and that revelation stunned her.

"I'm sorry, baby." Rory's voice was softer now. "Jess, please look at me and tell me you forgive me?"

Jess looked up and fell into Rory's dark-brown eyes. He was looking at her with such regret, and one hand was reached out toward her, hovering a few inches away.

"Please?"

She let go of Evan to take Rory's hand and he squeezed her fingers tightly but made no move to draw her out of the security of Evan's embrace. "So, what do you do for a living?"

"I'm a novelist. I don't tell people that because they get a bit weird about it."

"Why would anyone get weird because you write books for a living?" Rory asked, but behind her she felt Evan's chest start to vibrate as he began to laugh.

"I think Evan's guessed the answer to that already."

"So, sweetheart. Just how successful a writer are you? New York Times Bestseller? Midlist? I Googled you and nothing came up under your real name, so I'm betting you write under a pseudonym."

She blushed and laughed at the same time. "You Googled me? Vivian is right, I totally suck at this dating thing. And uh, to answer your question, I've had a few books on the bestseller list."

"A few!" Evan whistled low. "So you're sexy, talented, can cook, and you're famous? Rory, we totally scored. I don't know what we did to deserve her, but I'm never giving her back."

"I'm hardly famous," Jess protested. "I do all right, but I'm hardly one of the rock stars of the writing world."

"What do you write?" Rory asked, still holding her hand tight.

"Crime thrillers. A series of them, actually. Though since my mother died I've barely written a word until I came out here. I'm way behind on my deadlines and my publisher is having kittens about it."

"Wait, this is too good to be true. You write *crime*

thrillers? Rory loves those things. They're the only books he owns that aren't about fishing or sailing. What are the titles of some of your books?"

Jess was so relieved that neither of them was weirded out by the idea of her being a bestselling novelist that she didn't really catch what Evan had said until she'd already started to speak, and by then it was too late.

"I'm sure you've never heard of them. I write the *Frieze and Flame* series."

"Those were written by a man," Rory said and then frowned. "At least I always thought they were. J. J. Ford, right?"

Evan started to snicker. "J. J. as in Jessica James? Oh fuck, this is hilarious. I think Rory here is your biggest fan, and he didn't even know you were a woman!"

Rory stood up, let go of Jess and used both hands to dunk Evan, who went under still burbling with laughter. Jess nearly went under with him, and the three of them wound up scrambling for their balance as the jets pushed them toward the center of the tub.

Large, strong hands wrapped around her hips and she found herself face to face with a grinning Rory, who lifted her up and kissed her as he walked her back to the edge of the tub and settled her into one of the seats again.

"I love your books," he told her between torrid kisses. "And I promise I won't get weird about the fact you're an amazing writer. But there's a good chance that I'm going to want you to sign all my books. Hardcovers and paperbacks."

"I can do you one better, big boy. When I'm finished with this manuscript, I'll let you be the first to read it."

"Deal." Rory fished his dropped mug out from the

bottom of the tub and set it back on the tray. "Now, can we please take you back up to the house and make love to you? I want to wake up tomorrow and be able to tell everyone I'm fucking the creator of Crystal Frieze."

"Aaand you just went weird on us." Evan stood up, shaking his head. "Don't mind him, sweetheart. He's really harmless."

Jess looked at her two men and shook her head. "I don't think either of you is harmless. But I also know neither of you is going to hurt me. I trust you." She opened her arms to them both and they closed in on her, wrapping her in two pairs of powerful arms.

"Now, take me to bed."

CHAPTER TEN

EVAN BARELY GAVE Jess time to grab a towel from the stack before he gathered her into his arms and sprinted for the cabin, laughing wildly.

"Hey Rory, bring up our clothes, will you?" he called back as he made a beeline for the cabin, stark naked and with a giggling woman in his arms.

"He's going to kill you when he catches up!" Jess exclaimed as she threw her arms around Evan's neck and held on for dear life.

"You're worth the risk."

He didn't slow down until they reached the cabin and he had to put her down to open the door. The moment they were inside he lifted her again, this time coaxing her to wrap her legs around his waist. His hands curved under her ass, holding her up as he carried her down the hallway, stopping halfway to give her a slow, lingering kiss. He heard Rory open the door again as he and Jess staggered into the bedroom, and Evan swore as he realized Rory was only seconds away from catching up.

"I should have locked the door. Maybe that would have slowed him down," Evan muttered and lowered Jess onto her bed, his body covering hers briefly before he rolled them both over so that Jess was straddling his hips. His cock was hard enough to pound nails, and he had to bite back a groan as the hot, slick lips of her pussy parted to enfold the length of his dick.

"Fuck that feels good!"

"If you two started without me, there's going to be trouble." Rory stepped into the room, still naked and gleaming wet from their time in the hot tub. Evan watched Jess's eyes widened as she appeared to drink in the sight of him framed by the doorway.

"It was Evan's idea," she told Rory and bent down to kiss Evan before he could protest his innocence.

"Somehow it doesn't look that way to me," Rory drawled and made his way to the bed, sitting down beside Evan before reaching out stroke the bare curve of Jess's ass. "You're the one pinning him to the bed, baby."

She opened her mouth to argue but it was too late to stop Rory as he lifted his hand and brought it down sharply on one full cheek of her ass.

"Hey!" she yelled, her body jerking in surprise more than pain, and Evan lost the ability to think as her pussy convulsed and he felt the tip of his dick breach her channel. He made a strangled noise and both Jess and Rory looked down at him in concern.

"A little warning...next time, please," he panted and shifted his hips enough for Jess to realize just what had changed thanks to her response to Rory's punishment.

Rory's lips curled into a wicked grin and he raised his hand again. "Consider yourself warned." He smacked Jess again on her other cheek and the wet, slapping sound made her flex and jump again despite the warning. This time Evan knew what was coming and he arched his hips at the moment Rory struck, letting his thick cock slide inside Jess's sweet pussy.

"Holy fuck, so good!" Evan reached up to hold her wrists, keeping her in place as he gave another playful buck of his hips and pushed himself a little further into her slick cunt.

"What am I getting spanked for?" Jess demanded, turning her head to glower at Rory.

"Calling us cute and not being honest about your writing career, for starters." He stroked his fingertips over the pink flesh of her ass cheek and then smacked her again, lightly this time. "And that's for starting without me."

She jerked again and Evan groaned as he pushed his cock all the way home. "Thank you, bro."

Jess's inner muscles flexed around Evan's dick, gripping him tightly as she slowly rolled her hips. "Don't thank him yet. You aren't wearing a condom. And that means we need to get ourselves untangled and start this again."

"No!" Evan howled in protest. "Oh hell no, please don't say that. You feel way too damned good to leave right now, sweetheart."

Rory leaned in over them both and swept a tendril of hair out of Jess's eyes before kissing her and murmuring, "You have our word that we're both totally clean. Unless you're not on the pill, we are completely safe."

"I'm on the pill, and I had a full physical a couple of months ago." She went quiet, but Evan could still feel her pussy flutter and pulse around his cock. "And I haven't been sexually active in over a year, so yeah, I'm safe."

"Thank you, universe." Evan sighed and bucked his hips again, more insistently this time. He wanted her so badly it hurt, and he didn't want any barriers between them. "So what are you waiting for, sexy?"

"Well, for starters, don't either of you want to turn off the lights?" Jess asked and Evan felt her tense up, her entire body tightening as she looked at him with something like panic in her pretty eyes. He hated seeing her doubt herself, and lying there, staring up at her, Evan made himself a promise that he'd help Jess see herself the way he and Rory did, beautiful, glorious, and sexy.

"You're doing it again." Evan frowned and released her wrists to cup her cheek, drawing her down for another kiss. "You're beautiful, Jess. So beautiful you take my breath away."

"The lights are staying on, baby. I want to see you when we make love to you. I never want you to think you have to hide from us." Rory moved so that he was kneeling by Evan's shoulder and fisted his swollen cock, pumping it slowly. "Ride him, Jess. I want to watch." He grinned at her and winked. "At least for now."

"Not until I'm done here, thank you," Evan quipped and then groaned in pleasure as Jess rolled her hips and let him glide even deeper into her warm, soft body.

"You feel so good around me, so hot and tight. This is what I've wanted since you woke up in my arms yesterday." Evan lifted his head to kiss her, his tongue slipping past her lips to stroke over hers in long, lazy swipes that matched the easy rhythm of her hips. He never took his eyes off of her, loving the way her eyes seemed to shimmer between blue and the palest silver as she grew more and more aroused. She fit around his cock like a velvet vise, gripping him tightly as she grew wetter with every thrust and grind.

Evan changed his angle slightly and she moaned, her head falling forward and her eyes closing as she drove her hips down onto his.

"I think you found her sweet spot," Rory murmured. "Is he making you feel good, baby?"

"Yes!" Jess cried out and Evan thrust again, drawing another broken cry from her as he felt her body shudder. He had her on the edge of an orgasm, but he wasn't ready to let her go over yet. Instead he held himself still, letting her take control. She rode him hard, her skin flushed and her breath coming in short, sharp pants as she used him to advance her own pleasure. Her hot channel narrowed around his dick and he felt her pussy flutter and pulse as she tried to bring herself over.

Evan and Rory had never used their link during their few joint sexual encounters. It hadn't felt right, but tonight Evan didn't hesitate to share what he was feeling with Rory, letting his blood-brother experience a small measure of the glory that was Jess's body.

Rory swore and his cock twitched, making Evan grin.

"My turn's coming," Rory told them both as his hand moved hard and fast, stroking himself in time to Jess's hips.

"Her turn comes first." Evan slipped a hand into Jess's pussy and pressed his fingers hard against her clit. Jess came on a wail, her body shaking so hard Rory reached out to rest a hand on her back to steady her. Her pussy gripped Evan's cock so hard he saw stars, and he lost the last shreds of his control and followed her into the abyss in the thrall of a mind-shattering orgasm.

"Now that was memorable," Rory commented and Evan cracked open one eye enough to be able to spot his blood-brother grinning down at them both.

"You have no idea how memorable," Evan groaned and ran his hands down Jess's back. He could feel her heart hammering against her ribs as she sprawled on top of him, and part of him wanted nothing more than to keep her there, their bodies still joined, until morning. Evan had never been possessive before, but even though he couldn't wait to see Rory claim Jess, a tiny spark of jealousy flared to life deep in his heart at the knowledge she was destined for both of them. Jess stirred and lifted her head, and his heart stuttered in his chest as she licked her kiss-swollen lips and then smiled at him. She had to be their mate because there couldn't be another woman in the world who could make him feel this way. As Evan smiled back at her and stroked her cheek, he realized that if the price for having her in their lives was that he had to share her with the man he loved like a brother, then it was a price he'd gladly pay.

RORY LOVED SEEING Jess laid out in front of him, her bare limbs tangled up with Evan's and her entire body relaxed and boneless. Rory could still see the pink marks on her ass where he'd spanked her, and the memory of her reaction to his playful punishment made his dick throb and his balls tighten between his legs. He hadn't been this eager to bed a woman since he'd left his teen years behind, but he knew better than to rush. Human though she may be, Jess was going to belong to them, and Rory didn't want to do anything to jeopardize her acceptance of this unconventional love match.

When Jess lifted her head to give him a slow, seductive smile, he had to resist the urge to lift her off of Evan and drop her straight onto his cock. Instead Rory reached out and tugged her hair out of the scrunchie holding it captive, letting it fall around her face and over her shoulders like a cascade of silver and platinum that flowed down to touch the bed beneath them.

Rory wrapped his fist in her hair and pulled her head up to meet his as he leaned in and kissed her hard. Her lips parted at the first touch of his tongue and he delved deep into the sweet heat of her mouth. She tasted of chocolate and peppermint and he knew this night would forever be connected to those flavors in his mind.

Jess lifted herself up off Evan's chest and met Rory's kiss head-on, her tongue dueling with his in a give and take battle that made him growl in frustration. He needed to be inside her right *now*.

"Go on, beautiful." Evan released Jess to him with a low laugh.

"Come here, Jess. It's my turn now," Rory whispered into her mouth as Evan guided her to him, hands on her hips as he handed their women over to Rory for more loving. Rory's hand was still fisted in her hair as he drew her across the bed and into his arms, his lips never once breaking contact with hers. Slowly and gently he lowered her back onto the bed, giving her time to settle herself comfortably. Evan tucked a pillow beneath her head, and grabbed another one before giving Rory a quick nod.

"Give us a second here, baby," Rory told her and then slid an arm under her knees, lifting her lower body off the bed so Evan could get the second pillow into position beneath her.

"What are you doing?" Jess asked, lifting her head to give them both a confused look. "And while I have a chance to talk, I'd like to add that you do not get to be the boss of me, Rory Frazier."

"Uh oh, I think she called you out." Evan leaned back against the headboard and settled back with one hand behind his head, smirking.

Rory prowled up the bed and leaned over Jess, placing one hand on each side of her shoulders as he pressed his body down onto hers in a display of dominance that he simply couldn't control. "You're mistaken, Jessica James. I am definitely the boss of you, at least in the bedroom. In here, you'll do what I say."

He could see the flash of fear and uncertainty in her eyes and Rory brushed a tender kiss to the tip of her upturned nose and reined in his dominant side. "I won't hurt you, baby. Not ever. But if you backtalk me in the bedroom, you're going to make me nuts."

The fear faded and her lips quirked into a tiny smirk. "And what happens if Evan backtalks you? Do you spank him, too?"

"Oh, hell no! Don't you go giving him ideas!" Rory protested and threw up his hands in front of him, warding them off. "There's no way I'm going anywhere near his ass, thank you."

An idea sparked in Rory's brain and he brushed another kiss to Jess's mouth before making his suggestion.

"Tell you what. If Evan talks back to me, *you* can spank him."

There was no missing the sizzle of interest that flared in her eyes at that suggestion. "You have yourself a deal."

"Wait, what? Hang on a minute here. Don't I get a say?"

"You let him spank *me!*" Jess pointed out with a sweet smile and a dangerous gleam in her eyes. "I don't remember getting a say, so why should you?"

Rory was pleased to see that mischievous look, because it told him that once they put an end to Jess's doubting demons she was going to be able to hold her own with any member of the colony. She'd need that fire as his mate.

Evan was still sulking. "If you spank me, sweetheart, I'll find a way to get even with you."

"I can see this is going to be a relationship built on sex, laughter, and a continuous cycle of revenge, then," Jess giggled and Rory felt something stir inside him at the joyful sound. *This* was how he wanted the rest of his life to be.

"Not a bad start." He coaxed her legs further apart and let the thick head of his cock seat itself at the entrance to her pussy. "But so far, I'm not seeing nearly enough sex."

"You're being pushy again," she murmured and arched her hips, rubbing her slick lips against his dick.

Rory didn't bother answering her, but instead he let his body surge up and into her hot depths. He muffled his groan of pleasure against her mouth as her needy cunt wrapped itself around him and drew him in deeper. She took everything he offered her and when his balls hit her ass, he forced himself to go still. Jess was quivering around him, her pale eyes full of need as she squirmed beneath him, demanding more.

"Why'd you stop?" she asked, and he caught a note of doubt in her voice.

"Because this is too good to rush. We've waited a long time for you, baby. I want to remember this."

"Oh, okay." Her face lit up with a radiant smile and she wrapped her legs around his hips, drawing him in closer. "Just don't take too long."

"Brat!" Rory gave in and began making love to her in earnest, his body braced over hers as he drove himself in and out of her pussy. He made sure he angled his body so that his pubic bone hit her swollen little clit on every thrust, and soon she was panting and bucking beneath him. Her passionate responses kept pushing to the brink of his control, and as he started pumping into her hard enough to move them both up the bed, Rory knew he should ease back, but he couldn't.

Evan dropped his hand to Jess's head, protecting her from the headboard as Rory's control shattered and he fucked her hard. Her tits bounced with each thrust of his hips and she started chanting his name brokenly, spurring him on. Her cunt was so hot his cock felt like he was plunging it into a forge, and she reached up to wrap her hands in his hair, tugging at it so that there was a brief bite of pain as he bottomed out inside her again and again. The sensation of her hands in his hair nearly broke him, but Rory managed to hold back his orgasm until he felt the telltale flutter of her vaginal walls around his cock and heard her ecstatic cries as she climaxed. Only then did he give himself over to the moment, grinding his body against hers as he sent jet after jet of his cum into her body.

"Mine," he growled and slumped over her, his mouth tracing down her jaw to seal her mouth with one final kiss.

"Ours," Evan corrected him and laid a hand on Rory's shoulder, his other still resting on the crown of Jess's fair hair.

Jess turned her head and broke the kiss and looked up at them both, flushed and panting from her latest orgasm. "Are you two always going to be this possessive?"

"Yes," they answered together and Jess laughed.

"Good. I just wanted to be sure."

Rory eased himself away from Jess and settled down on the opposite side of the bed from Evan, leaving her sprawled between them. There wasn't much extra room in her queen-size bed, and Rory was already trying to figure out how to convince her to come home with them, hopefully to stay. Rory didn't care what his father or anyone else thought about him and Evan taking a human mate. As far as Rory was concerned, it was a done deal.

CHAPTER ELEVEN

"YOU NEED TO TELL THEM, RORY." Evan was sitting at the table, making short work of yet another lunch of grilled ham and cheese sandwiches as the two of them argued. He knew why Rory didn't want to go to his parents about Jess, but they couldn't continue on the way things were. *Not that things aren't damn near perfect these days.*

Since the night Jess had cooked them dinner, the bonds forged between the three of them had only grown stronger. In the tradition of the selkie people, he and Rory had started making a point of keeping an eye on Jess, and she was usually in the company of one or the other of them. He wasn't sure she'd noticed yet, but if she hadn't figured it out, she would soon. It was an ancient practice, and a necessary one for a race whose women were renowned for their beauty and wifely attributes.

The selkie legends made constant mention of the fact that fishermen would try to steal a selkie woman's pelt, thus preventing her from returning to the sea and keeping her tied to him as wife and mother to any children they might have. In an attempt to safeguard their women, selkies had long ago devised a three-way marriage, ensuring that no mated selkie female was ever left unguarded. Despite the fact that their arrangement with Jess hadn't been formalized, they were already treating her as their mate.

"You know that's not going to go well," Rory said as he set his plate of sandwiches down on the table and joined Evan to eat.

"Uh, yeah. Your dad was ready to it lose it over the idea of you and I mating with someone who wasn't of the right bloodline. He's going to go off like a thermonuclear warhead when he finds out Jess is human. But we can't tell her who we are without his permission, and there's no way I'm going to ask her to consider making this a permanent arrangement without her knowing the truth. I won't lie to her, Rory."

"I don't want to lie to her, either. She doesn't give her trust easily. If she ever thinks we betrayed her or lied to her…" Rory trailed off and shook his head.

"She'd be gone, and we'd never get her back again." Evan finished the gloomy thought and they both stared at their meal for a long moment.

"We need her," Rory finally spoke. "It's been less than a week and I hate it when I'm not with her. The bonding process has already started."

"It's the same with me." Evan looked up to grin at Rory. "And I think it's affecting Jess, too."

"That's not possible. She's human. Everyone knows it takes humans longer to form the bond, and that's even after they've gone through the bonding ritual."

Evan ran a hand through his hair, sweeping the bangs

away from his face as he wondered how to say what was on his mind. "Yeah, I know." He looked up at Rory and decided to get straight to the point. "The thing is, I don't think she *is* human."

Rory snorted. "Yeah, okay. So what is she? A pixie? A runaway wizard from Hogwarts?"

"I think she's one of us."

Rory's head snapped up and he stared at Evan like he'd grown a second head.

"Not possible. Have you ever known a selkie to drown? If she'd had a drop of selkie blood in her, she'd have changed forms instinctively."

"Not if she didn't have her pelt," Evan reminded him and Rory furrowed his brow in thought.

"So the reaction we're having to her might be real?"

"You mean the fact we wanted to fuck her the second she came on board the *Storm Lord* and we don't want to let her out of our sight? Yeah, I'd say that's very damned real. It's exactly the way the records describe a reaction to a true mate, and there's no record of anyone having a true mate bond with a human."

"I cannot imagine growing up not knowing what you were or who your people were. Why would someone do that to her? And where the hell is her pelt?" Rory stood up and stomped across the kitchen and Evan could almost see the thunder clouds gathering over his blood-brother's head.

"Just the idea of someone doing that to her pisses me off!" Rory yanked open the fridge door and grabbed two beers, twisting the caps off and kicking the door shut behind him. He handed one to Evan and then threw his head back and downed a good portion of the contents before sitting down again.

"We don't even know for sure that's what happened, it's only a theory."

"No, it makes too much sense. I think you're right, Ev." Rory took another drink and slammed the bottle down onto the table with enough force to make the table legs shake. "Her family owns that cabin right? And it's right next door to our lands. Maybe there's information about them, something we missed?"

Evan shook his head. "I checked. Summer visitors only since they bought the property more than sixty years ago. The James family is completely human."

"So that leaves her mother." Rory sighed. "I really don't want to make J.J. cry by asking her for her mother's family history."

"Hang on, our serious conversation is going on hold for a second. When did you start calling her J.J.?" Evan watched in amazement as Rory's face actually darkened as he blushed. Blushed! Jess might never realize the depth of the changes she was having on the both of them.

"Well, it's sort of been in my head since I found out she writes as J.J. Ford. It just came out yesterday while we were hanging out. I think it suits her."

"That is fucking adorable. I am going to tell your mom."

"Fuck off, Ev. You tell my mom one word of what's going on I'll toss your delicate ass off the dock the next time it snows."

The two of them lapsed into silence, drinking their beers and considering what they were going to do about Jess. Finally Evan cleared his throat and said, "I don't think we can talk to Jess about this until after we've dealt with your father. We can't ask her all about her background and then not be able to tell her why."

"When we do tell her, do you think she's going to be able to deal with it?" Rory asked, new worry lines creasing his brow. "How did some of the others manage the whole, 'Hey babe, we're really glad you're good with living in a permanent three-way relationship, oh and by the way we may have forgotten to mention the fact we're seal shapeshifters, too' conversation?"

"Maybe we should ask them." Evan arched a brow at Rory. "You're technically their prince, so you could swear them to secrecy.

"Good thinking. I'm sure my mom will be happy to help, too, but I'm not sure how well-behaved Dad is going to be at first. Torin is going to love her, though." Rory shrugged. "I guess two out of three isn't too bad."

"You're forgetting about your little sister. Katelyn is going to be thrilled we're finally giving her a sister-in-law. Maybe this'll be enough to bring her back home to stay."

"Not likely, she's still not forgiven Dad for trying to mate her to that pair from the Haida Gwaii colony. Are you going to tell Cameron?"

Evan grinned at the mention of his little brother. "I already emailed him a few days ago and let him know there was a potential change in my marital status. Once he got over the shock, he emailed me back and let me know he's going to try to book off once we actually get this figured out and set a date. He's not due to be going back out to sea until early next year, so it should work out."

Rory suddenly laughed and raised his beer in a toast. Confused, Evan followed suit, tapping his bottle to Rory's.

"So what are we toasting exactly?"

"To the fact that you and I casually discussed the fact we're getting married, and we haven't even discussed our plans with the bride-to-be yet."

"So, I guess that makes it unofficially official, then?" Evan asked.

"You think it's time? Even without telling her the whole story?" Rory didn't look completely certain.

"I think we need to tell her how we feel. If she decides to walk away when it's all said and done, then at least we know we tried."

"You know Dad's going to hit the roof when he sees her wearing that, right?"

"It's our choice, not his. I'm never planning on letting her go, Rory. Are you?"

"No."

"Then I think we should plan something special for tonight, and tomorrow we can go tell your mom, dad, and Torin the good news."

Rory nodded and finished the rest of his beer before asking, "Do you think she'll like it?"

"Have you ever met a woman who didn't like jewelry?" Evan asked, laughing. "No, wait, I'm betting you have never given a woman jewelry before."

"Why would I spend that kind of money when I knew they weren't the ones I was going to be spending my life with?"

Evan groaned. "Let's make a deal right now that you leave the big, romantic gestures to me and you stick with whatever it is you're supposed to be good at."

"I'm good at the stuff that doesn't require me to be in touch with my inner goddess," Rory shot back.

Evan choked on his mouthful of beer as he tried to laugh and swallow at the same time. "I never, ever want to meet your inner goddess. She's probably six feet tall with a mustache and legs hairier than a sasquatch."

"All right, Mr. Romance. Do you any ideas on where to take Jess tonight?"

"Of course I do. You're going to hate it, though. It's going to require you parting with some of our hard-earned coins."

Rory grunted. "She's worth it. Are you going to share with the class or am I going to be left to guess?"

"Let's go find that necklace first, and then I need to make a few phone calls. Once I know if this will work, I'll let you know."

Rory grimaced. "The necklace is in the attic. I stored it in the fireproof safe, along with our pelts. I guess we should bring those down, too. She's going to want to see them eventually."

JESS HAD BEEN deep in her manuscript when Evan had called and asked her if she had plans for dinner. When she'd said no, he'd cryptically told her to be ready for pick up at five o'clock, and told her to dress for a night out. As she went through her minimally stocked closet for the fourth time, she wondered again what the hell her men were up to.

"I really need to go shopping for more clothes. Either that or I need to have Viv ship me another box or two of the stuff I put into storage. I didn't pack with plans to be dating when I got here."

She finally decided to wear the one dress Vivian had insisted she pack with admonishments that no woman should be without at least one little black dress.

"Thank you Viv, I owe you…again."

Jess was still fussing with her outfit when she heard the guys' truck roll up the driveway. The dress ended above her knees and the V-neck was deep enough she felt half-naked as she tried to simultaneously tug her hem down and her neckline up. As a knock sounded Jess looked down and realized she'd forgotten her shoes, again.

"One second!" She dashed back to the bedroom and grabbed her heels from beside the bed, where she'd left them expressly so she didn't forget to put them on. "I'm losing my mind," Jess muttered and headed back to the door, shoes in hand, to let her men in. The moment she opened the door she was grateful she'd opted to wear the dress.

Both of them were dressed to kill, and her mouth watered as she dropped her heels and opened her arms to greet them both with a hug.

"You guys look amazing!" She curled her fingers around Rory's deep-burgundy tie as she stood on tiptoes to kiss him and then turned to Evan, grabbing his blue silk tie before tugging his head down to her level before kissing him, too.

She felt a hand travelling up her stocking-clad thigh and laughed as she swatted at it. "Hey! No rumpling the outfit before we even get out the door."

"But you look way too sexy to take out in public, sweetheart." Evan grinned at her. "Maybe we should cancel and stay in."

"Maybe we should. I'm going to need a stick to beat off

the throngs of women who are going to try to get your attention tonight." Jess let go of their ties but stayed comfortably settled between them, loving the sense of security they gave her whenever they held her this way.

"Hmm. Other women you say? When you put it that way…" Evan winked this time and Rory rolled his eyes.

"Don't pay him any attention. We've got the only woman we want right here."

"I'm glad to hear it," Jess laid her head on Rory's chest and beamed up at him. "So where are you taking me? Evan wouldn't give me any hints."

"Ever heard of the Wickaninnish Inn?" Rory asked.

"Heard of it, I can't even pronounce it!"

"Wick-an-inn-ish Inn." Evan repeated the word incredibly slowly and she stuck her tongue out at him.

"So you're taking me to a tongue twister?"

"No, but I'll twist tongues with you anytime you want." Evan waggled his blond brows at her and she found herself rolling her eyes at the same time Rory did.

"What's got into you tonight, Ev? You're full of sass and vinegar."

"I'm looking forward to taking our beautiful girl out for a meal that you don't have to cook yourself or Captain Grilled-Cheese Sandwiches over there didn't make for you." Evan stepped back and offered Jess his arm. "Shall we, milady? Your carriage awaits."

Jess pointed to her shoes with a sheepish smile. "I just need to get these on, and my shawl."

Rory let her go and slipped past her to grab her shawl and purse from the chair nearest the door, and Jess gripped Evan's arm for balance as she stepped into her heels. She felt the heavy pashmina she'd chosen to wear being draped over her shoulders, and a shiver ran down her spine as Rory's fingers brushed the nape of her neck as he drew her hair out from underneath the shawl and released it to fall down her back again.

"Did I mention you look breathtaking?" he whispered near her ear and the delicate caress of warm air made her shiver again as thrill bumps chased across her skin.

"If you keep talking like that, we're not going to make it to dinner."

"Come on you two, I promise this is worth leaving the house for." Evan jangled his truck keys for emphasis.

He and Rory offered her an arm at the same time, and instead of choosing, Jess slipped an arm around each and nodded. "All right, then, you may escort me to the carriage."

CHAPTER TWELVE

As THEY WALKED into the hotel lobby, Jess gasped softly, and both Rory and Evan seemed to relax as they realized she was pleased with their choice of dinner spots. The entire inn was built onto a large, rocky headland and was tucked into the old growth forest that surrounded the area. It was beautiful, inside and out, and Jess was amazed to find such an elegant retreat so far from what she'd always considered civilization.

Her surprise must have shown on her face, too, because Evan glanced down and gave her a wink.

"See? We can be sophisticated when the situation calls for it."

"It's just not very often we have a reason," Rory added, his fingers squeezing her hand as he led her further into the building.

She spotted the sign for the dining area and took a step in that direction, only to have Evan and Rory shake their heads. "Evan's got something a little more intimate in mind for dinner," Rory told her and drew her to a halt as

Evan went to the front desk and began speaking to the clerk there.

"More surprises?" she asked Rory.

"My lips are sealed. You're going to have to wait and see."

Evan rejoined them a few minutes later and handed Rory and Jess both keycards. "I'm going to go get our things out of the truck and I'll join you in a few minutes." For a second he looked unhappy, but then he gave Jess a lopsided smile and shrugged very slightly. "Officially we have two rooms. You and Rory are in one, and I'm booked in one down the hall. This is one of those times when discretion is needed."

Jess's heart twisted as understanding dawned and she gave Evan a subtle wink and a smile as she whispered, "Out here, we'll behave, but once you're in our room where you belong, I say discretion be damned. This is all completely amazing, and I can't wait for you to join us."

His eyes lit up at her words and he nodded. "I grabbed your overnight bag from our place, sweetheart. You won't even be missing your toothbrush. I'll see you guys shortly."

He left them and headed back outside, and Jess couldn't help but notice the way every woman in the lobby watched him go, all of them wearing identical expressions of appreciation.

She didn't even realize she'd made a sound until Rory laughed and tugged her into his arms for a slow, heated kiss that made her knees weak. She had to grip his shoulders to stay upright, and when he lifted his lips from hers he managed to whisper near her ear. "Relax. He didn't even notice them. But feel free to growl like that any time you want, I like it."

Jess startled and stared at him. "I growled?"

"Oh yeah, like a terrier guarding her favorite bone."

"I didn't even realize. I saw them watching him and I..."

"You didn't want anyone else moving in on what's yours," Rory finished for her. "No need to explain it to me, I'm feeling exactly the same way right now."

Jess laughed. "Lucky for you, no one's looking at me," she said dismissively and was startled by the intent look Rory shot her.

"You don't think so?" He leaned in close and kissed her again. "Right now there are at least three men watching us and wishing they were me right now. I think it's time to get your hot little ass behind closed doors before I need to deck someone."

"Really? Where? Are they cute?" Jess asked and then burst out laughing as Rory glowered at her and then scooped her into his arms.

"That's it, we're going up to our room and when we get there, you're paying for that little remark!"

"Rory, put me down! People are staring!"

"I thought that's what you wanted." Rory's long legs carried them over to the elevator in no time at all, and Jess peeked over his shoulder at the people watching their little scene unfold.

"I was teasing you!" she protested and then buried her face against his jacket as they stepped into an open elevator car. The moment Jess heard the door close she wriggled, trying to get Rory to put her down, but his arms tightened around her, holding her firmly in place.

"Rory, put me down, please," she asked, feeling more than a little foolish.

"Not a chance. If I put you down, you might decide to head back downstairs and check out the competition." She heard the light, teasing tone in his voice and silently hoped that meant he wasn't serious about punishing her for her earlier remark.

She lifted her head and smiled. "There's not a man in the world that could compete with what I've already got."

"Damn skippy." Rory turned his head and captured her mouth with his. His kiss was pure male, forceful and demanding nothing less than her complete surrender. The door opened and Jess barely noticed as he carried them down a long corridor, his lips still on hers and their tongues tangled as his powerful arms kept her pressed against his hard chest.

When Rory stopped to work the keycard against the lock, Jess came back to her senses and looked around, grateful the hallway was empty and no one had seen the rest of their display. When the door swung open Rory carried her inside, and Jess looked around them in amazement.

"This is our room?" she asked, staring out the huge windows that overlooked the rocky shore beyond the inn. "It's stunning!" A gas fireplace was situated between two windows that spanned nearly all of the space from floor to ceiling. A straight-backed chair made of driftwood sat next to a simple desk, and a few soft chairs sat in the corners of the room. The rest of the space was dominated by a king-size bed that faced the fireplace.

"It is, isn't it?" Rory set her down carefully on her feet and stripped off his jacket, tossing it onto the bed with a careless flick of his wrist. He walked over to the driftwood chair and pulled it out from the desk, turning it around so that it faced into the room. He sat down on it and crooked a finger at Jess. "Come here."

Her heart beat faster as she stood her ground and shook her head. "I want to look around our room."

"Jessica James, come *here*!" This time there was no mistaking the commanding tone of his voice. Rory pointed to the floor directly in front of him and Jess found herself standing there before she had time to think about it. Her pulse was racing now, and despite being more than a little uneasy at what she knew was about to happen, she was almost quivering with anticipation at the same time.

Rory slid his hands up her stocking-clad thighs, pushing the fabric of her dress aside as he worked his way slowly toward her waist. Jess reached down to try to rearrange her and he stopped and shook his head sharply.

"You are to stay still and not say anything unless I ask you a direct question. Do you understand?"

"Yes." Her answer came out as more of a squeak and she forced herself to stop moving.

"Good girl."

She bit back a retort and concentrated on not moving. Now he'd ordered her not to, she was almost compelled to do *something*, just to defy him.

His callused fingers brushed higher and he smiled slightly as he found the lacy trim of her panties. "You won't need these," he said and tugged them down her legs, drawing her stockings down at the same time until all of it lay in a heap around her ankles. "You can step out of those, but then I want those sexy heels of yours back on your pretty feet."

Jess did exactly as he told her, her cheeks hot as she stripped the tangle of fabric off her feet and then stepped back into her heels. Rory leaned in close, his face nuzzling her lower belly and then drifting lower as he inhaled.

"You're turned on, baby. I can smell it. Is this making you wet?"

Not sure if she should answer aloud, Jess nodded.

"Say it. I want to hear you tell me your pussy is wet just thinking about me spanking your sweet ass."

"I—yes. Yes, I'm turned on," she stammered and he lifted his head to stare into her eyes.

"Say 'yes, I'm turned on thinking about you spanking me.'"

Jess swallowed and opened her mouth to speak, but nothing came out.

"Jess, I gave you an order." Rory's voice had dropped to a low rumble and his dark eyes narrowed as he continued to stare at her intently. Her pussy was soaked and she could feel her insides quivering with anticipation as she finally found the courage to speak.

"Yes, I'm turned on by the thought of you spanking me." He rewarded her with a slight smile and a nod.

"Now I want you across my lap, head down." Rory patted his lap and waited for her to obey.

Jess did it, her eyes closed and her entire body tense as she tried to find a comfortable position without wiggling too much.

"Take a breath, baby. This isn't the executioner's block you're bent over." Rory stroked her back and she exhaled with a loud *whoosh*.

He stroked her a few more times, and she managed to relax slightly by the time he reached down and tugged her dress up to her waist, exposing her bottom. Jess stiffened up all over again and Rory chuckled.

"Take a deep breath and then hold it to the count of three, and then you may exhale."

She sucked in a lungful of air and held it as he counted.

"One. Two. Three." Just as she started to exhale his hand came down on her bare ass and she yelped, struggling to get up out of his lap as she sputtered in shock.

"Be still!" he snapped and she stopped cold as his command cut through her surprised reactions.

"Now, was that so bad?"

"No. I mean yes. I mean well, I don't know." Jess huffed from her facedown position.

"I'd never deliberately hurt you, Jess. You know that. But downstairs, when you made that crack about the other men, you made me more than a little crazy."

"Sorry," Jess murmured. "I really was only teasing you."

Rory smoothed his hand over the spot he'd spanked. "I know, baby. Next time remember that I don't have much of a sense of humor when it comes to the idea of you being interested in anyone else. You're mine."

"Actually, she's ours." Evan's voice joined in the conversation and Jess jerked her head up, mortified that he'd walked in on her like this.

"Ours, right." Rory accepted the correction and reached over to gently push her head back down. "We're not done yet, Jess. Stay still."

"And what did our sweet little girl do to deserve a spanking? I was only gone five minutes, if that!" Evan walked past Jess and she could follow his feet as he crossed the room and sat down on the bed, dropping their bags to the floor.

"She wanted to know if the men looking at her tonight were cute."

"She did? Well then, I see why she's got her cute ass on display."

"You should have seen her when she spotted a couple of women checking you out when you went for our bags. She *growled*, Ev."

"Really?" There was an odd, thoughtful tone to Evan's question and Jess wished she could look at him and see his expression, but she didn't dare raise her head.

"So are you done? Or am I still in time for the pre-dinner entertainment?"

Jess muttered a curse under her breath and then bit back another one as Rory's hand swatted her ass again.

"I heard that. I told you not to speak unless asked a question."

Her ass tingled and her clit was throbbing as Jess gasped and said, "Sorry," the apology slipping out before she realized he hadn't asked her a question.

The next smack came lower on her backside, close enough to her pussy that she actually felt her vaginal walls clench at the combination of pain and pleasure that flooded her body.

This time when Rory stroked over the tender spot where he'd spanked her he let his fingers keep going until they brushed over the lips of her pussy. "You are so wet. Did you enjoy that, Jess? You must have."

"Y-yes," she confessed, her entire focus on the delicate caresses he was giving her labia.

"Tell me who you belong to."

"You and Evan."

She nearly sobbed with relief as Rory slipped a finger inside her slick folds and stroked her swollen clit.

"Yes, you do. And we belong to you. Now, do you want to get off my lap, or do you want to come first?" Rory's finger stroked over her clit again and Jess moaned in response.

"I'd say that was a vote for getting off before getting up," Evan said and she heard the bed frame creak as he shifted his weight. "May I?"

"She's all yours." Rory moved his hand away from her pussy and she moaned again at the loss of contact.

Jess needed to come so badly she was shaking with frustration as she watched Evan's feet stroll slowly across the room and out of her field of vision.

Warm hands settled on the twin globes of her bottom and she was too horny to care that she was bare-assed and bent over. All thoughts about chunky thighs and unsightly bulges were completely forgotten as she waited breathlessly for Evan to touch her.

"So pretty," Evan complimented her as his fingers stroked over still sensitive skin. "Pink's a good color on you, sweetheart."

Warm breath fanned over her bare flesh and the ache in her pussy grew even worse as she felt his lips brush over the back of her thigh.

"Spread your legs for me." His knees moved between her legs, helping her open for him and then his mouth was on her clit and Jess had to muffle her scream of relief. Evan's tongue went straight for her clit, drawing the hard pearl of delicate nerves out from beneath its hood of flesh, and Jess curved her back and tried to arch herself against his mouth.

"She's not going to last very long, is she?" Rory groaned and started stroking her back along her spine, his fingers leaving trails of fire in their wake.

"Does that feel good, Jess?"

"Oh god, yes, so good," she managed to moan in response, her entire body trembling on the cusp of a cataclysmic release.

"Make her come for us, Ev."

Evan didn't say a word, but his mouth and tongue worked in concert, teasing, sucking, and laving at her clit and pussy. A finger pushed into her cunt and then a second one joined it and Jess moaned as her channel clenched hard around Evan's invading digits. He curved his fingers and began tapping on the spot just above her clitoris. That sent Jess's over the edge and she came so hard that her vision filled with dancing lights and she barely heard herself scream their names.

When she came back to her senses she was being carefully lifted up and carried to the bed, her two men holding her together as they gently lowered her to the soft mattress. One of them tugged her dress back down over her hips as the other stroked her hair, and she didn't bother to open her eyes to know which one was where. It didn't really matter. They were both taking care of her, and Jess had never felt more pampered and adored than she did right at this moment.

She let herself drift for a while, and when she opened her eyes again they were both beside her, watching her with loving expressions that made her heart melt. Without even thinking about it Jess reached for them both, stroking their faces as tears started rolling down her cheek.

"I love you both so much," she told them and the next thing she knew she was caught in between two hard, muscular bodies as they both tried to hug her at once.

"We love you, too, sweetheart. That's what we brought you here to tell you." Evan nuzzled her neck as he shared his heart with her.

"We both love you so much. You're the most important thing in our world," Rory told her and then kissed away the tears running down her face.

"Aw hell, is she crying already?" Evan asked and reached up to wipe away the tears Rory had missed. "Don't cry. We're not done being romantic yet!"

"There's more?" Jess looked at them both, amazed and grateful that she'd found these two incredible men and that they truly loved *her*.

"We were going to wait until after dinner, but I don't want to wait anymore." Rory sat back and took one hand while Evan took the other. The two looked at each other, and then Rory looked at her and smiled. "We want you to come live with us, permanently. We want you to be part of our lives. I know it's only been a short time, and we shouldn't be moving this fast, but we're sure this is right. We've been sure since we fished you out of the ocean. You're it. The one we've been waiting for."

"I—I don't know what to say."

"Say yes," Evan squeezed her hand. "Admit that you've been feeling the same thing we have. It's like a magnetic pull that started the minute we met. You're the first thing I think about when I wake up in the morning."

"And you're the last thought in my head when I go to sleep," Rory added.

As Jess looked at her two men and felt the love she held for both of them in her heart, she knew that there was only one answer. It didn't matter how insane it was or that it was too soon, or that she was committing to a relationship not many would ever really understand or accept. "Yes. Oh yes. You've been all I can think about since I woke up on your boat. You've both made me so happy that I'd be crazy to say anything else. Yes, I love you and I will move in with you and we'll find a way to make this work. I can't imagine my life without you in it. Both of you."

Rory kissed her long, hot, and hard and then slipped away as Evan dragged her into his arms for a kiss of his own. She felt Rory leave the bed and reached out for him, not sure where he was going.

"I'm coming back, baby. I just need to get something out of my bag."

Evan hauled her up into his lap and cupped her cheeks in his hands as he kissed her again, laughing the whole time. "You've made us very happy, sweetheart. I promise we'll take such good care of you you're never going to regret this."

Rory rejoined them on the bed, settling himself so that he was facing them both. "This is for you, Jess." He handed her a hand carved wooden box with a fitted lid.

She opened it carefully and her jaw dropped as she saw what was inside. Nestled on a bed of faded blue velvet was a white-gold pendant made in the shape of a three-sided Celtic knot. The mazelike pattern formed a triangle that pointed downward, and dangling from the point was a single pink pearl the size of a small grape. The upper points of the pendant were fastened to a finely crafted chain that was also made of white gold. It was the most beautiful thing she'd ever seen. Jess's lifted it out of the box and held it up to the light, blinking away the tears that filled her eyes as she stared at it.

"I've never seen anything more incredibly beautiful," she finally whispered tearfully. "Thank you."

"Here, let me put it on you." Rory took it from her and drew it down over her head, carefully drawing her hair out from under the chain and settling it so that it lay against the points of her collarbone.

Evan's voice murmured near her ear, "It's a traditional gift among our families to present the woman with a courting gift like this one. If she agrees to wear it, then it acts as an engagement ring of sorts, telling everyone that you are with us. Each family group has a slightly different pattern, usually based on a combination of both *their* parent's patterns." Evan leaned around so he could look at it. "In this case, though, the pattern is the traditional Frazier family one. The pearl however, was my grandmother's."

"So this is a family heirloom, made up of both your families?" She touched the pendant and smiled, ignoring the tears still tracking down her face. "I love it even more than I did before."

Evan kissed her cheek. "When my parents come back from Scotland and finally get to meet you, they are going to love you. My mom would be pleased to know you're going to be wearing her mother's pearl. It was her favorite piece of jewelry."

Jess kissed Evan and then turned her attention to Rory. "What about your family? Are they going to like me?"

Rory gave her a smile that didn't quite reach his eyes. "We'll find out tomorrow night. We're all going over there for dinner. My mom is going to adore you, Torin will, too. My dad might need a little time and a lot of that patented Jess charm. But what will matter most to them is that I'm happy."

"He means that *we're* happy." Evan chuckled. "Bro, you really need to remember she's *ours*."

"He's going to have a very long time to get used to the idea. I'm not going anywhere," Jess declared and beamed at them both.

"So, now that I'm a teary-eyed mess with a sore ass, what's for dinner?"

CHAPTER THIRTEEN

DINNER WAS AN UNIMAGINABLY DELICIOUS EXPERIENCE, and Jess made a note to bring Viv back here as part of the "why I'm staying in Tofino" tour package. Not that Jess really thought Vivian wouldn't understand once she laid eyes on Rory and Evan. More likely after that introduction, Vivian would be looking for her own reasons to stay in town.

They'd ordered in room service straight from the five-star dining room and when Jess had confessed that she'd never had fresh-from-the-sea seafood, they'd made sure to get a wide variety for her to try. They ordered bacon-wrapped scallops, shrimp and crab and poached salmon, too, and every dish was better than anything she'd ever had back in Toronto.

They had spread out the dishes on the bed in an extravagant picnic, picking off of each other's plates and feeding each other morsels of food until all three of them were sated and still, too content to move.

"That was the best meal I have ever eaten," Jess declared as she finally got up and started putting the empty dishes back onto the cart. "Thank you both, so much. I feel like the most pampered woman on the planet."

"The night's not done yet," Rory commented from his position on the bed, his hands crossed behind his head and a look of regal satisfaction on his face.

"Did you see the bathroom yet, or the private balcony? Or did tall, dark, and bossy over there not let you explore before he had you over his knee?" Evan sat up and started helping Jess clear away the remains of their meal.

"We have a private balcony?" Jess perked up and looked around. "Where?"

Evan laughed and pointed to a doorway on the far side of the bed. "Right over there. Really, Rory, would it have killed you to wait two minutes so she could appreciate the view?"

"Yes," was all Rory said, looking completely unrepentant.

"I was guilty of some serious teasing." Jess winked at Rory and was rewarded with a sensual smile that sent tendrils of heat curling around her womb and making her thighs damp.

"If you start encouraging him, he's going to go all alpha male on you and then I'm going to sit back and say 'I told you so,' and not lift a finger to save your cute little ass," Evan warned her and then slid an arm around her waist. "Come out here and take a look at the view with me."

The air outside was bitterly cold and smelled of salt and seaweed. The wind whipped around them both and she leaned into Evan, cuddling up to him for warmth and the pure joy of having him touching her.

"There's a storm coming in tonight. Later on it should be quite a show." Evan gestured to the breakers rolling in, already huge and topped with heavy white foam. "And tomorrow there'll be another storm, when you meet Rory's father. He's a lot like the storm, all blow and froth and screaming wind. So tomorrow, sweetheart, you and I need to be like the rocks." His hand moved to point out the dark mass of stone that the waves crashed over time and again, only to retreat back into the sea. "Rory is like his dad. Let the two of them rage at each other. They've been doing it since the day Rory was born. Don't let it bother you. Stay close to me and let everything wash over you."

"He's going to hate me that much?" Jess's heart hurt at the idea of being rejected before she even had a chance to defend herself.

"No, sweetheart. He's going to hate that Rory and I are choosing for ourselves, instead of following tradition. When he gets past that, he's going to like you just fine."

"What tradition? Why do I get the feeling there's more going on here than either of you have told me? I keep catching snippets of conversation, half-spoken sentences and veiled references to things I don't understand." She turned to face Evan and tipped her head up so she could look him squarely in the eye. "What aren't you telling me?"

"I can't talk about it. If I could, I would, but I can't. Not yet, anyway. I know that sounds insanely cryptic and I'm sorry, but there are some things I can't tell you yet. Things *we* can't tell you yet."

Jess took a step back, her arms wrapping around herself as she struggled to understand. Loss and hurt filled her along with a healthy dose of confusion. "So you love me, but you won't tell me what's going on? You two asked me to move in with you. You want me to make a life with you, but you're both keeping secrets from me. What kind of a life will we have if we're starting out like this?"

Evan reached out for her with both hands but Jess shook her head and took another step backward, fighting to keep her tears in check.

"I want you to tell me what's going on, Evan."

"Tomorrow night we'll explain everything, I promise. There's a whole bunch of tradition and other crap going on because of who we are and how we live. We have to try to do this the right way." Evan crossed the short space between them and wrapped her in his arms before she could move away again. "We've already made our decision. We want you, Jess. If Rory's father can't accept that, then we're keeping you anyway, traditions be damned. You are who we've been waiting for all our lives, and we're not giving you up."

Jess wanted to curl up in Evan's arms and trust him, but she wasn't ready to let it go yet. She'd had enough of secrets and lies. Faithless boyfriends, her father's secret affairs, her mother's cryptic notes about coming here to find her happiness, it was all getting to be too much. Even with the comfort of Evan's heart beating by her ear and the strangely soothing effect his spice and citrus scent always had on her emotions, Jess couldn't give in and trust that everything was going to be all right. She'd tried that before, and so far her batting average was abysmal.

As if he could read her mind, Evan hugged her and pressed a kiss to her hair. "I know this isn't perfect. But you have to give us credit for trying at least. We wanted to make tonight special and to give you that necklace so you knew we were serious. Tomorrow, when you walk into Darius's house wearing that, he'll know we're serious, too. The three of us are going to be together, sweetheart. We just need to weather the storm first."

"Well, at least you're being honest about not being totally honest with me," Jess finally murmured and wrapped her arms around Evan's waist. "And dinner was amazing, and so is this place. So I will agree to give you two partial credit."

"I know this is a lot to take on trust, but it's going to work out." Evan's voice softened to a whisper. "I love you, Jessica James. You're the only woman I've ever said that to, and you're the only one I ever will. We were meant to be together."

"I love you, too. I'm just...scared." She finally confessed to the tiny seeds of fear that had sprouted the minute they'd asked her to move in with them.

"Don't be. Trust the way you feel, sweetheart. Deep down you already know we're supposed to be together. You can feel it, just like we can."

"Right. Why do I suddenly feel like I'm caught in a scene from *Star Wars*? Any second Obi-Wan Kenobi is going to appear and tell me to trust my feelings and use the force."

Evan cracked up and hugged her tight. "Well, you may be onto something there. Darius does bear a striking resemblance to Darth Vader."

"You're not really inspiring a lot of confidence here, Ev."

"Sorry. But now you've got me thinking about it..." Evan started laughing again and this time Jess joined him. By the time they had stopped snickering the wind had picked up and Jess was starting to shiver from the cold.

"Let's get you back inside and warmed up." Evan lifted her into his arms and carried her effortlessly back into their room. Jess idly noticed that Rory had moved the cart with their dishes out of the room, but he was nowhere to be seen.

"Where'd Rory go?" she asked, scanning the room.

"He's in the bathroom getting set up for the next phase of the evening," Evan answered automatically and then added. "Uh, I mean that's what we planned, so I assume that's where he is."

"That's another thing I've noticed. I swear you two have complete conversations without ever saying a word. I know you've been friends for a lot of years, but it's the slightest bit freaky."

"Rory, she's calling us freaks now. Want to spank her again?" Evan called out as he passed the bed and headed for the bathroom.

"Hey! No fair taking comments out of context," Jess protested as the door opened and a warm cloud of fragrant steam surrounded them.

"Freaks, huh? And why were you calling us..." Rory stepped into view and then trailed off and frowned as he saw her still reddened eyes. "Why does it look like she's been crying? What the hell did you say to her, Ev?" Rory lifted her out of Evan's arms and cradled her against his bare chest.

"I...uh...was trying to explain a few things about tomorrow." Evan ran a hand through his hair, leaving it rumpled and spiked up in spots.

"And you made her cry? For fuck's sake, you're supposed to be the sensitive one."

"It's okay, he made me laugh, too." Jess nuzzled her face into Rory's neck. "Why are you half naked?"

"I ran you a bubble bath." Rory turned her around so she could see the massive two-person tub that dominated the bathroom. It was full of fragrant bubbles, and when she breathed in again she recognized the scent. It was the same tangerine and vanilla as the body cream she'd worn the night they'd first made love. The fact they'd gone to the effort to track that down helped her let go of her doubts. If they loved her enough to find her favorite bath gel, surely they loved her enough to keep their promises to her.

"I hope I'm not going into that massive tub alone," she purred and kissed Rory's neck again, enjoying the way the scent filled her nose even over the smell of tangerines.

"I was hoping to be invited to join you," Rory murmured.

"What about Evan?"

"It's Evan's turn to get things organized. This is our time." Rory lowered his head to brush a kiss over her mouth. "And I promise I won't make you cry while you're with *me*."

"I heard that!" Evan called from the other room, where he had already retreated to leave them their privacy.

"Stop eavesdropping and get on with your part of the plan!" Rory called back and then gently lowered Jess to the floor, keeping his arms around her as he leaned in and kissed her again. She let her lips part, inviting his tongue to dance with hers as her fingers stroked through the dark hair on his chest. His skin was warm and damp from the steam, and as she stroked her chilled hands over his nipples she felt them pebble and tighten in response.

"You need to get warmer," Rory whispered against her mouth and began sliding his hands down to the hem of her dress, easing it up over her hips and up to just below her breasts. Only then did he break their kiss and lift his head as he skinned the garment over her head and let it drop to the floor.

"I'll need that to wear home!" Jess went to pick it up and found herself held where she was. "No, you don't. Evan and I packed for you from the things you left up at our place. Leave it be, J.J. Tonight everything is taken care of. You don't need to worry about a thing."

"I've never…" she started to explain but he laid a finger on her lips and smiled.

"I know. You've never had someone take care of you, not since you left home. You've got us now, though, baby. You're not on your own anymore."

A wave of emotion crashed down over Jess and she felt more tears stinging at her eyes. "You're going to make me cry again," she warned him.

"No tears." Rory started kissing his way down her throat to her shoulder, his hands reaching around to undo the clasp on her bra and smoothing the straps down over her arms until he could draw it away and drop it onto the floor by her dress. He handed her a hair clip and watched with heat in his deep-brown eyes as she quickly twisted her hair high up on her head and fastened it there with the clip.

"All right, beautiful. Let's get you into the tub and then I'll join you." He offered Jess his hand and she used it to balance herself as she stepped up to the edge of the tub and then down into the bubble filled depths.

"It's the perfect temperature." She slid into the water with a sigh and then waved him closer. "Come on, there's more than enough room for you in here with me. I'll even let you scrub my back."

"I'm going to do more than wash your back. I've got plans that include washing every inch of you."

Rory's voice was rich with sensual promise and Jess shivered in anticipation at whatever he had planned. She'd spent time alone with both of them over the course of the last week, getting to know them better, but until now she'd never made love to either of her men without the other being there, too. She had a feeling that was about to change.

She watched as Rory stripped off his dress pants and the black boxer briefs he was wearing beneath. His cock was already stiff and leaking a few droplets of pre-cum and she felt a needy ache in her pussy as she saw him so hard and ready for her. She wanted him inside, stretching and filling her. The sight of his naked body was a source of constant wonder to her. He was all strength and power, a dark god who could have had anyone in the world, but he'd chosen her. Jess reached up to touch the pendant that hung at her throat and smiled as Evan's words came back to her. The pendant was a symbol of their intentions and their desire for a future with her. Jess realized that every time she started to doubt herself all she had to do was touch it and she'd be reminded her two men loved her.

"It looks beautiful on you," Rory told her as he stepped into the tub and settled his large frame beside hers before lifting her up into his lap. "I knew it would."

"I love you," she said as she let his hands guide her to

where he wanted her to be, lying with her back to his chest, her legs falling outside of his and her head resting on his shoulder.

"I love you, too. You have no idea how glad I am you got caught in that rip current and nearly drowned."

Jess laughed. "What a romantic way to put it."

"We were there to save you, and we always will be. You're ours to protect and love now, baby. I was starting to wonder if we'd ever find you." Rory's voice was thick with emotion and he buried his face into her hair, holding onto her tightly. As he took a deep breath she heard him groan softly and he reached between them to free his cock so it nestled along the seam of her pussy. "God, you smell so good."

"It's funny, but I never really noticed how someone smelled until I met you two. Just catching a whiff of your cologne helps me relax." She closed her thighs slightly, squeezing his dick between them. "And maybe it makes me a little horny."

"Only a little?" Rory stroked his way down her belly to cup her pussy in his hand, his fingers drifting through her trimmed curls. "I bet I can make you feel more than a little horny."

Jess sighed and let her legs fall open, craving his touch. "I bet you can, too."

"Mhmm, but not yet." He lifted his hand away and Jess mewled in protest.

"First I get to bathe you, then I'm going to make you come, and then I'm going to fuck you." Rory snagged a washcloth and squirted more of the bath gel onto it, working it up into a thick lather. "And once we do that,

I'm going to dry you off and carry you back out, and then Evan and I are going to fuck you again."

Rory's words were turning Jess's mind to mush and jacking her arousal up to a pussy-melting eleven out of ten. Needing some relief, she reached between her legs and pressed her fingers against her clit, only to have Rory's fingers curl around her wrist and move her hand away.

"Don't even think about it. You're going to wait for me." His lips drifted over the curve of her ear and he blew across it before whispering, "I want you so badly right now I hurt, and I want you feeling the same way."

Jess whimpered as Rory began running the washcloth over her stomach, moving in slow, lingering circles across her skin. He left no part of her untouched, and by the time the cloth reached the swell of her breasts Jess was panting softly. Rory's cock bumped and rubbed along her labia, and every touch made her clit throb in response. The sensual caress of soap and cloth made her hyperaware of her body. The heat of the water, the quiet fizzle of the bubbles as they popped and released more scent into the cloud of steam that filled the room, and the way the hairs on Rory's chest tickled her back, all came together in a sensory overload that had her reeling.

As the cloth swirled over her breasts her nipples hardened into tiny buds and she lifted her head to watch a wave of goosebumps flow over her skin.

"Lie back and close your eyes. We're about to get to the good part," Rory instructed and she complied. If there was any mercy in the world, he'd be getting to the good part very damned soon, before she started begging. Jess wasn't sure how far off that point was, but she knew that it wouldn't be long.

Rory finished washing her breasts and worked higher, lifting her arms one at a time to wash all the way to her fingertips and then back to her shoulder. "Close your eyes tight, I'm going to wash your face."

She felt the gentle touch of the cloth and kept her eyes closed as he carefully washed away every trace of her earlier tears. As he finished he turned her head toward him and brushed a tender kiss to her mouth. "You can open your eyes now, J.J."

He was still watching her as she peeked up at him, and Jess felt herself getting lost in the depths of his eyes. Tonight there was no mask in place and she could see his feelings for her clearly, his love and his desire gleaming so brightly there could be no mistaking it.

"I have a request to make before this goes any further," she said, smiling.

"And what's that?" A flicker of concern passed over Rory's features as he cupped her cheek with his hand.

"If I'm dreaming, please don't ever wake me up."

"Now you're getting sappy." He chuckled and kissed her again as the washcloth slid down her stomach again and he rubbed it against her pussy, his index finger pressing the cloth between her folds with gentle pressure. "I think we need to finish getting you cleaned up."

"I think you're using this whole washing thing as an excuse to put your hands all over me, Mr. Frazier."

"Hmm, you've finally figured it out." He drew the cloth over her clit with enough force to make her gasp. "Want me to stop?"

"No!"

"I didn't think so."

Rory drew his knees up and out, forcing her legs to part wider until her entire pussy was completely open to his touch. He pushed his stiff dick to one side as he washed her carefully, and then moved his hand around to begin the process again with her bottom. As he pressed a finger to the rosebud of sensitive flesh he found there he told her, "Tonight we want to take you at the same time. Evan in your pretty pussy and me right here." He pushed the tip of his finger in the slightest bit and Jess quivered. "Would you let me do that?"

"Y—yes," she stammered and rocked back against his hand, her pussy clenching at the thought of her two men claiming her together.

"We don't have to, baby. Not if you don't—"

"I want to," she interrupted him and then blushed. "Please? I really want that."

"I knew you were the perfect woman for us," he said and then groaned as his cock twitched and hardened again. "Do you like it that way? Have you been keeping secrets from us?" He teased at her rosebud again, wiggling the tip of his finger until he was inside her ass up to the first knuckle.

Jess moaned and nodded, too embarrassed to speak but too turned on by what he was doing to deny it.

"You should have told us, baby."

"Too embarrassing."

"Sex is nothing to be embarrassed about. You are gorgeous, and we want to do anything and everything you'll allow us to do." Rory withdrew his finger and washed his hands with the cloth before dropping it onto the floor outside the tub.

"Now, I believe I promised you an orgasm before I fucked you, didn't I?"

"Yes, please." Jess squirmed, trying to bring more of his cock into contact with her aching clit.

"Since you asked so nicely..." Rory finally reached between her legs and rubbed her clit between his thumb and forefinger, sending a surge of molten lust coursing through her. Her hips bucked and she moaned as he tweaked her clitoris again. After all the teasing, she was already primed, and at his next touch Jess felt the first tingling rush of her impending release start to spread outward from her womb.

Rory fucked her with his fingers, pressing hard over her clit and then past it to slide into her slick channel. As her hips jerked against his hand he sped up the pace until the water in the tub was splashing over the sides at her frantic motions and she was racing toward the peaks of ecstasy. Jess was splayed out, her legs caught and her body held captive so that she was entirely at Rory's mercy. He pushed her body to new limits and she reveled in the freedom of having finally given herself over completely. There was no need to reciprocate, or even consider her lover's needs, there was only pleasure and her reaction to it. She took everything he gave her as he focused his entire purpose on one thing, bringing her to orgasm.

When Jess's climax finally hit her body arched up out of the water and she cried out Rory's name as his fingers continued to pluck at her tender flesh, stretching out her orgasm until she was quaking and limp.

He gave her only a few short minutes to recover her senses and then he gently flipped her over so that she was face-to-face with him, her legs straddling his hips as he leaned against the backrest and braced his feet against the far end of the bathtub. Behind him, Jess could see the Pacific rage and churn as the promised storm hit them full-on.

She turned her gaze back to Rory and realized a storm just as powerful was brewing in his dark eyes, and she leaned in and kissed him, her arms twining around his neck as he drew her down onto his cock and filled her until there was no room for anything between them. Skin to skin they moved, rocking slowly in an easy give and take that left no room in Jess's mind for anything else. Rory's cock stroked over the magical spot that made her gasp, and he groaned as her cunt squeezed tightly around him, milking him hard as she bucked and tried to get his cock to touch that spot again.

"Found your sweet spot, did I?" Rory's hands tightened around her waist and she let him take over as he guided her into the right position to hit her G-spot again.

"Yes!" Jess moaned as he found the right angle and started fucking her faster, sending jolts of pleasure through her body with every thrust and grinding her clit down against his pelvis before he lifted her up and then plunged into her again.

Her mouth found his and their kisses fell into the same rhythm as their bodies, tongues twining and parting in time to each penetration of her quivering pussy. Jess felt his thighs tense and his cock thickened inside her as he pushed them both to the brink of orgasm and then felt herself tumbling over it. Rory was not far behind her, pumping his cock into her body as he groaned her name and finished with a triumphant shout.

Jess slumped over him, and it was a minute before she

regained enough of her bearings to realize there was a lot less water in the tub than there had been before. She shivered, her wet skin now exposed to the air.

"Cold?" Rory asked and sat up a little, looking around them. "Oh shit. Uh, baby? I think we need to cut short the cuddling and go mop up the floor."

"Oops," Jess peeked over the edge of the tub to the large pool of sudsy water now flooding the tiled floor. "Hey, Evan? Could you come in here for a second? Rory made a mess and he's going to need a hand cleaning it up."

Evan opened the door and stepped into the bathroom, right into a pool of rapidly cooling bathwater. "Oh for the love of…" He stared down at his soaking wet sock. "I can't take you two anywhere nice. All right, I'll start mopping up in here. Rory, you get to call housekeeping and ask for more towels."

CHAPTER FOURTEEN

Jess grabbed one of the massive, fluffy robes hanging by the bathroom door and slipped out past Evan and back into the main room. While she and Rory had been bathing, Evan had been busy. The blinds had been drawn on all the windows, and the only light in the room came from the fire that was cheerfully blazing in the gas fireplace. A bottle of sparkling wine was chilling in a bucket of ice, and as Jess crossed over to the bed she spotted a negligee laid out across the coverlet. It was a concoction of lace and sheer fabric, all done in the softest shade of apricot she'd ever seen.

Jess lifted it off the bed and laughed as she realized that she could see right through it, but instead of worrying about it she shrugged out of her robe and slipped it over her head, letting it flutter down around her. She tugged the spaghetti thin straps into place over her shoulders and then glanced down to see how it looked. It fell to just above her knees and the plunging neckline was deep enough that she felt like her breasts were on display.

"It's supposed to look this way," she muttered to herself and made herself stop playing with it. Needing to distract herself, Jess went and draped her bathrobe over the back of one of the chairs and then rummaged through her purse until she found her hairbrush. She went to stand by the fireplace as she unclipped her hair and brushed it out as she listened to her two men bicker and joke with each other as they finished cleaning up the bathroom.

So this is what love feels like.

Jess knew she was smiling as she finished brushing the tangles from her hair. The guys' laughter filled the room with as much light as the fire, and she was content to bask in the warmth of it all.

When Rory walked out of the bathroom she looked at him and smiled, and for a moment she didn't understand why he stopped dead and stared at her.

"Ev? You need to come out here," Rory called to Evan and then raked his eyes over Jess from head to toe. "You look—"

"Holy shit, there's a goddess in our room," Evan broke in and leaned up against the doorjamb with a look of smug approval. "We did good. Didn't we?"

Jess nodded and did a slow pirouette so they could see her from all angles. For once there wasn't so much as a whisper of doubt in her mind, and she soaked up their admiration like a rose after the rain. "It's beautiful, thank you."

"No, you're beautiful. That just enhances everything." Evan was already walking toward her as he talked, and as he got closer Jess could see his dress pants were soaking wet and marked with traces of soap suds.

"You're a bit of a mess, lover. I think you need to get

out of these wet clothes." Jess reached out and tucked her fingers into the waistband of Evan's pants, pulling him closer even as she started working on undoing his button and fly.

"You help him get sorted, baby. I'm going to go call housekeeping. We are officially out of dry towels."

Jess gave Rory a nod and then dropped to her knees at Evan's feet, tugging his pants down to low enough he could step out of them. Evan gripped the mantel for balance and then groaned as Jess leaned in and nuzzled his cock through the thin fabric of his silk boxers. She pressed her mouth to the thick shaft, running her tongue over the silk until she felt him shudder. Without moving her mouth she slipped his wet socks off and dropped them on the floor before running her hands up the back of Evan's newly bared legs.

"You look so fucking beautiful right now, sweetheart." Evan stroked her hair, wrapping a strand around his finger before releasing it again.

"Thank you." Jess leaned back and smirked as she looked up at him. "You look really handsome in that shirt and tie, but I think you'd look better without them."

"You don't have to tell me twice."

"Bullshit, I have to tell you things twice all the time. You never listen to me the first time," Rory commented from the far corner of the room as he put down the phone. "And if the only way I can get you to listen to me is to tell you to get naked while getting up close and friendly with your dick, then I'm fine with having to repeat myself."

Rory came to stand near the door, his hand already gripping his cock as he stroked himself, his eyes on Jess. "Suck him off for me, baby. But make it quick, housekeeping's coming with our fresh towels, and no one gets to see your sexy ass naked but Ev and I."

"Agreed." Ev winked at her and lightly bumped her chin with his groin. "So by all means, let's get on with the fun before we're interrupted."

"Pushy, pushy. How did I get so lucky as to fall for not one, but two pushy alpha male types?" Jess muttered as she eased Evan's cock out of his underwear and brushed a kiss to the already moist tip.

"You didn't," Ev groaned his words, his hips already jerking slightly in anticipation of what she'd do next. "Rory's the bossy one, sweetheart. You and I will keep him happy by doing what he says…most of the time."

Jess winked up at Evan and parted her lips to take in as much of Evan's cock as she could. She let her jaw relax as he slid into the warm recess of her mouth, teasing the tip and then the underside of his thick shaft with her tongue. She finished tugging his boxers down to his ankles and then reached up to wrap the fingers of one hand around the base of his cock, her palm brushing his balls.

"Jess!" He let out a strangled moan of her name and rocked his hips, pushing himself all the way to the back of her throat. "I'm not going to last long if you keep that up."

Jess hummed in satisfaction at his reaction and began working his cock over eagerly, sucking and tonguing him as she worked every inch of his impressive length in and out of her mouth. Her fingers pumped in time to the movements of her mouth, and she felt a thrill of power as she felt Evan's legs tremble with the effort of staying upright.

Evan buried one hand in her hair, holding her close without restricting her ability to move too much.

"That's right, baby. Just like that, you're going to make him lose his mind any second," Rory encouraged her and she glanced over to see him standing with his legs spread and his cock a deep shade of red as he stroked himself off. Acting on instinct Jess reached out her free hand, gesturing for Rory to join them by the fire.

He was beside her in a second, and she took over jerking off his beautiful cock, smoothing her hand over the head and down, mirroring what her mouth was doing to Evan.

"Holy fuck, I...yes!" Rory groaned and Evan managed a broken chuckle.

"Tell me about it," Evan said and then Jess felt his balls tighten against her palm as he started to come.

Jess kept her hand busy stroking Rory as she let Evan fuck her mouth, relaxing and letting it happen as he cradled her head with one hand and rocked his cock against her lips and tongue until he came with an explosive, "Yes!"

His cum filled her throat so she swallowed, licking and sucking until he started to soften, and then she released him with a sly smile up into his face.

"I love all of you, sweetheart. But right now I'm particularly fond of that amazing mouth of yours." Evan leaned on the mantel and winked at her. "If you hurry, you can probably break both of us before housekeeping gets here."

"You don't have—" was all Rory managed to say before Jess turned to him and sucked his thick, heavy cock into her mouth with a moan that she knew vibrated right through him. Between her hand job and his arousal at watching her suck off Evan, Jess was confident that Rory was already primed and nearly ready for his own release. She cupped his balls in her hand and toyed with them as she pleasured him with her mouth and fingers, stroking and sucking as she let him in all the way to the back of her throat and then swallowed several times in rapid succession. She heard Rory growl her name and his hips jerked of their own accord as he plumbed the depths of her mouth with his cock. Rory's hands dropped to the crown of her head and his shaking fingers wrapped around her hair as he came on a rumbling groan. He tasted subtly different than Evan, the smoke and cedar taste of Rory's mouth echoed in the taste of his seed. She swallowed him down and nuzzled her nose against his skin, reveling in the way she had brought both of them to orgasm. She felt sexier and more alive than ever before, and as she lifted her head to look at her two men she knew in a flash of insight that this was where she was supposed to be, and these were the men she was destined to love.

They reached down together and helped her to her feet, strong hands stroking and guiding her back to the bed. Jess felt like she was in a bit of a daze, like the world was glowing around the edges and slightly out of focus. As she lay back onto the covers, one of them slipped a pillow under her head and the other drew her new negligee down her legs.

"You are the most incredible woman," Rory whispered tenderly and brushed his lips over her forehead before retreating back toward the door. "You stay there and relax, baby. I can hear the squeak of the housekeeping cart coming down the hall."

"Mmmkay," Jess murmured and turned her head as

she felt Evan's hand stroke her cheek and come to atop the pendant they'd given her earlier.

"I don't know what we did to deserve you, but I'm grateful." His smile warmed her heart and then he waggled her brows at her. "Especially for your sweet, amazing mouth. Where the hell did you learn to suck cock like that?"

Jess giggled and felt her cheeks get warm as she looked up at Evan. "You're going to laugh at me."

"Not a chance, sweetheart. Just please don't tell me you practiced on the entire high school basketball team or something, because then Rory and I would need to go kick some serious ass."

"Nope. Never practiced. I like reading romance novels, and um, some of them have some pretty vivid imagery."

"You learned that from a *book*?" Evan gave her a look of disbelief and then ducked behind the bed as a knock sounded at their door and housekeeping announced themselves.

"You are going to need to show me some of these books later," he whispered to her and then grinned as he gestured to his still-naked body. "They don't get to see me naked, either."

RORY HATED the fact Evan had to duck out of sight behind the bed. He hated the fact that they'd had to book two rooms just to keep up appearances instead of proudly escorting Jess to their room together. He'd seen other members of the colony make an effort not to draw attention to their alternative living arrangements, but he'd never had to experience firsthand until now. Now that he had he knew for certain that he didn't like it one bit.

He took the towels from the hotel employee and sent her on her way with his thanks, and the moment she was gone he locked the door and dropped the bundle of fresh linens onto the nearest chair.

"I don't care if this place is burning down around us, I don't plan on opening that door again until checkout time tomorrow," Rory said, already undoing the knot on his robe's belt. It shouldn't have been long enough for him to be ready to take her again, but he could feel his cock hardening as he drank in the sight of his mate as she lounged on the bed, her luscious curves barely covered by the negligee they'd managed to find in town. Rory hadn't even known there were stores in town that sold that sort of thing, but now that he did, he had plans to shop there more often. Jess looked gorgeous dressed in that little bit of nothing.

He dropped the robe on the floor at the foot of the bed and joined Jess, stretching out beside her as he moved her to the middle of the bed and into his arms. Evan took his place on the other side of her and Jess sighed in contentment as she nestled between them.

"I've never felt this good before." Jess lifted her arms and reached out to lay a hand on each of their stomachs. "All warm and sort of gooey."

"We made her gooey, Rory. I'd say that was mission accomplished." Evan chuckled from his side of the bed.

"Not quite yet," Rory reminded him and Jess's eyes widened a little.

"Oh, right. I recall someone promising me something…

new." Jess's plump lower lip disappeared between her teeth and Rory's cock roared to life with a vengeance.

Rory and Evan had discussed it while they'd been in the bathroom cleaning up, and they already knew how this was going to play out. Rory could still recall Evan's look of shock when Rory had told him that not only was their sweet Jess willing to try taking them both on at once, she was downright eager.

"You're sure, sweetheart?" Evan asked, and Rory could already hear the lust in his blood-brother's voice.

"I'm sure." Jess turned her head and gave Evan the same sexy smile she'd given Rory earlier. "I've done this before."

"What!" Rory and Evan both sat upright and stared down at her, and Evan's jealous expression was a match for the emotion roiling in Rory's stomach. There was no way she would have kept that from them, was there? Ugly feelings reared up and filled Rory with bitter envy.

Jess looked at them in confusion, completely taken aback by their reaction. "What is it? What did I say that's upset you?"

Rory leaned over her, his heart slamming against his ribs as he hovered a few inches above her face, staring down into her wide, blue eyes. "Who were they? The ones you shared before you came to us?"

"What?" Jess frowned and then shook her head. "No! Never. Not like that. I meant I had a boyfriend who liked anal. That's what I meant!"

Rory felt the fury in him die down as he looked down at Jess and saw the worry in her eyes.

She whispered, "I've never been with two men, ever.

Never loved anyone the way I love the two of you. I want to do this because it's us, the three of us together."

"Damn right it's the three of us, and there won't be anyone else for you, not ever. You're ours, Jess." Evan's hand closed over her fingers where they touched his stomach. "I will share you with Rory because that's the way it has to be, but I will never, ever share you with anyone else."

Jess nodded. "And you two belong to me. I can't be hurt by the women you had before me, shared or not. That was the past, but if you ever touch another woman again, I'll never forgive you."

Rory chuckled as his tension eased, and his laughter brought the others out of their distress as well. "And here I thought I was supposed to be the pushy, possessive one. You two are as bad as I am." He stroked Jess's cheek. "There will never be anyone else for us, I swear it."

Jess nodded, but there was uncertainty in her eyes and Rory knew before she said a word that they were finally going to hear at least part of the reason she was so quick to close herself off.

"My father once made that vow to my mom. They were happy together, but one day it wasn't enough anymore, and he left. He married someone else and was busy celebrating his new life while his former wife lay dying. She started fading the day he left, and not even my love could keep her here." Jess looked at them both and there were tears in her eyes. "So how do I know that one day one of you won't decide you want to forget the promise you made here tonight?"

"That'll never happen, sweetheart." It was Evan who

spoke the words, but Rory hoped she understood they came from both of them.

"How can you be sure about that?" she asked, reaching up to wrap her soft fingers around Rory's hand as he touched her face.

"It's something else that you'll have to take on faith for now," Evan told her and Jess's lower lip popped out into a faint pout.

"You two are asking for a lot of faith right now," she muttered. "All right, then, until tomorrow, but then I want some answers. No, tomorrow night I want *all* the answers."

Rory's heart melted as he pictured a little girl with his dark hair and her mother's ice-blue eyes using that pout against him one day and he leaned in to kiss Jess's sweet mouth, teasing his tongue over her lower lip.

"Don't pout, baby. It makes me crazy when you do that," Rory whispered when he finally lifted his head.

"Nice going, hotshot. Now she knows how to make us *both* crazy!" Evan grumbled and playfully shoved Rory aside to kiss Jess as well.

As Rory watched Jess respond to Evan's kiss, an idea started forming in his mind and he changed position so that he was down near Jess's sexy little feet. While she was still distracted he lowered his head and ran the tip of his tongue along her pink-painted toenails, eliciting a soft squeal of surprise from Jess.

He lifted her foot in one hand, cradling her heel so that he could slowly nibble on each of her toes and working his way very slowly along the instep and up to her ankle. Rory could see that Evan was taking advantage of her distraction to advance his own agenda, and as Rory watched, Evan kissed his way down to her breasts and nuzzled at them through the filmy fabric that covered them.

Rory continued kissing his way higher, sampling the soft skin of her calf and then slowing down to tickle the back of her knee with his tongue. Jess giggled and parted her thighs wider, inviting him to move higher up her leg. Her scent filled his senses and Rory was nearly overcome by his need for the woman lying open and pliant beneath him. She smelled of citrus and vanilla and a subtle musk that called to him like no other woman ever had. He'd first scented her in the water that day they'd saved her from drowning, and the part of him that was more animal than man had known even then that she was meant for him, his mate. She was his and Evan's, because that was the only way to keep her safe. After they were fully bonded, her life would be linked with theirs, and if they lost her, there would be no one else, ever.

Rory brushed his mouth over the soft, succulent flesh of her inner thigh and let the perfume of her arousal wash over him. Without realizing what he was doing, his kisses grew rougher, and he nipped her tender skin hard enough Jess yelped in surprise.

"Sorry, baby," he apologized, already kissing her better.

Evan's voice sounded in his head and Rory realized that the link between them was growing stronger, and that it had been ever since they'd pulled Jess out of the water. *"Easy, bro. We can't bind her to us without her knowing what that would mean. It wouldn't be fair."*

"I didn't mean to." Rory sent the thought back, chagrined that he'd let his instincts rule his reason. Selkies

hadn't lived as animals for centuries, but still the instincts were there, right below the surface.

Forcing himself to be more patient than he wanted to, Rory brushed a final kiss to Jess's thigh and then started the entire process with her other foot, nibbling on her toes until he was rewarded with a low, thrumming moan of pleasure. As he worked his way higher he let his eyes lift so that he could watch as Evan tugged the floating scraps of fabric off their mate, leaving her bare to their gazes.

As Rory drifted more kisses up Jess's thigh she moaned again and Evan chuckled. "You should see the expression on her face, Rory. I think she's getting impatient."

Rory lifted his head and found himself staring into a pair of crystal-blue eyes that were nearly burning with need.

"I want to come and so far neither of you boys is getting the job done," Jess complained, grinning at them both.

"Did you just call us *boys*?" Rory asked, meeting her gaze briefly before lifting his eyes to Evan's and sending him a quick mental picture of what he wanted.

"Uh oh, not a good idea, sweetheart. Now you've got him riled," Evan chuckled as he reached for both of Jess's hands and took them into his own. Rory watched as Evan slid himself in behind Jess, cradling her between his legs as he drew her back against his chest, his hands still holding her wrists as he crossed their joined arms across her body.

"Thank you, Ev. That will do nicely." Rory lifted Jess's legs over Evan's so that she was spread-eagled on the bed, laid out like a feast for him to devour. Her eyes went round and her mouth popped open into an expression of surprise as Rory prowled his way up between her thighs. "You wanted to come, baby, and that's what you're going to do." He ran his finger down her gleaming, wet slit and then parted her labia so that she was completely exposed to his gaze. "You'll come so hard you're going to see stars, I promise."

He heard the air whoosh out of her lungs as she tugged at Evan's grip and realized she wasn't going to be allowed to move.

"Spread her legs for me, Evan. I want to see her pretty pussy."

Evan stretched his legs out farther, until the angle was just past the point it would be possible for Jess to be able to free herself.

Having her helpless and open like this was testing the limits of Rory's control. His cock was harder than granite and he wanted nothing more than to cover her body with his and fuck her until she screamed his name. But that wasn't going to happen, at least, not yet. First he had to remind their newly blossoming vixen who was in charge in the bedroom, and then...Rory's balls tightened as he thought about what would happen next, when she was riding Evan's dick as Rory took her from behind and they fucked her together.

That image was seared into his brain as he buried his head between her thighs and focused in on her clit. He nibbled, sucked, and lashed at the tiny cluster of nerves without mercy. He wanted to hear her beg him to let her come before he'd let her go over.

"Oh god! Rory!" Her words spurred him on and he felt her entire body go taut as she teetered on the edge of orgasm.

"I don't think he's quite ready to forgive you for calling us boys yet," Evan pointed out and Rory could hear the laughter and the lust in his blood-brother's voice.

Rory plunged two fingers into her channel and was rewarded with another wild moan. Lifting his mouth just enough to form words he muttered, "Not even close."

"I'm so screwed," Jess whimpered as Rory's mouth latched onto her clitoris again, drawing the hypersensitive flesh into his mouth. He shifted his hand and curved his fingers until the tips brushed over her G-spot and he felt her body spasm in response.

"Not yet you're not, but I think you're going to be, very soon," Evan whispered.

Rory let himself get lost in the heady perfume of her arousal until her cream soaked his chin and his hand and dripped from her swollen pussy. He reveled in her body and the way she responded so quickly to every touch of his hand and mouth.

Only when she was completely mindless with pleasure did she finally say the words he'd been waiting for. "Please, Rory. Please let me come."

Rory smiled as he took her to a new level of pleasure and let her come at last. As she came undone beneath him her cries of release were the sweetest music he had ever heard. Dazed, she lay panting in Evan's arms as Rory moved up the bed to kiss her, letting her taste her own essence on his tongue.

"Remind me not to call you *boys* again," she whispered breathlessly, her lips still moving against his. "At least not until I've had a month or two to recover."

CHAPTER FIFTEEN

THE THREE OF them stayed piled together in a blissful tangle for a while, until Jess's breathing returned to normal and her limbs once again moved when she asked them to. She was sandwiched between her lovers, her arms around Rory's shoulders and Evan's arms draped atop of hers, holding them all together. She could feel both their erections pressed against her body, and she knew the minute she moved she was going to have one of her favorite fantasies come true. Well, it was a very recent fantasy, but that didn't stop it from being one of her favorites.

She stroked the back of Rory's neck and his head lifted immediately so that his dark-chocolate eyes met hers. "Hey, sexy," Jess murmured as she ran her fingers over his lips and was gifted with a slow, sensuous smile that sent a fresh set of tingles down her limbs.

"You ready for us, baby?" Rory asked, lust sparking in his gaze.

"I want you both so much." Jess turned her head so she could see Evan. "Make love to me, please?"

Both men groaned in agreement and Rory lifted himself up and to one side, sprawling his big body down one side of the bed as Jess and Evan untangled themselves. Still feeling the pleasant afterglow of her most recent orgasm, Jess gave Evan enough space to shift himself to the middle of the bed and stretch out on his back. As his blond head hit the pillows he patted his chest and winked at her.

"Come on up, sweetheart."

Evan's hands wrapped around her waist and half lifted her up and over his body so that she was straddling his hips. His cock was pinned along the seam of her pussy and as she leaned down to kiss him they both moaned when even that small movement pressed their bodies together.

"Need you," she whispered into Evan's mouth as their lips met. His tongue mated with hers, stroking and thrusting as she rocked her hips and ground her clit against the hard shaft of his erection. Evan's hands were still on her hips when she felt another hand slip between them, lining up Evan's cock so that he could thrust up into her. Evan's entire body shuddered as he drove himself high, hard, and deep and Rory withdrew his hand without comment. Instead he came around behind her and stroked his fingers over the curve of her ass and along the backs of her thighs. The contrast of Rory's light touches and Evan's powerful thrusts were making it hard for Jess to remember to breathe, never mind think.

"Let it go," Rory told her in a tone as gentle as his

caresses. "You don't need to do anything but let us love you."

Evan groaned in agreement even as his hands tightened on her hips, guiding her into a slow, rocking rhythm that sent shimmering threads of bliss coursing through her core. Rory's hands left her body and then she felt something cool and slick being poured onto her skin. Goosebumps washed up her back and then Rory's hands were back, warming her as they traveled across the slickness and carried it down to the rosebud of her anus.

Evan's constant give and take made it easy for her to relax as Rory's fingers breached her narrow opening, stretching her carefully as he introduced more of the lubricant. The initial burning quickly faded and Jess let herself be distracted by the pleasure of Evan's cock stroking deep inside her pussy. Jess let her head drop to Evan's chest as she rode him, forcing herself to relax even more as Rory stretched her even further as he penetrated her with a third finger. Bright pleasure and dark pain blended into one exquisite, overwhelming sensation and Jess moaned, clamping her inner walls around Evan's cock.

"I think she's ready," Evan groaned as her body squeezed him tighter.

"Just breathe and trust me," Rory told her and withdrew his fingers.

Jess felt more cool liquid being spread over her skin and then Rory moved up close enough that she could feel his thighs against hers. The head of his cock pressed up against her opening and she breathed out slowly as he pushed his way past the tight ring of muscle. Her vaginal muscles tightened up around Evan's dick again and he stopped moving, letting her adjust to this new experience.

Rory eased himself inside with painstaking gentleness, going so slowly that Jess felt nothing more than minor discomfort. Finally she grew impatient and wriggled her hips, drawing a raw-sounding groan from both men.

"Baby, if you do that again I'm not going to be able to hold back," Rory warned her.

"I don't want you to hold back, I want both of you. It's all right Rory. This is what I need."

"Fuck!" Evan swore as she rocked her hips forward slightly, taking him deeper. "I don't know how long I can last, either. This is too good."

Jess saw the look of adoration Evan was giving her and it warmed her soul.

"Now you're truly ours," Rory declared and let himself slide in the last inch, until he was completely buried inside her. "So tight!" he groaned and Jess tensed her body, feeling every inch of her two men as they filled her so full she could barely breathe.

She wasn't sure how they did it, but somehow her men moved in concert, Rory withdrawing slightly as Evan drove himself as deep as he could, and then Evan's hips were pulling back as Rory moved to fill her. Back and forth they went and Jess could do nothing but hang on, her world so full of sensation and pleasure that she felt like she was drunk with it.

Soon her pussy began to clench and she knew she was on the verge of coming as her two lovers began to accelerate their pace. Groans and soft cries of need filled the air and she was no longer sure who was saying what. She was not sure of anything except the slow-blooming flower of passion that unfurled deep inside her and then carried her away on a wave of pleasure so deep she lost herself completely. Jess barely heard her men call her name as they both came within seconds of each other, jetting their hot streams of cum deep into her body.

Nearly senseless with pleasure Jess collapsed onto Evan's broad chest and waited for the room to stop spinning around her.

"Fucking hell, that was incredible." Evan's arms came around her as he spoke, cradling her gently against his chest. "You okay, sweetheart?"

"Mmhmm," Jess murmured. "Better than okay. *So* much better."

She felt Rory brush his lips over her back and then he was carefully withdrawing from her body. "I love you," was all Rory said as his weight shifted and she felt him leave the bed. She managed to lift her head enough to watch him walk to the bathroom, and it gave her more than a little satisfaction to see he wasn't quite steady on his feet. Once she heard the sound of water running she turned back to Evan and grinned.

"I think we broke him."

Evan burst out laughing. "No, sweetheart, we didn't. *You* did. You broke both of us." He pressed a very soft kiss to the tip of her nose and then stretched out with a contented sigh. "I've been used and abused and I've never been so happy in my life. Thank you."

Jess gingerly moved off of Evan and was not surprised when her legs gave out and she flopped face-first onto the bed. "I think I broke me, too."

Evan was up in a flash and hovered over her, a look of

worry on his handsome face. "Are you okay? We didn't hurt you, did we?"

"I'm not hurt, just weak in the knees." She rolled over and gave him what she hoped was a reassuring smile. "I'm weak in the knees, and pretty much everywhere else, too."

"What's wrong?" Rory came out of the bathroom still gloriously naked and Jess couldn't help but wonder how she managed to get so lucky as to have not one but two gorgeous guys in love with her.

"Nothing's wrong. But I may need you two to carry me out of here tomorrow morning. I'm spent!" Jess announced and threw a hand over her eyes for emphasis. "If this is the way things are going to be between the three of us, I'm never going to need to go to a gym again. I'll end up skinny just trying to keep up with you two."

Rory rumbled in protest and came to sit beside her on the bed. "Don't you dare get all scrawny on us, baby. We like your curves."

Evan nodded. "You're beautiful just the way you are." He reached down and stroked her breasts. "I'd be very unhappy if you took these beauties away from me."

Jess burst into a fit of giggles. "All right then, no diets, but only because I couldn't stand to make either of you unhappy."

"Thank you." Evan kissed her sweetly and then left the bed, padding over to the bathroom. "And don't think I don't see you ogling my ass there, sweetheart." He tossed the words over his shoulder before closing the door and leaving her and Rory alone for a moment.

"Lie still and let me clean you up a bit." Rory held up the washcloth he'd brought with him and Jess smiled at his thoughtfulness. "You're sure everything's fine?" he asked as he started gently running the cloth over her inner thighs. "That was…I guess intense is a good word to describe it."

"It was amazing, and wonderful. I'm not hurting at all," Jess reassured him and then decided to ask the question that had been in her mind since he'd first suggested they make love together. "Is it always like that? I mean, that intense?"

Rory's hand stilled and he lifted his head to stare into her eyes. "Evan and I have shared women before, but never like that."

"Never?" Jess's heart swelled at the realization that no matter how much her men had experienced before she'd come into their lives, this was the one thing she had with them that no one else ever could. It was a first time for all of them.

"Never. We wanted to wait for the right woman. That's why we were so worried we'd hurt you. This was something we'd never done before."

"Well, you did it perfectly." Jess threw her arms around Rory and tugged him down on top of her, kissing him happily. "I love you so much."

"Oh sure, I leave the room for three minutes and you two are at it again!" Evan grumbled as he rejoined them. "I thought you were worn out, sweetheart?"

"It was a temporary energy surge." Jess reached out for Evan and drew him in so she could kiss him, too. "Rory just told me this was a first time for all of us, and I was trying to show him how much that meant to me."

"It meant a lot to us, too." Evan glanced at Rory, who nodded and stood, scooping Jess up off the bed as Evan pulled down the covers so they could all get in and get comfortable.

Jess found herself once again snuggled between her two favorite bookends, her head on Rory's chest and Evan spooned up behind her, his hand resting on the curve of her hip.

As Rory reached out and turned off the light, a gust of wind slammed into the windows and room was filled with the sound of rain splattering against the glass. Jess burrowed deeper under the covers and held onto her two men. She knew that for tonight at least, they were safe from the storm.

EVAN LISTENED to the storm that raged outside, the violent wind and rain counterpointed by the soft breathing of the woman he held in his arms. As she settled into a deeper sleep she let out a tiny snore and Evan smiled to himself. He had it bad if he even found Jess's snoring adorable, but he was more than okay with that idea.

As Evan lay there in the darkness he sent out a tendril of thought to Rory, and found his blood-brother's mind as awake as his own. *"So, we're committed now. How are you feeling?"*

A touch of laughter accompanied Rory's reply. *"I thought I'd be having second thoughts by now, but I'm not."*

"After what she just did with us? We'd be insane to be reconsidering. She's the most amazing women I've ever met."

"And she's all ours or she will be once we get through tomorrow. If my father doesn't accept her, we're keeping her

anyway, right?" Rory asked for confirmation, but they'd had this conversation many times before.

"She's worth it, Rory. There are others who could lead the colony, but there's no one else I want to share my life with." Evan let his feelings bleed into the thoughts he was sending to Rory, making his opinion as clear as he could.

"Then we're in agreement." Rory's thoughts went silent for a moment and then he added, *"Do you think she's going to accept us after all of this is over?"*

"I still think she's one of us, or at least she's got a bit of selkie in her bloodline somewhere. Once she gets over the shock of it all, we'll be able to figure it out together. She loves us, bro. I don't think she's going to walk away from that. Not even after she finds out we're a bit more myth than men."

"If Aaron and Rick could manage to bumble it as badly as they did and still keep Jenny, I think we have a good chance," Rory said and both men shared a silent laugh. The selkie men Rory had talked to had claimed they did a great job of explaining themselves to Jenny, to whom they had now been married for more than twenty years. Jenny's version of events, though, had brought tears of laughter to Evan's eyes as she'd gone into detail about where her men had gone wrong and what Evan and Rory could do better when their time came.

"She has to stay." There was an unfamiliar undercurrent of fear in Rory's thoughts. *"I don't want to go back to the way things were before we fished her out of the ocean."*

"Neither do I," Evan answered. *"So let's make sure that doesn't happen."*

CHAPTER SIXTEEN

THE THREE OF them made the short drive to Rory's parent's house in relative silence, and Jess couldn't help but notice that both of her men seemed to need to be in constant contact with her. Holding her hand, touching her leg, or stroking her cheek, they were always finding ways to connect with her, as if they needed the reassurance almost as much as she did.

Jess knew this wasn't going to be an easy visit, though she was still unclear as to exactly why Rory's father was going to object to her relationship with his son and Evan. *I suppose I'm going to find out soon enough.*

As if sensing her thoughts, Evan turned and pressed a kiss to her temple and his arms tightened around her waist as he held her in his lap. When this ordeal was over with, she really needed to talk to the guys about returning her little rental car and buying something more practical, preferably a vehicle all three of them could fit into without her winding up in someone's lap.

As Rory slowed the truck down Jess couldn't help but gawk at the massive log house that rose up into view.

"That's where your parents live?"

"That's the traditional home of the colony leader and his family," Rory confirmed as he drove up the circular driveway and parked outside the front door.

"Wow," Jess muttered. "And here I thought all log cabins were supposed to be rustic." The house was situated on a bluff overlooking Kismet Cove, nestled into the edge of the rainforest so that it was sheltered from the worst of the wind. The moment the door opened she could hear the wind whistling between the boughs of the evergreen trees and making even the largest of them creak as they swayed. Evan handed her down to Rory, and then climbed down out of the truck to join them. They both took one of her hands as they made the short walk to the doorway.

Jess's heart was beating faster and she could have sworn she could hear mocking laughter being carried on the wind that swept around them. *Now I'm imagining things, great.* A shiver chased up the back of her neck and she squeezed her fingers tighter around Rory and Evan's hands. Both of them looked down at her, and she took comfort in the adoration that was so evident in their gazes.

"Ready, sweetheart?" Evan asked and then dropped a kiss to her cheek as he whispered in her ear, "Remember, we're the rocks. Rory and his father are the storm."

Jess nodded. "Let's get this over with."

Rory raised his hand to knock and then stopped, turning to kiss her thoroughly. "I love you. That's all you need to remember tonight."

"I love you both," she told them and then quickly

smoothed her hands over her top. It was the same one she'd worn the night she'd made them their thank you dinner, and she'd hoped it would bring her some of that same luck today.

Rory knocked and the door was opened almost instantly. Standing there was a woman only an inch or so taller than Jess, and Jess knew right away that this had to be Rory's mother. She'd given her son his stunning smile.

Rory opened his mouth to make introductions when his mother got an odd look on her face and grabbed Jess by the shoulders and then dragged her into her arms for a hug that nearly squeezed the breath from Jess's lungs.

"Mara?" she queried and there was shock in her tone. "Mara, it's me, Emma. How can you still look so young?"

Grief welled up inside Jess and she clung to Emma in confusion. How could this stranger know her mother's name?

Emma gripped Jess tightly for a moment longer and then seemed to find her composure and released her, taking a step back. "I'm so sorry, dear. Of course you can't be Mara. But the resemblance is uncanny. Tell me, who are you and how is it you're involved with my boys?"

Rory and Evan stood in the hall and stared, both of them clearly as confused as Jess was.

"I'm Jess. M-Mara was my mother. Mara Silk. Did you know her?"

"Your mother? Of course! You look just like her, but I'm sure you knew that. Same beautiful hair, same eyes, you could be her twin! I haven't seen her since we were girls, but there was a time I was your mother's closest friend. How is she? Where has she been? I've never stopped thinking about her and wondering if she'd come home."

"She…she died," Jess blurted out. "Six months ago. I grew up in Toronto. She never said anything about living out here, only that this is where she met my father."

"Mom, slow down." Rory slipped an arm around Jess's shoulders, supporting her. "Jess's dad just signed over their family cabin to her a few weeks ago. Jess has come out here for the winter to finish writing her book and get away for a while. Are you saying you knew her mother?"

"Knew her? We were best friends. She's the only daughter of Jack and Alicia *Silk*, Rory. Mara disappeared one night after things got a bit…heated at home. That was during your grandfather's time." Jess glanced up at Rory and watched his eyes widen as if suddenly understood some great secret she wasn't privy to.

"Holy shit, bro. I told you she was a true mate!" Evan whooped and slapped Rory on the back.

"True mate? You three?" Emma beamed and glanced down, finally spotting the elegant pendant Jess was wearing. "Oh that's wonderful! Your father is going to be thrilled. Thrilled! Why didn't you tell us earlier?"

"We didn't know, mom." Rory started to explain but then Emma was babbling and Jess was struggling to understand what the hell was going on. True mate? One of us? Why hadn't her mother told her she had grown up here?

"…Imagine you two finding a true mate, and one of the missing bloodlines at that. You can't know how hard it's been for us selkies since your mother left, Jess. She wasn't the only one to run, you know. We all lost friends back then, and now here you are, back and going to be bonded to my boys!"

Jess found herself caught up in another hug. "So tell

me, do you look like your mother in your seal form? She was always considered one of the most beautiful selkie women around. Did she tell you that?"

"Selkies? My mother was a selkie? That's insane! They're just myths! Ancient legends and folklore!" Jess stumbled backward out of Emma's arms, her head spinning. *Are they all crazy?*

Evan caught her and tried to draw her into his arms, but Jess was too overwhelmed to let him. She spun away from him and backed up until she was plastered against the wall and she could see all three of them. "You're saying that you're all selkies? Seals?"

"Of course dear, just like you are." Emma gave her a puzzled look and Jess realized that the kindly woman believed every word she'd said.

"Mom, stop it! She doesn't know who she is!" Rory roared, his voice reverberating down the hall.

"Don't you dare yell at your mother that way! I taught you better than that!" An older version of Rory stormed down the hall toward them, as fierce and wild as his son.

"Not now, dad!" Rory turned to Jess and she could see the fear and worry in his eyes. "Jess, it's going to be okay, please. Just trust us, okay?"

Tears blinded her and Jess shook her head again and wailed as confusion and hurt tore her heart in two. This couldn't be happening. This had to be a nightmare.

There was a crash and the floor shook, and through her tears Jess could see that Rory's father had thrown her lover up against the wall. "You will not take that tone with me, boy, now or ever! Now what the hell is going on here and why were you yelling at your mother!"

"She's Mara's daughter…"

"Dad, let me go or so help me…"

"She doesn't know who she is…"

The voices were a jumble of noise and Jess couldn't take it anymore. She bolted deeper into the house, needing to find someplace quiet where she could think and be alone for a minute. The hall ended and she found herself in a bright and cheerful kitchen with a tile floor so smooth she nearly lost her footing as she came careening into the room.

"I see Darius and Rory are off to a fine start." A man's voice came from nearby and Jess squeaked in shock as she spun around to see who else was here.

"Whoa! You're going to wind up flat on your ass on the floor, and then the boys are going to blame me for scaring you, though I'd say they were doing a damn fine job of it already." A kind smile and red hair registered in Jess's mind and she realized she had met Rory's second father, Torin.

"Hi," she managed weakly and reached up to dash the tears from her cheeks with an unsteady hand. "I don't think I can stay here. Please, can you tell me how to get back to the truck without them seeing me?"

Torin looked thoughtful and then sighed. "They really screwed up this time, didn't they?" He jerked his head down the hallway to where a cacophony of raised voices was still easily heard. "And they say redheads are the ones with the nasty tempers. Not in this household. I'll tell you how to get back to the truck, but you need to promise me something." His gaze dropped to the pendant at her throat. "Don't run far, all right? If you love them enough to wear that, then you love them enough to give them a chance to make up for whatever idiotic thing they've managed to do."

Jess nodded. "I promise I won't go far. I just can't stay here."

"Fair enough." His eyes narrowed and then widened. "Oh hell, I think I can guess what at least part of the problem is. You're a Silk. You look like your mom, and your uncle, too, though I must say you're a far sight prettier."

"I—I have an uncle?" Jess's head was starting to ache from all the new information she'd been bombarded with in the past five minutes.

"You have an uncle, and grandparents…and you don't know anything about any of this, do you? Well, fuck the proverbial duck, no wonder you're upset. All right, you're coming with me, and I think we both need a drink." He winked at her. "I'm going to get my ass kicked for this, but if anyone says anything, you tell them I went with you to make sure you didn't do anything rash. Deal?"

"Okay." Jess nodded, still reeling from the realization that these people knew her mother, not to mention the fact they all believed they were shapeshifters straight out of legend. A legend her mother had taught her about as a child…

She found herself following Torin out a back door and down a few stairs. He helped her clamber into another truck and then they were gone before she could really think about what she was doing.

"I'm Jess, by the way."

"Torin Sheils. It's nice to meet you, Jess, though I suspect the circumstances could have been better for you. Now we're clear of the chaos, would you please tell me why my blood-brother and his son were bellowing like a pair of bulls during mating season?"

"Emma thought I was my mother and uh, Rory got protective and very loud when I got upset, and then things sort of got out of hand. I didn't even know my mother was from this area or…well anything."

"You do look just like Mara. She is your mother, right?"

"Yes." Jess glanced over at Torin and her heart leaped into her throat as she finally realized who and what she was speaking to. "So you're one of them? I mean, you think you're a selkie?"

"I don't think I am, I know it. Born and raised." He shot her a sideways look. "And your mother never told you about us." It wasn't a question, so Jess didn't feel she needed to answer it. "You didn't know about Rory and Evan either?"

"That they believe they're monsters that can be summoned to sexually satisfy any lonely woman who knows to shed her tears into the ocean? No, I didn't."

Torin barked with laughter. "Well, I see you know at least a little bit of our mythology, anyway. But to clarify, mated selkies are immune to that sort of summons. If they bond with you, that's it, they're locked in for life. And for the record, we're not monsters. We're just not human all of the time."

"So you—I mean—all of you are, uh real?" Jess stammered, trying to decide if even asking that question meant she was delusional too.

"We're very real, I promise you. I know this is a lot to take in, but you're not crazy, and neither are we."

Jess nodded and a scrap of memory suddenly fell into place. "So the day Evan and Rory pulled me out of the water, I didn't imagine that a seal swam up and tried to help me?"

"If the seal was dark brown, then it was Rory. If it was more golden, that would have been Evan." Torin was so matter-of-fact about it that Jess couldn't help but believe him, no matter how strange it was to consider.

"Wow. So…selkies. Huh." She hugged her purse to her chest. "This has been a very weird day." That was when the rest of what he'd said sunk in. "You said selkies are locked in for life?" Jess turned to Torin. "But what happens if one of us wants to leave?"

"Once you're bonded, you won't want to leave. At least that's what happens when one of our kind bonds to other selkies. Humans can bond, but it's weaker for them." He glanced over at her again, his eyes kind. "Your mother didn't tell you any of this?"

"She never told me anything about her past, only that things had been bad at home and she'd eloped with my father to get away."

"She married a human then?" Torin mused.

"My father was spending the summer in the cabin next door to your land. It belongs to his family. Or it did. Mom had him give it to me as part of their divorce."

"They're divorced? Did your mother come back with you then?"

"She died," Jess confessed and felt tears welling up in her eyes yet again.

"Damn it, I put my foot in that, didn't I? Sorry. I should have guessed."

"Why would you have guessed she died?"

"Because, little one. That's how it works. If she was bound to your father, then she couldn't live without him.

That's one of the reasons we live in trios. If one of us dies, then the others can go on. But no bonded selkie can live on if both their mates are gone. They fade away quickly once that happens."

Jess burst into bitter tears as yet another revelation struck her. If her mother was truly a selkie, then she had known she was going to die from the moment her father had decided to leave. She'd known, and that's why she'd arranged everything and sent Jess back to Tofino as her dying wish.

"He killed her!" Jess howled as fresh grief tore through her. "My stupid, selfish father and his stupid midlife crisis killed her!"

"Oh hell." Torin pulled the truck over and opened an arm, and Jess unclipped her seat belt to sob against his shoulder. "They really made a complete mess out of this, didn't they? Your father couldn't have known what his leaving would do. If your mother didn't tell you, do you think she'd tell *him*? Of course she didn't. And your mother didn't do you any favors, either. You've been walking through life thinking you're a duck when you're really a swan. She should have done better by you, no matter what it was that sent her running from here."

Torin patted her shoulder awkwardly for a few more minutes until Jess felt a little better.

"Clean yourself up and I'll take you into Breakers and then I'll buy us both a drink or three. I think we're going to need it. You've got questions, and any minute now Tweedledum and Tweedledummer are going to start calling in a frantic huff because they've figured out you left."

"They can call all they want. My phone is staying off

for a while," Jess declared as she slid back over to her side of the truck and put her seat belt back on. Once she was settled in her seat she started rummaging through her purse for a mirror and some makeup to fix some of the worst of the damage. Torin started the engine and pulled back onto the road, heading for town.

"Do you know where your pelt is?" he asked, and his voice was softer now.

"My pelt? You mean I actually have one? I can change into a seal?" Jessica felt like her head was going to explode from all the new information being crammed into it.

"Yes, you have one, somewhere. Or you should. If you don't remember turning into a seal then your mother must have taken it from you right after you turned for the first time. You'd have been six or so."

Jess felt her stomach twist and she gripped tightly to her purse as she fought to cope with this new revelation. "So I'm a selkie, even though my dad was human?"

"There's always a chance that the human side will be dominant, but that's fairly rare unless the child is several generations removed from their selkie parentage. Your mother was a pure-blooded selkie, so I'd be very surprised if you took after your dad's side.

He looked thoughtful for a moment. "If the boys didn't know who or what you were, why did they give you that pendant? Did they explain what it means?"

"They said it meant that I was the woman they'd chosen to be with." She smiled a little. "And they may have suggested that Darius wasn't going to be very happy when he saw me wearing it. But they promised me that after tonight they'd explain everything. I guess they don't need to bother now."

"Don't you let them off that easy!" Torin snorted and shook his head. "You have an entirely new life ahead of you if you want it, and those two chowder-heads are the best ones to explain it to you. They have a vested interest in making you want this life, so I'd say they should make for absolutely *inspired* guidance counselors."

Jess giggled and Torin shot her a pleased smile. "That's better. There'll be time for tears later on, but for right now, better to laugh and have a drink."

"Or three," Jess muttered.

CHAPTER SEVENTEEN

It was only a matter of minutes before they reached the outskirts of town and Jess glanced around, noting a few landmarks so she'd be able to come back here on her own. So far she'd not made it out to experience Tofino's nightlife, and this Breakers place might just be the way to change that.

They swung into a crowded parking lot and Torin somehow managed to ease his truck between two other jacked up behemoths.

She hopped out and had just enough room to squeeze herself down the side of the truck. She brushed the dirt off her jeans as she waited for Torin to join her, and he gave her a wink before offering her his arm. "Anyone so much as looks sideways at you, little one, you let me know. The boys would have my hide if I let anything happen to you, and this place can be a little…rough."

"Sounds about perfect for my current mood, then," Jess retorted and took his arm. "I am in dire need of tequila right now."

Torin looked down at her and grinned. "Tequila? Oh my dear girl, you've made my day. I was expecting you to order a nice, ladylike wine cooler."

"Oh, hell no! I passed the wine stage right about the time Evan started high fiving Rory and talking about true mates."

Torin's jaw dropped and stopped them both dead in their tracks outside the main door. "True mate. You're their true mate? They knew that and they didn't think to look into your family heritage? I take back what I said about them being inspired guides. They're too stupid for the job. If they even *suspected* that's what you were then they should have realized you weren't human and proceeded accordingly."

He scrubbed a hand through his red and silver hair and shook his head. "I imagine they were too busy chasing you around the bedroom to think too much at all."

Jess blushed. "Something like that, yes."

Torin gave her a brazen grin. "There's a good reason we selkies are in such demand as lovers, then and now. You best get used to it." He winked. "We get better with age, too." Torin pulled open the door before she could answer and a wash of warmth and raucous music poured over them. Nickelback's "Burn It to the Ground" was blaring out of a number of speakers, and the bar's small dance floor was completely packed, despite the fact it was still only early evening.

Jess followed Torin through the crowd and they found themselves a pair of stools tucked up against the back corner of the bar. The nearest speaker was far enough away that conversation was difficult but not impossible, and Jess hopped up on her seat with a nod of approval.

It didn't take long for a bartender to spot them, and Jess couldn't help but notice he was mouthwateringly gorgeous. He gave her a friendly grin and leaned in close enough for her to hear him clearly.

"What can I get you, sweet thing?"

Torin snorted with laughter. "You can save your breath, Byron. This one's spoken for. Byron, this is Jess." Torin turned to Jess. "Jess, this is Byron Triggs, he and Tucker own Breakers."

"It's nice to meet you." Jess beamed at Byron. His gaze dropped to the pendant at her throat and he whistled low in his throat. "It's the end of the world as we know it. Rory and Evan have fallen."

Jess touched the pendant and nodded. "I'm afraid so."

"Then for you, milady, the drinks are on the house. What are you having?"

"Tequila shots, plural. Please."

Byron arched a blond brow. "Tequila shooters and you're here without either of your men in attendance. I smell a story."

Torin leaned forward slightly. "Before you forget to ask me, pup, I'll have a Guinness."

"Tequila and a Guinness, coming up." Byron grabbed a mug and stepped down the bar to the beer taps, leaving the two of them alone for a minute.

"So Byron's one of you?" Jess asked the moment she confirmed they were alone. "How many of you are there?"

There's an entire colony of us, living here in secret." Torin touched his finger to his lips to remind her to be discrete. "Byron and Tucker are a bonded pair, the same as Rory and Evan."

"What?" Jess groaned as she realized there was even more information she was missing.

"Rory and Evan are bonded?" She frowned. "What exactly does that mean? They told me they weren't into each other...uh...that way."

Torin threw back his head and brayed with laughter loud enough several other people turned to stare. When he finally regained his composure he grinned at Jess. "Please be sure to ask for clarification when they get around to that part of the explanation. They deserve it for the way they messed this up. Some bond pairs are bi, some aren't. Different folks and different strokes and all that. As for what bonding means, it means that those two are linked by a bit of magical weirdness that I don't rightly understand, just like Darius and I are linked to each other as well as to Emma. Torin lifted his hand, palm up to show Jess a thin white scar that crossed his palm. We're blood-brothers, literally. The boys will explain it, but you make sure they answer all your questions to your satisfaction, or you can call Emma or me and ask us."

Jess snickered. "Oh, don't worry. I will."

"I think you're going to be exactly what those boys need in their life," Torin told her as Byron returned with their drinks. He set the dark ale down in front of Torin and then placed two shooter glasses on the bar for Jess along with a bowl of limes and shaker of salt. "I figured you'd be needing at least two drinks before you're going to feel like telling me where your lesser halves are tonight."

"Don't you have a bar to tend?" Torin waved Byron off with a laugh. "Shoo, pup, this may be the last chance I have to get to know this lovely girl before her men come and whisk her away on me."

"All right, I'm going!" Byron threw up his hands in mock surrender and backed away. "Just wave when you're ready for a refill."

"Thanks." Jess waved and reached for her drink. She didn't bother with the salt before she downed the first shot, though she did bite into the lime wedge once it was gone.

"So, is there anything else I should know before I let Tweedledum and Tweedledummer take over as my tour guides on this bizarre adventure I'm on?"

"You mean anything critical? Not really. Though I can tell you that now that your lineage is known, Darius is not going to have any issue with the fact the boys chose you for their mate. There's an old law on the books that states that colony leaders are only supposed to bond with mates from the oldest bloodlines. Needless to say, if you'd been human there was going to be one hell of a fight between Darius and his son. As it turns out, you're from one of the right bloodlines."

"Wait a second. Darius is the colony leader, so what does it matter if Rory...mates with me or not?" Jess stumbled over the odd wording.

"Darius is the colony leader *now*, yes. But one day that job will fall to Rory." Torin sighed and moved the second shot glass closer to her. "You're going to want to drink that, girl. Your Rory is the local equivalent to a prince, and that makes you a soon-to-be princess. Congratulations, you're selkie royalty."

"Fucking hell." Jess groaned and downed the second glass without hesitation. "I'm going to have to work on the guys' communication skills. They skipped over a lot of very important information."

"I can drink to that." Torin tapped his mug to her empty shot glass before downing a measure of the contents.

The second shot burned a lot less than the first one, and Jess knew she was already heading toward a pleasant buzz. Not surprising considering she hadn't eaten anything since breakfast at the hotel. She'd been too nervous about making a good impression tonight to eat anything else. *So much for first impressions.*

A mountain of muscle moved into her field of vision and Jess looked up, and then up some more until she finally found a face. Holy shit, this guy's huge! was the first thought to cross her mind, followed by the realization he looked a little familiar.

"So you're the one?"

"I'm the one...what?" Jess asked, puzzled.

The stranger reached out one massive arm and gestured to the pendant around her neck. "Byron said Rory and Evan's doom was at the end of the bar, doing tequila shots." His stern features softened as he smiled slightly and a dimple appeared in his right cheek.

"Oh! Uh...I guess so. You must be Tucker." Jess managed to focus her attention on Tucker's face and not on the broad expanse of muscle and sinew moving beneath his dark-blue shirt. He had slate-gray eyes, an unshaven jaw and jet black hair cut short, but what drew Jess's attention was the eyebrow ring that sat over his left eye. Her first thought was that he was the kind of man you never wanted to bump into in a dark alley. As she noticed the tribal style tattoo that ran down his neck and vanished beneath his shirt, Jess's second thought was to wonder if the tattoos showed up when he was in seal form.

"Jess, this is Tucker Pine, Rory's cousin." Torin made the introduction. "Tucker, this is Jess Silk."

"Silk?" Tucker's brow shot up in surprise. "Any relation to Martin Silk?"

"She's Mara's little girl." Torin's voice was barely loud enough to be heard over the music.

Tucker nodded to Torin and set another shot glass of tequila in front of Jess. "Welcome home, Jess. I hear you had a bad day. Byron says he'll be back for the details after you finish this."

"Thank you, and tell Byron thanks, too," Jess said smiled up at Tucker. He nodded and headed down the bar to another waiting customer. As he turned she caught his face in profile and realized that was why he looked familiar. He looked a bit like Rory and Darius, only a whole lot bigger. She tossed back the shot he'd left and then turned on her stool to face Torin.

"So, is he a seal, or a sea lion? He's huge!" She threw her arms out wide and it dawned on her that the tequila had finally kicked in.

Torin sniggered into his ale. "I see you're feeling better."

"Much, thank you." Jess reached out and patted his arm. "This was exactly what I needed. A little more time here and I'll be ready to deal with everything." She turned back toward the bar and glanced down at her purse, wondering if her voicemail was full of messages yet. She was betting it was, but she wasn't quite ready to turn her phone back on and face reality. Fifteen more minutes, then I'll call them, she promised herself.

Torin finished his ale and stood. "I need to visit the facilities, you stay put. If you need anything, wave Tucker or Byron over, they'll keep an eye on you while I'm gone."

Jess nodded and he stepped into the crowd, vanishing from her sight within seconds. She would bet her next royalty check that while he was gone, Torin was going to call Rory and let him know she was okay. She was more than fine with that idea, because if Torin called them, she wouldn't have to. She was already feeling a bit guilty for running away, even though she knew it was the smart thing to do. She had needed a bit of time and space, and Torin had given her both.

She waved to Byron and mouthed a request for him to bring her a glass of water. He grinned, gave her a thumbs-up, and then finished filling the line of empty beer mugs he had sitting on the counter. Jess knew he'd bring her the water once he was done with the order he was working on.

"What the hell do you have that I don't?" A woman's voice snarled from behind Jess and she spun around too quickly for the amount of tequila she'd consumed. Her brain took a second to catch up to her body, and the sensation was far from pleasant.

"I'm sorry, were you speaking to me?" Jess asked.

"Holy shit, they really did pick you over me." A tall, leggy woman with dark-brown hair was standing inside Jess's personal space, and she was staring at the pendant with outright jealousy.

"If I had known Rory's taste ran to sea cows, I'd have skipped a few workouts and had a dozen hot fudge sundaes before making the trip down here," the woman snarked and leaned in close enough that Jess could smell the almost toxic blend of booze and perfume that clung to the woman.

"Who the hell are you and what are you talking about?" Jess finally asked, sitting up straighter on her barstool.

"I'm Renee, the one Darius Frazier wanted for his son, Rory. I'm the one who was supposed to be wearing *that*." Renee reached out and flicked a finger against the pearl that hung from the bottom of the intricate Celtic knot.

"Keep your hands to yourself," Jess snarled as she swatted Renee's hand away.

A malicious sneer twisted Renee's features into something quite ugly as she eyed Jess. "The boys didn't want me to keep my hands to myself. I got to touch them *all* over. They wanted to test out the goods before buying."

Jess hopped off the stool and managed to land squarely on her high heels. "Sweetie, I wouldn't be bragging about that. If they tried out the goods and then sent you packing, you clearly failed to meet their standards." She moved into Renee's space, staring daggers at the other woman. "I'm already having a very bad day, so do me a favor and take your skanky, scrawny ass off to some other part of this building, or better yet, some other part of the country."

"Fat, short, and rude, too! The Frazier clan must be so pleased to have you joining them," Renee taunted her, and Jess literally saw red. It was like a crimson filter dropped over her eyes and she went on the attack.

"I'm only rude when I'm accosted by lying, jealous bitches who don't know how to lose graciously. Rory and Evan are *mine*. You had your shot and they decided they could do better, and now they have. Get over it and get out of my face before *my* men arrive and they toss you on your bony butt for giving me grief!"

Renee screeched and lunged for Jess, but before Jess could even lift a hand to defend herself Renee stopped dead in her tracks and then levitated up and backward. At least that's how it looked until Jess realized that Tucker had grabbed hold of her would-be assailant and was half carrying her toward the door as Renee pitched a fit.

"I see the boys are going to have to keep a close eye on you." Torin stepped into Jess's line of sight and shot her a rueful grin as he walked her back to her barstool and lifted her onto it with a strength that surprised her. "I let you out of my sight for five minutes and look what happened!"

"She started it," Jess muttered and tossed back her hair, still too angry to think straight yet. "She got in my face, called me a *sea cow* and told me she'd had sex with *my* guys."

Torin took his seat and sighed. "I warned Darius she wasn't a good match for Rory and Evan, but he's got a bit of an obsession about bloodlines and was blinded to the fact she's a stone-cold bitch."

Jess growled in disdain. "He thought that was Rory's type? Does he know his son at all?"

"You're not the first to ask that question, odds are good you won't be the last. Emma and I try to steer him the best we can, just as you and Evan will be there for Rory. Some days we do better than others."

Byron walked over to them and shook his finger playfully at Jess. "Less than an hour in my bar and you're starting trouble. I'm not sure if I should be giving you a warning or an award for telling off that nasty bit of trash the way you did."

"The only award I want is that glass of ice water I asked for before the wicked witch of the west coast tried to drop a house on my head. Please, Byron?"

"My pleasure." Byron winked at her and reached below the counter to pull out a glass of ice water complete with a twist of lime. "I made this for you, but by the time I got down to this end of the bar you were already tearing a strip off of Renee. I was about to come to your rescue, but Tucker beat me to it." He gave Jess a sad puppy face. "Do I still get partial credit for good intentions?"

"Of course you do. Maybe next time you'll get there first," Jess told him and laughed.

"Next time? You're already planning a next time?" Torin groaned and dropped his head into his hands in mock despair.

"My best friend is coming to town next month, and she is a total trouble-magnet. I might as well prepare these kind gentlemen in advance, don't you think?"

"Your *friend* is the trouble-magnet?" Byron gave her a knowing look. "And what was that a few minutes ago?"

"That was...an anomaly." Jess grinned. "I'm very sweet, ask anyone."

Torin and Byron both rolled their eyes. "Is this what I have to look forward to when we find our mate, Torin?" Byron asked.

"Afraid so, pup. The benefits are worth it, though."

"You might want to remind Rory and Evan about that benefits thing." Byron stared at something beyond where Jess as seated and she knew without looking around that her men had arrived at the bar. She could *feel* them, a comforting presence that wrapped around her like a warm blanket.

229

"You called them," Jess said to Torin, not even bothering to make it into a question.

"They needed to know you were all right."

"I know. I'm glad you did." Jess gave Torin a smile, winked at Byron, and then spun around on her stool for the second time that night, nearly making herself dizzy yet again. She wound up nose to chest with Rory, who had her up off the stool and in his arms before she could say a single word.

"Don't you ever take off like that again, baby!" Rory crushed her to him so tightly all Jess could do was make a strangled squawking noise as he buried his face into her hair.

"Are you all right? When we realized you were gone, we nearly lost our minds." Rory squeezed her even harder and Jess could have sworn she heard her ribs creaking. "Jess? Why aren't you answering me? Are you still mad?"

"Bro, I think you hugged the stuffing out of her, along with all the air in her lungs." Evan stepped in close and stroked the back of Jess's head. "Hey, sweetheart. I'm so sorry we screwed that up. What say we get you out of here and we'll go somewhere to talk?"

Jess managed to turn her head and nod slightly, and then Rory was easing up his grip and she sucked in a long breath.

"I'm sorry, too," Rory said, his breath hot on her ear as he leaned down so she could hear him.

Jess got her breath back and wriggled herself out of Rory's arms so she could step back and look at them properly. "You should both be *very* damned sorry! You knew there was something about me and you didn't say anything! And then you started yelling, and Evan was cheering, and your father is so...loud! And you were both so busy being a family that you forgot I was even there."

Both men opened their mouths to argue and Jess held up a finger. "Don't you dare try to deny it. How long was it before you realized I was gone?"

Evan looked utterly sheepish. "It took Emma and me a few minutes to get Darius and Rory calmed down, but right after that we went looking for you."

Rory growled low in his throat and glared at Torin. "The minute we realized Torin's truck was gone, we knew he'd absconded with you. Neither of you were answering your phones, though, so we had no idea where you'd gone."

"Torin was the only one smart enough to realize I needed to get out of the house and away from everything long enough to deal with the bombshells dropped on me tonight." Jess looked from Rory to Evan and back again. "For two men who promised to take care of me, you both really fucking sucked at it tonight."

"We *fucking* sucked?" Evan repeated her wording and then narrowed his gaze as he leaned and took a closer look at Jess. "Torin, how much did you give our girl to drink exactly?"

"*I* didn't give her anything. *She* charmed Byron and Tucker into three shots of tequila, on the house."

"Three?" Rory choked and wrapped an arm around Jess's shoulders. "You haven't been here more than thirty minutes!"

"I'm going to kill Byron," Evan muttered.

"Byron was sweet, and Tucker tossed Renee out on her scrawny butt before she could claw my eyes out, so you are not going to say a bad thing about either of them!" Jess declared.

"Son of a bitch! Renee's still in town? You met her?" Rory was almost howling with frustration now and Jess suddenly found everything incredibly funny. *That's the third shot of tequila kicking in.*

"Met her, called her a skanky bitch and got her thrown out. Now, can we please go home? I'm not done being mad at you, and it's too loud in here."

"That's the best idea I've heard since we got here." Evan scooped her into his arms and Rory started clearing a path toward the doors. Jess leaned back and waved good-bye to an amused-looking Torin. Behind him Byron waved back, and Jess started giggling again.

"Don't you dare wave at Byron, sweetheart. As it is I'm going to have to kick his ass later for flirting with you and giving you free drinks," Evan told her in the gruffest voice she'd ever heard him use.

"Oh, don't worry about him. He knows who I belong to." Jess tapped her pendant. "And he told Tucker, and someone told that bitch Renee, and when we get out of here you're going to have to explain how you forgot to mention anything about Darius wanting you two to join up with that witch!"

Evan groaned. "Believe me, sweetheart, that was never going to happen."

"Damn straight," Jess muttered as they walked outside into the cold and much quieter night. "You're both mine, and I'm keeping you."

CHAPTER EIGHTEEN

As the truck rolled to a stop outside Jess's cabin she lifted her head from Rory's shoulder. Rory hugged her again. He hadn't let go of her from the moment Evan had passed her into Rory's waiting arms. Not that she ever wanted to go through that kind of day again, but one thing that had come out of it was a strong affirmation that she, Rory, and Evan were destined to be together.

Evan snickered as he opened the driver-side door and let himself out. "I'll give you a hand, Jess. That tequila's made you a little unsteady."

"I'm not unsteady," Jess argued.

Rory opened their door and held onto her as Evan made his way around and helped her to the ground.

"You're right. You're not unsteady. You're tipsy." Evan's arms came around her and she snuggled into him, letting his familiar scent work its strange magic. "But that'll pass soon enough. I'm going to make you some dinner and maybe Rory will give you a foot rub."

"Sounds good to me." Jess's words were muffled against Evan's chest, but she was too comfortable to move.

Rory came up behind her, his hands on her shoulders and his breath warming the back of her neck. "Give Ev the keys and we'll get you inside."

Jess fished her house key out of her purse and handed it over to Evan, and with a light kiss to her cheek he was gone.

Rory turned her around gently and drew her into his arms. He bent his head and brushed a tender kiss to her lips, letting his mouth linger over hers. "I love you. I'm sorry things didn't go the way we planned today, and you have my word that no matter what, from now on nothing is going to distract me being there when you need me."

"I'm going to need both of you to get through this. I have a lot of questions, but first I want to get changed and relax. It's been a spectacularly insane evening."

Rory lifted her into his arms and carried her inside, straight through the living room and down the hall to her bedroom. He put her down by the bed and immediately set to work undressing her, swatting her hands out of the way every time she tried to help.

Once she was dressed again Rory got her to sit down at the edge of the bed and eased a pair of thick socks onto her feet before he curved his arms around her waist and lowered his head to her lap. Stunned to silence by the gesture, Jess sat there and stroked Rory's hair, removing the fastening so she could run her fingers through its entire length. After a few minutes Evan's blond head popped into the room, but when he saw what was going on he swallowed whatever smart comment he was about to make and blew Jess a kiss before heading back to the kitchen.

When Rory finally spoke, his voice was husky. "There was a moment, right after we realized you'd left, when I thought maybe you'd changed your mind about us. It nearly killed me to even think about." He lifted his head to look into Jess's eyes and she was overwhelmed by the force of the emotion burning in his gaze. "I never want to feel that way again. So when you're ready, and when all your questions have been answered, I want us to be bonded completely."

Jess nodded. "I want that, too. I'm not even sure exactly what it entails, but I want it. I want forever with you and Evan."

"We'll talk about that later tonight." He swept her hair back from her face smiled. "Right after we sober you up."

"I think I'm more or less sober now."

"After three shots of hard liquor on an empty stomach, I doubt it. Let's get some food into you, and then I know you'll be fine." Rory stood up and reached his hand out for her, helping her to her feet.

They headed back to the living room, hand in hand, and Jess's stomach growled as she caught wind of something delicious wafting out of the kitchen area.

"You're making me breakfast for dinner?" she asked, beaming. "You're making me chocolate chip pancakes! They're my favorite!"

"See, I told you it was important to know this stuff," Evan told Rory. "I've got bacon, sausages, scrambled eggs, and pancakes."

Jess let go of Rory's hand and went to hug Evan. "I

love you both, but right now I'm afraid Evan is my favorite. Sorry, Rory."

"Oh sure, thrown over for pancakes." Rory threw up his hands in mock surrender. "I see how this is going to be. You stick with breakfast boy over there then, J.J. Clearly you don't need one of my foot massages."

"That's not fair!" Jess laughed and kissed Evan on the cheek. "Syrup's in the cupboard, sexy. Thank you so much, this will be perfect."

Then she followed Rory over to the couch and flopped down, lifting her sock-covered feet into his lap the moment he sat down. "Yes, please."

"Fickle creature," Rory teased and tugged her socks off.

Jess let her eyes close and groaned in encouragement as he started working the sore spots on her arches with strong fingers. She could hear Evan puttering around in the kitchen, and as normalcy returned to her world it was easy to let go of the worst parts of her day and hang on to the good things. Jess let her thoughts drift where they may, and she found herself remembering some of the stories her mother had told her about selkies as a little girl. That's when it hit her.

"The box!" Jess yelled and sat up, startling Rory. "I completely forgot about the box. How could I be so stupid?" She scrambled up off the couch and stood up, looking around the room until she spotted the heavy wood and metal box her mother had asked Jess to bring to Tofino with her. Without explaining herself, she bolted across the living room and tossed aside the various papers and assorted junk she'd managed to pile on top of it in the short period of time she'd been in residence.

The moment she had unearthed it Jess hauled it out

of the corner, only to realize Rory and Evan were crouched beside her and were helping her manhandle the bulky container out into the middle of the living room floor.

"What the hell is in this thing, bricks?" Evan grunted and then stiffened as he took a closer look. "Holy shit. Rory, is this what I think it is?" He rapped a knuckle on one of the bands of metal that crisscrossed the entire surface of the box.

"Iron," Rory confirmed as she touched another one of the bands. "The whole thing is wrapped in iron."

The two men exchanged knowing looks then looked at Jess with pity in their eyes. "So what's the big deal about iron?" she asked as she worked to undo the ancient latches.

"It's got magic dampening properties," Rory told her.

"Did you say *magic*? As in abracadabra and hocus pocus, magic?" Jess demanded as she managed to wrench the second latch open and lifted the lid.

"What did you think selkies were, sweetheart? A human-seal hybrid? An alien DNA experiment gone awry? We are magical creatures, and iron is one of the few things that messes with our mojo."

Evan and Rory stared into the box, and Jess heard them both sigh sadly as they looked at the contents.

"This must have been your mother's pelt." Rory started to reach out to touch it but then withdrew his hand. "She locked it away in an iron box so she could never change forms."

"What the hell happened to her that she'd do that to herself?" Evan asked in a voice thick with emotion.

"I don't understand," Jess whispered as she very

carefully touched the dried and brittle fur. "You both sound almost horrified at the idea she did this."

"Until you've experienced it for yourself, you won't understand completely. But what your mother did to herself would be a bit like cutting out a part of her soul on purpose," Evan explained and she felt both of them rest a hand on her back as she leaned closer and lifted the pelt up out of the box. It weighed almost nothing despite its size, and Jess realized it was completely dried out. It was pale silver and marked with darker rings of gray and Jess laid it gently on the floor in front of them. If they could have spread it out, it would have been large enough to cover a human being.

"It's beautiful," she said and stroked the fur very carefully with her fingers.

"Jess, look." Rory lifted a hand and pointed into the box. "That's got to be yours."

Lying at the bottom of the box was a second pelt, almost identical to her mother's in color and markings. Jess held her breath as she reached in and gingerly lifted it out, cradling silver fur in her hands. It was soft and pliant to the touch, and an undeniable sense of *rightness* flowed through her as she held onto it.

"This is me," she breathed in awe. "I can feel it."

"She had to have taken this from you when you were only a child." Evan sighed. "You probably don't even remember changing."

Jess blew out a long breath. "How does this even work? Was I born human or..." She lifted the pelt slightly. "This?"

Rory explained. "Pups are born with the same form as their mother at the time of their birth, and then they stay in that form for the next six years or so. Seal-form selkies need to imagine a human shape and the pelt comes off. For human-form selkie children, it's the reverse.

"The change from human to seal is instinctive, especially when we're in the water. Take a selkie child of the right age out into the water and tell them to imagine their seal form while playing and splashing around, and it usually doesn't take very long for them to change forms. After that, the pelt is hidden in a safe place and the child learns to summon the change at will."

"What do you mean, hidden?" Jess asked, feeling lost. "Don't we need it to transform? I don't understand."

Rory answered her. "A selkie doesn't need to have their pelt physically with them to transform. It's more a symbol or a talisman than an actual pelt we wear. We just need to summon the power it holds."

"Power," Jess breathed the word. "You're talking about actual magic again. Do you have any idea how hard it is to accept all this?"

"We know," Evan murmured. "You keep asking questions, Jess. I promise, this is all real. We're really selkies, all of us."

"So why can't I change?" she asked, looking at Rory.

"Well for starters you didn't know you could. How could you summon an ability you didn't know you had? Plus, your pelt was contained inside an iron box."

"And that was enough to stop the...magic?" Jess stumbled over the last word.

"It would be enough to stop any of us from being able to transform," Evan chimed in. "You've read the legends, right? Sometimes humans would find a selkie's pelt and use iron to block the magic so the selkie couldn't transform and effectively became a slave to the one who possessed their pelt."

So we hide our pelts very carefully." Rory explained. "We keep ours tucked away in a fireproof safe. We'll keep yours there too, when you're ready."

"I think that's a good idea."

Both of them leaned in close and Jess basked in the warmth of their presence, grateful they were here with her. Her mother had to have known that by sending Jess back to Tofino, all of this would have come out eventually, and Jess was thankful that she had Rory and Evan's love and patience while she muddled her way through all these revelations.

Jess unfolded her pelt so she could see the silver and charcoal coloring more clearly, and a folded note fell onto the floor. Her name had been clearly written on it in her mother's elegant handwriting.

"Mom." She whispered the single word and felt tears pricking at her eyes again. "She always did like getting in the last word."

I think you've spent enough time kneeling on the floor." Rory was already moving and helping Jess to her feet as he spoke.

"I'm going to make sure I didn't burn dinner. Give me a minute." Evan kissed her cheek and then jogged back to the kitchen.

Rory settled her in the middle of the couch and sat down beside her, drawing her up against his chest and curving one strong arm around her waist. "How are you holding up?" he asked and she heard the concern in his tone.

"All things considered, I'm doing pretty well. I haven't

run screaming out into the woods yet, so I'd say I'm coping nicely."

"When you're ready, Evan and I will help you learn to take your other form. Now that you know what we are, there are so many things we can tell you that we couldn't before."

"Just remember that after today, we're not allowed any more secrets. I don't think I can take any more dramatic surprises in this lifetime."

"I think we've covered all the big ones. The rest we can show you as you get used to the idea that you're not who you thought you were."

Evan came around the couch and joined them, cuddling up close to Jess. "Read the letter, sweetheart. Then we're going to put this soap opera on hold and go have something to eat."

Jess laid the pelt in her lap and unfolded the note.

My darling Jess,

I hope that by the time you are reading this, you've already found at least some of the answers to the questions you always wanted to know. You always wanted to know where I was born, who my family was, and why you never saw any of your relatives. I'm sorry that I never gave you the answers you deserved. At the time I believed it was for the best, but now I know I should have given you at least some of the answers you wanted. Now it's too late and I fear you'll have to find out for yourself.

Once you've read this letter I want you to go find Emma Frazier. She lives up the road from your cabin in a place called Kismet Cove. There was a time when she was my dearest and closest friend, and I know she will be able to help you make sense of what I'm going to tell you.

Before I married your father, my name was Mara Silk. My parents were Jack and Alicia Silk. They are very likely still living at Kismet Cove. Before you go to speak to them, please, talk to Emma and show her this letter. She'll understand what is needed.

Jess, be wary of your grandfather. Don't let him try to take control of your life in any way. He is the reason I left home all those years ago, and he may still be a threat to you now. He ordered me to marry against my wishes, and when I refused to agree to the marriage he beat me and made it clear to me I had no choice in the matter. I was already in love with your father, and rather than face a lifetime of unhappiness with my father's choice for me, I ran to your father's cabin and begged him to take me away. We eloped that night.

I had to keep you safe, and to do that I made decisions that weren't really mine to make. I denied you your heritage, and I will always regret that I wasn't brave enough to tell you the truth. I hope one day you will forgive me for keeping secrets from you, but I truly believed it was necessary. Be happy, my beautiful daughter.

Love always,
Mom

JESS READ the letter and then read it again, and when she was done there were several tearstains on the paper. "Well, at least I don't have to worry about granddad trying to order me around like he did mom. I have you two to protect me from him."

Rory reached around and took the letter from her and

handed it to Evan. "I read it over her shoulder, but you really need to read this, too," was all he said to Evan before turning his attention back to Jess.

"Baby, your grandfather passed away a few years ago, so you'd be safe from him no matter what. Your grandmother and her other mate, Michael, are still alive and living here, though. They'll be very happy to meet you, they're good souls."

Evan sucked in a breath and handed the letter back to Jess as he finished reading it. "It's what everyone suspected was happening back then. I guess now we have proof."

"Proof of what?" Jess demanded.

Evan was the one who answered. "About the time your mom took off, other younger members of the colony started disappearing, too. Rory's grandfather and some of the other parents of the time were obsessed with improving the bloodlines. There was a lot of talk of forced pairings and other nastiness, but the ones who were involved all left the colony so there was no one to confirm anything. Instead of improving the bloodlines, the colony lost nearly half a generation. We're still recovering from that imbalance."

"So my mom wasn't the only one."

"No, she wasn't. But that exodus is one of the reason's my father is so hung up on our mating to someone of the right bloodline. He's better than my grandfather, but he was still influenced by the bastard. When it's my turn to lead, things are going to be different." Rory made the last line sound like a vow, and Jess turned her head to kiss his cheek. "Yes, we will."

"Spoken like a true princess-in-training," Evan said

approvingly and patted her knee. "So, can we please eat now? Jess still needs to sop up the last of that tequila, and I'm starving. Breakfast was a long time ago."

"I think food is a great idea." Jess sat up and smiled at her two men. "Then I want to take you two to bed so you can make me forget all about this day, selkies, and most especially Renee."

"Yeah, about her—" Rory started to speak and Jess put a finger to his lips to silence him.

"I know you didn't sleep with her, no matter what she said. I know my boys, and she was not even close to your type."

"So what is our type?" Evan helped her to her feet and then hauled her into his arms for a slow, lingering kiss before she could answer.

When he finally released her she took an unsteady step backward and bumped into Rory, who turned her around and kissed her just as intently as Evan had. By the time he lifted his head to breathe Jess's head was spinning and she knew the answer to Evan's question.

"*I'm* your type. And I happen to be one of a kind."

CHAPTER NINETEEN

AFTER DINNER RORY waved them off, claiming that since Evan had done the cooking, it was only fair someone else did the dishes. Evan sent his blood-brother a silent message of gratitude and snagged Jess's hand, leading her away from the kitchen before she could even consider offering to help.

He led her down the hall to the bathroom and kicked the door closed behind them. He'd been waiting for his moment to get Jess alone, and he wasn't going to waste the time Rory had given them.

Evan tugged her into his arms and held her close, letting her soft warmth and soothing scent ease some of the anxiety he'd felt since he first realized she'd run away from them, hours before. He knew her upset was his fault, and every time he looked back at the scene at Darius's home he wished he could go back and undo the moment he'd gloated over confirmation Jess was a selkie.

"I'm sorry I was an idiot before. I should have found a way to tell you what we suspected about your family.

Vows of secrecy or not, I will never forgive myself for the way you found out about everything."

"You mean the way you cheered and did a victory dance?" Jess's asked, her tone at its drollest.

"Uh, yeah. I'm aware that wasn't my finest moment. I am really sorry, sweetheart."

"So sorry you're currently apologizing to me in the least romantic room in my house?" Jess's crystal-blue eyes were dancing with mirth and Evan knew she'd forgiven him. "Well, I figured as part of my apology I'd offer to wash your hair for you, starting at your toes and working my way up."

Jess inhaled sharply and he got to watch as a wave of desire transformed her expression from humored to aroused between one heartbeat and the next. Her skin flushed and her sweet mouth parted a little so that the tip of her tongue could dart out to lick her lips. The pulse point at her throat started to visibly jump, and Evan felt his cock thicken and swell in response to every signal her body was giving his.

"You are so beautiful." Evan felt the heat of his desire merging into the deeper warmth that was his love for Jess and he leaned in to kiss her. Her lips were still sticky with traces of maple syrup and he paused to savor the sweetness, nibbling at her lower lip until she grew impatient and stretched upward to kiss him fully on the mouth. That simple act set Evan's blood blazing and he hauled her up against his body as he let his mouth brand and plunder hers. He needed this, to be lost in the scent, the flavor, and the feel of the woman he and Rory had found and intended to claim forever.

Jess moaned as she ground her soft body against his

dick, her fingers already working to unfasten his pants and free him from the too-tight confines of his briefs. As her warm hand wrapped around his cock Evan shuddered and rocked his hips, pumping his dick in and out of her grip.

"This is not what I had in mind," he murmured against her lips and then lifted his head, backing up a half a step so he could try to regain control of the situation. "Not that I'm complaining, mind you, but I'd rather we got naked and wet first."

Instead of answering, Jess followed him and grabbed hold of his shirt so she could lean up and kiss him. The moment he responded to her Jess closed her teeth on Evan's lower lip and sucked it into her mouth and Evan felt his determination waver as all his willpower and most of the blood in his body raced to his dick.

She released his lip and fisted his cock before finally whispering, "We could skip the shower and go straight to bed instead."

Evan pondered for a moment, and then pulled away from her with a shake of his head. "Nuh-uh. There's something I've wanted to do with you since I first saw this incredible shower, and now's the perfect time."

"Now you have my attention." Jess smiled up at him, her eyes glowing with a heady mix of lust and love that made Evan's head spin. *Mine.* The single word reverberated through to his very soul.

"Ours." Rory's mind touched his, rife with amusement and the faintest hint of reproof.

"Nosy bastard, get back to washing those dishes," Evan grumbled and then realized he'd spoken aloud.

"What was that about?" Jess demanded.

"Uh, that was Rory." Evan's mind raced as he tried to figure out a way to explain things without upsetting her yet again.

"I gathered." Jess released his cock and snuggled herself back into his arms. "I was right, wasn't I? You two can talk to each other without speaking."

"It's part of the bond we have, yes. And once you're fully bonded with us, you will be able to do it, too."

"I want to do that soon."

"What, the telepathy thing? You will, sweetheart."

"I want us to be bonded and the sooner the better. I don't want any more surprises or any other women trying to claim my place. I want both of you." She looked up at him and her face was full of determination and there was a stubborn set to her jaw. This was a woman who knew what she wanted, and Evan rejoiced at the fact that what she wanted was a life with him and Rory.

"Rory's the next leader of the colony, sweetheart. There is going to be one hell of a party the day we're formally bonded. It'll take a few weeks to get organized." He brushed a kiss over her lips and grinned down at her. "I promise we'll keep you very busy in the meantime. We need to move you in with us and get you a car, and you and Emma need to plan everything. And I need to get my family back here. You haven't even met them yet. Oh yes, you're going to need all that time to get prepared."

"*I'm* going plan this?" She grinned back at him. "Oh, no. *We* are going to plan this. I'm not doing this alone, buster."

"If you can get Rory to help pick out flowers and a menu, then that will be proof positive that you are the perfect partner for us."

248

Jess smirked and started skinning off Rory's T-shirt. "I have ways of convincing him that you don't have at your disposal."

"Like what?" Evan asked and then lost his train of thought as Jess cupped her breasts in her hands and toyed with her nipples until they were swollen to hard nubs.

"Like this."

"Brat!" Evan swatted her on the ass and laughed as she squealed and backed away from him. "Go get the shower turned on. I need to get naked here and then I'm going to show you what happens to bratty mates."

Jess deliberately wiggled her ass at him as she turned on the water and adjusted the temperature. "I thought Rory was the one with the thing for spankings?"

"He is. But there's more than one way to skin a cat."

Or in this case, tease a pussy.

Evan shucked his clothing and left it in a heap on the floor. The only thing he was interested in right now was getting Jess's naked body wrapped around his. He stepped into the shower with her and slid his hands around her waist, one hand cupping the heavy weight of her breasts while the other dove straight down to part the lips of her pussy so he could stroke her clit. Hot water streamed down over them both and he held her there, her back pressed to his chest as he buried his face against her neck and inhaled.

"I am never going to get tired of the way your scent makes my dick hard."

"Is that a selkie thing? Because the way you and Rory smell makes me feel like I've come home."

"It's because we're true mates. We're perfectly matched. It means that you, Rory, and I were meant to be together." Evan ground his hips against Jess's backside, letting his cock run up and down the seam of her ass. "It's rare, because not everyone is lucky to be as compatible as Rory and I. The elders have to take their best guess and hope."

Evan bit down on her shoulder and the taste of her skin, warm and sweet, filled his mouth. "You taste good, sweetheart, but I need more."

He turned her around and backed her up against the wall of the shower, ignoring her hiss of complaint when her body hit the cool tiles. He reached up blindly and grabbed the shower nozzle, moving it over so that the steady flow of steamy, hot rain fell over them in their new position. Only then did he indulge himself in a long, slow tour of Jess's body, starting with her lips and working his way down to her breasts. She moaned and arched herself against him and he turned his head to suckle one plump nipple into his mouth. As he nibbled and sucked at one breast his hand worked its way slowly lower, until his fingers were resting in the patch of trim curls that guarded her cunt. Jess's entire body shuddered and she rolled her hips, rubbing herself against his hand as her fingers tangled into his hair and tugged his head closer.

"Evan, I need you."

He let her breast go with a slight pop and looked up to grin at her. "I can see that, sweetheart." He dipped his fingers into her pussy and rubbed over her slick folds. "I can feel it, too." He worked his hand further between her thighs and stroked the length of her pussy, deliberately avoiding her clit.

"I want you to put your hands behind you and hang onto that soap dish handle." His cock jumped as she did what he said and the change in position thrust her breasts out further so they were brushing his chest. "Perfect. Now, don't let go."

Evan lowered himself to his knees, ignoring the odd sensation of having the river rock tiles press into his shins as he positioned himself in front of Jess's pussy. Leaning in, he nuzzled her curls as he used his free hand to lift and guide her leg so that it was draped over his shoulder.

"Now that's a beautiful view," he breathed while lust spiked through him and made his dick harder than marble. "Wet, soft, and all for me."

He buried his face between her folds and lapped at her honey-soaked flesh, letting her scent and flavor fill his head until he knew it was branded into his memory forever. He tongued the entrance to her pussy until she was vibrating with the need for more.

"Your mouth feels so good on my pussy," Jess whimpered and Evan's cock surged to nearly painful levels of hard. If she started talking dirty, he was going to lose his mind.

"I need you to fuck me, Ev. I want something inside me so I can come. Your tongue, your fingers, your cock...I don't care. Please?"

Fucking hell, she was killing him. Hearing his sweet little mate use words like "pussy" and "cock" had his blood turning to lava in his veins. Instead of giving her what she wanted Evan sought out her tender clit and drew it into his mouth so he could lash it with the tip of his tongue. The moment his tongue made contact with that hard little pearl Jess's thighs tensed and her broken cry of encouragement filled the shower. Her hips rolled so she could grind herself into his mouth, and Evan finally fulfilled her wish, spearing two fingers into her channel and then groaning as her inner muscles clamped around him, squeezing him so tightly he was tempted to pull her down on top of him and fuck her on the floor of the shower.

Again he sucked on her clit and Jess's pussy responded with another powerful pulse. He slid a third finger into her and hummed in satisfaction as she writhed in pleasure and moaned his name. Determined to make her come hard, Evan began fucking her with his fingers, his pace almost punishing as he pushed himself deep into her body, his fingers curved so that he struck the area above her clit with every thrust and withdrawal.

Hands and tongue worked together to send her racing headlong toward a release, and he played her body until she was trembling, her toes arched and her head thrown back against the tiles.

"Evan, please!" she begged and squirmed, riding his fingers. "Please, I need to come."

With her sweet pleas ringing in his ears, Evan gave her what she needed, driving her body past the breaking point so that she came on a scream, her body's nectar flowing all over his hand and mouth as she shuddered into a glorious orgasm. She looked like a goddess as she lost herself to her passion, sleek with water and flushed with the heat of her passion.

Still on his knees, he waited for her release to end before carefully cupping handfuls of water to wash her clean and then standing up to gather her into his arms. "I love you." The words he'd never said to anyone else came so easily when it came to this wonderful, caring woman.

"I love you, too," she murmured in a shaky voice and

looked up at him, her face glowing and her silver-blonde hair plastered to her skin. He remembered the day they'd pulled her out of the ocean, and how much had changed since the last time he had seen her looking this way.

As she reached for the tap he took her hand and stopped her. "I was going to wash your hair for you."

"Another night." She gave him one of her heart-stopping smiles. "I want to take my boys to bed now."

"I'd be a fool to argue with that plan."

"Yes, you would, and despite the fact that Torin refers to you two as Tweedledum and Tweedledummer, I would like to believe my mates are very smart men. After all, they did choose me."

"Yes, we did," Evan agreed as she turned off the water and he reached for the towels. "It might have been the smartest thing either of us has ever done."

JESS TOWELED OFF and scooped Rory's shirt off the floor as she left the bathroom, making sure she wriggled her hips as she bent over to gather up both of their clothes.

"Just this once, I'll clean up after you," she sassed Evan. "But don't get used to it."

"What, famous writers don't do laundry?"

"She does her own laundry. All other chores still need to be negotiated." Jess walked into the bedroom and dropped their things onto a chair. She wanted nothing more than to crawl into bed between her two men and make love to them before falling asleep in their arms.

"Fair enough, just please take Rory's turn at cooking. You're ten times the cook he'll ever be."

"Says the man who once screwed up boxed macaroni and cheese," Rory grumbled as he came in behind them.

"That was ten years ago!" Evan protested.

"How do you screw up packaged pasta?" Jess asked, bemused.

"Uh…" Evan shrugged and looked sheepish.

"You drink half a bottle of vodka and then you decide the correct cooking method is to dump the packet of powdered stuff straight into the boiling water along with the pasta," Rory explained as he skinned his shirt over his head and tossed it onto the pile of clothes Jess had put on the chair.

"That sounds disgusting, more like cheese and pasta soup. Really bad cheese soup." Jess dove into the middle of the bed and stretched, wriggling her toes as she snuggled down beneath the comforter.

"It wasn't *that* bad. Once I added ketchup it was edible."

Jess burst out into horrified laughter. "You added ketchup?"

"I was improvising!" Evan slid into bed beside her and hauled her into his arms for a laughing kiss. "

"Worst thing he ever cooked." Jess heard Rory unzip his pants and soon his naked body was spooned up behind hers as he dropped a kiss to her bare shoulder.

"But as recall, you ate your share rather than try to cook something for yourself," Evan muttered when he finally lifted his mouth from Jess's.

"Yeah, well I had drunk the other half of that vodka and I was pretty sure I wasn't going to manage to do any better than you had."

Two sets of strong, male hands started stroking over

Jess's body, palming her breasts and touching every inch of her until she was squirming between them, needing more than just their touch. Taking the initiative, Jess reached out and took a cock in each hand, giving both shafts a slow, lingering caress.

"Now that I have your attention," she purred, "I'd like to request that one or both of you fuck me, please."

"She said please again," Evan groaned. "I love it when she does that."

Rory reached around to pinch a rosy nipple and Jess groaned as splintering shards of pleasure flowed from her breast to her pussy.

Rory glanced at Evan and this time she knew they were discussing their plan of attack.

"I cannot wait until I can listen in on these conversations," she grumbled. "It's really unfair that you two can do that and I can't."

Without saying a word Rory moved her so that she was angled across the bed and then slid his hand from her breast to her knee, lifting her uppermost leg up and back until it was draped over his thigh. As he reached between them to position his cock against the entrance to her pussy, Evan sat up and adjusted his body so that Jess's head was cradled on his inner thigh, his cock a few inches from her mouth.

"Patience is a virtue," Rory teased her as he eased his impressive girth into her channel, pressing in only little before stopping.

"Don't stop. Please don't stop." The words tumbled out of Jess's mouth as her cunt ached with the need to be filled. She wriggled and tried to press him deeper but he arched his hips back, denying her what she needed.

"She's talking too much. Ev, do something about that would you?"

Jess looked up and saw Evan grinning at her. "Good idea. Open your mouth for me, sweetheart."

The second her lips parted Evan dropped the tip of his cock into her mouth and she ran her tongue over the slit and gathered up the pearls of pre-cum she found there. Evan's fingers tangled in her still wet hair, drawing her head closer so she could take in more of him. She let him in all the way, relaxing her throat and taking him inch by slow inch. She swirled her tongue over his shaft, teasing and encouraging him she could feel his cock touch the back of her throat.

She hummed softly and Evan growled low in his throat in response. His fingers tightened their grip on her hair and she felt his cock jerk and thicken as she pushed him to a new level of arousal.

That was the moment Rory finally moved, plunging his cock deep into Jess's pussy in one strong, steady thrust that had her moaning around Evan's dick. Jess closed her eyes, reveling in the exquisite joy of the moment. Before Evan and Rory, Jess could have never imagined being in love with two men at once, but now this was the only way she wanted to live. She was cherished, loved, and more sexually satisfied than she had ever been in her life.

Rory buried himself so deep Jess could feel the crisp hair of his crotch brush against the back of her thighs. His hand found her breast again, and he began plucking and teasing at her nipples in a slow, sensual rhythm. His hips rolled and retreated at the same gentle pace, filling and stretching her with every delicious movement.

Jess began to work Evan's cock with the same slow

rhythm and soon their bodies were synchronized, all of them experiencing the sweet pleasure of their joining at the same time. Evan stroked and tugged at her hair while Rory's hands toyed with her breasts, and Jess reached up to cup Evan's balls in her palm, rolling them lightly between her fingers until she felt them tighten and his cock twitched within the heated confines of her mouth.

Evan groaned and Rory shuddered behind her before muttering, "Holy fuck, Ev. Are you trying to break me?"

"Just sharing the love, bro."

Rory leaned in and blew a puff of air over Jess's ear. "Evan is letting me feel what you're doing to him right now, baby. I can feel your mouth on him, sucking him off. He's going to come soon, because that talented tongue of yours is making him crazy."

Jess moaned as a roaring wave of lust washed over her and she tightened her inner muscles around Rory's cock.

"I think she likes hearing about it." Rory nipped her earlobe and rocked his hips in harder. "Did you like that? Do you want to hear more?"

Jess moaned again and Evan swore. "Oh fuck yes. Now Rory's sending me what it feels like to be fucking you right now. Your pretty cunt is clamped so tight around his dick he's seeing stars, baby."

Jess made her vaginal muscles pulse and drew back on Evan's cock enough she could flick her tongue over the head. Both men stiffened and groaned at the same time, and she knew they'd both experienced what the other one was feeling. Rory abandoned his slow, controlled lovemaking and began thrusting into her body eagerly, his hand leaving her breasts to cup her pussy, holding her in place as he fucked her hard. His fingers spread her labia and found her clit, rubbing it hard enough that Jess cried out and jerked her hips, grinding her pussy against his hand.

Evan groaned as her cries reverberated against the hard shaft of his cock and Jess struggled to split her focus between the incredible sensations blooming in her womb and the need to bring Evan to orgasm before she came. She licked and sucked, bobbing her head and swirling her tongue as her fingers toyed with his balls until they drew up tight against his body.

"That's it, baby, just like that!" Evan groaned and Jess knew he was at the jagged edge of his control.

"Make him come, Jess." Rory ordered and lifted his fingers from her clit. "First Ev can come, then you, and then me."

Jess hummed in ascent and Rory's hand returned to its place between her thighs, rubbing circles around her clit as she swept her tongue over the head of Evan's cock and down the sensitive underside. Evan's hips jerked and he arched upward as he came, a wild cry on his lips as his head fell back and his hot seed flooded her mouth.

"Now it's your turn," Rory whispered and shifted the angle of his thrusts so that his cock hit her most sensitive spots on every pass. His fingers strummed and rubbed her swollen clit until Jess was trembling with the need to come. She lifted her head and released Evan's cock so she could take a ragged breath and then sobbed as Evan reached out to cup her breasts, her nipples diamond-hard points against the palms of his hands as he kneaded and stroked. Completely overwhelmed, Jess came apart, her senses reeling, spinning as her orgasm hit. Lights flared behind closed lids, a roaring sound filled her ears, and Jess could barely hear her own ecstatic cries as she was swept up in a heady rush of emotional and physical reactions.

Rory gave a strangled roar and came, pumping his seed into her body in hot jets. His fingers stilled but he kept his hand cupping her pussy, holding her tightly against him as he ended on a low, shuddering groan.

Jess's world finally faded to gray and silence replaced the roaring in her head, and she lay still, too stunned to even try to move.

"Did you feel that?" Evan whispered, and there was a strained note to his voice that made Jess force her eyes open to look up at him.

"Feel what?" Her words came out in a husky rasp.

"You, sweetheart. I felt you come," Evan was looking down at her with a look of shell-shocked awe on his handsome face.

"How could you have? We haven't...I mean..." Jess frowned. "Is that possible?"

Rory nuzzled her neck. "It must be possible, because I felt it, too. It was incredible. We really make you feel that good?"

"You two always make me feel that good." Jess blushed and then laughed. "I will confess that was slightly more incredible than usual, though."

"We're good, bro." Evan smirked. "Really damned good."

"So how come you two could feel me and I couldn't feel you?"

"I haven't the slightest idea how we could have felt you, but we did." Rory relaxed his hold on her, gently separating their bodies and untangling her legs from his before leaning over to kiss her cheek. "Maybe it's something about that true mate thing, or maybe we're just blessed."

"So, if you two felt that, can you read my thoughts now?" Jess asked.

Both of them went quiet and Jess knew they were trying to read her. After a few seconds Evan shook his head. "I'm not getting anything. How about you?"

"Nothing," Rory said. "So whatever that was, it isn't a full bond." He shifted and Jess felt him tense slightly behind her.

"What's wrong?" she asked Rory.

Silence greeted her inquiry and Jess looked up at Evan, hoping he knew what was going on.

Evan gave his blood-brother a knowing look and sighed. "So much for postcoital bliss." He sat up straight, arranged a pillow behind him and stretched out on the bed, gesturing for Jess to join him. "You might as well get comfy, sweetheart. This is going to take a bit of pillow talk, and unless I miss my guess Rory isn't going to be talking much."

"There's nothing to talk about," Rory snapped before rolling over and sitting up, his back to them both and his feet on the floor.

Jess realized Rory was about to walk out, and she reached out to lay her hand on his back. "Rory, please don't leave me." Jess hadn't meant to say those words, but as she spoke them she finally understood that was what she was most afraid of. Too many people had left her over the years, so many that in the end she had only trusted her mother and Vivian, and then her mother had been gone, too.

"I'll never leave you." Rory's voice was raw and he

reached back to take her hand without turning his head. "But I don't know if I can talk about this either."

"You're going to have to," Evan said. "You've been putting this off for years, but you can't put it off any longer. It's time you let it go, Rory."

"You don't know what you're talking about!" Rory snarled.

"Bullshit! I know exactly what's going on." Evan snapped back at him and Jess sensed that things were on the verge of falling apart.

"Well I don't know what's going on," she whispered as she reached for Evan's hand. "Would someone please enlighten me?"

CHAPTER TWENTY

Rory didn't want to do this. Not now. Jess had already been through enough today. She'd just found out that all three of them were selkies for fuck's sake, she didn't need to hear about the fact her future mate was a head case, too.

"Rory, please talk to me." Jess's soft fingers gripped his hand so tightly he idly wondered if she was cutting off the circulation.

"It's nothing. I've just never really been thrilled about the idea of having Evan in my head all the time, and now you're going to be there, too."

"You don't want me to be linked to you?" Jess asked and he could hear the pain in her voice. "I want you and Evan to be able to see into my heart, so you'll know how much I love you both. My mother could never have that with my father, and in the end it killed her. I want more than that. I want to know you better than anyone else in the world. Just this one time I want to be selfish and have it all. I want both of you with no secrets and nothing held back."

Jess sniffled and Rory realized she was crying. His heart ached and he turned around to see his mate curled in Evan's arms, her cheeks wet with tears and her eyes full of pain and fear.

"Jess." He said her name and stopped, not sure what to say or how to explain why he didn't want to let her in. He had never let Evan in completely, but if he bonded with Jess, there was no way he'd be able to keep her at any distance. She had already broken through every wall he had, save one.

"Tell her, Rory. We've been dancing around this subject for years. You think I don't know what's going on?" Evan pushed at him. "I've been in your head for over fifteen years. I know what your problem is. I've been waiting for you to finally admit it."

"You want me to tell her I'm dangerous? That I don't trust myself and that deep down I'm a dark, violent son of a bitch that's descended from a long line of the same. There you go, I said it! Now when she runs, it's on both our heads."

Jess stared at him with tears still on her cheeks and he felt her grip tighten on his hand, and then she did the last thing in the world he expected. She burst out laughing.

"And all this time you've been telling me *he's* the delicate one," Jess sniggered and inclined her head toward Evan. "Did you hear yourself, Rory?" Jess scooted out of Evan's embrace and crossed the bed so she could wrap her arms around his neck and snuggled herself into his lap, still laughing softly.

"I got news for you, buster. You're not that scary. You're not your grandfather. Not even close. And Torin explained to me that Evan and I are supposed to balance you out, the same as you do for us. Yes, you're bossy, but I happen to think that's sexy. You're going to be a leader one day, and that means you're supposed to be stubborn and bossy, right? So sometimes you get off on spanking me and ordering me around. It might be a little kinky, but that hardly makes you a monster. It just means things in our bedroom are never going to get boring."

"But—" Rory tried to interject and Jess laid a finger across his mouth and shook her head.

"You hush, I'm not done talking yet."

"Yeah, you hush, big guy!" Evan snickered and then fell back on the bed, laughing hard.

"You behave yourself, Ev. I'll be back to talk to you about the fact that you let him carry this around for years and never helped him before now."

"Me? Aw man. We're *guys*, Jess. We don't talk about this shit. That's why I was waiting for you." Evan waved his hands vaguely. "It's not my job to deal with the touchy-feely stuff."

Jess turned back to Rory and kissed the corner of his mouth, the tears and hurt of before fading now. "I'm not afraid of you, Rory Frazier. The only way you could ever hurt me would be to leave me. I've had too many people walk out of my life, and I don't think I could bear it if I lost you or Evan. Nothing else scares me the way that does. So I want to be bonded to you both, soon. That way I know that there's no way I can lose you until we're old and gray."

"I love you." Rory gathered her into his arms and hugged her hard as relief slowly undid the knot in his chest. "I'm still not sure you're going to like what you find in my mind, but..."

"But I'm going to be in there anyway, so you better get used to the idea," she informed him pertly despite the fact that her voice was muffled against his chest.

"Just go easy on him in the beginning. He's been locking away parts of himself for a long time, Jess." Evan moved over so that he was curled around Jess's back and then clapped a hand down on Rory's shoulder and looked straight into his eyes.

"I love you like a brother, and we both love Jess. This is everything we ever wanted, and a hell of a lot more besides. Let it go, Rory. Stop worrying about your temper and your need for control and be happy. For some insane reason, she loves us the way we are."

Evan slapped Rory once on the shoulder before leaning back. "There, touchy-feely crap done. Can we please go back to cuddling now?"

"I think so," Jess said, looking relieved and slightly emotional as she looked from Evan to Rory.

"Ev, I love you, too. Now let us never speak of this again." Rory grinned at his blood-brother and then kissed Jess until she was breathless. "I love you more, though, baby," he whispered as he lifted his head to breathe, and she giggled.

"Love you, too."

JESS WAS BACK on the beach outside the cottage, but it was summer and as she glanced down at herself she recognized her pink-and-green swimsuit as one that she'd outgrown before she'd turned seven. The sun was beating down and the sand beneath her bare feet was almost too hot to walk on, so she skip-hopped

all the way down to the water's edge. Here the sand was cool and wet and the waves washed up to her ankles, tickling her toes. She started to play tag with the incoming waves, seeing how close she could get to the receding water before another wave washed up the beach and sent her scampering inland. When she saw the seals watching her from just offshore, she waved her hand and called out, excited to see them again.

Jess knew for certain that she was dreaming when time jumped and she found herself waist-deep in the ocean, standing on tiptoes to try to stay upright as her life jacket buoyed her up over each wave, making it impossible for her to stand up. As she tipped into the ocean the seals appeared at her side and she reached for one, stroking it just as she remembered doing as a child.

As the seals pulled her deeper into the water, she laughed and squealed, just as before, but this time part of her mind struggled to remember something. Something important that she knew she should recall but couldn't quite grasp. She returned to the dream as the waves closed over her dream-self's head and the sting of salt water hit her eyes and filled her mouth and nose.

Panic set in and Jess struggled to regain her balance, but the seals had her lifejacket tight in their jaws and they wouldn't let her up to breathe. Jess fought and flailed, but the waves kept closing over her head. That was when the world went dark and something happened. Something she hadn't remembered before. Her world shifted and she felt a difference to her body, to the way she moved. Jess opened her eyes and discovered that the saltwater no longer stung her eyes. She wriggled free of the life jacket, which suddenly didn't fit her at all well, and swam into the open water. As her head broke the surface she screamed in terror, but this time Jess realized her screams were within her mind, and no sound came from her *throat but a frightened bark as she tried to clear the water from her lungs.*

As her mother splashed into the water and sent the other seals diving for cover, the truth was revealed to Jess for the first time as she finally saw what had really happened that day so long ago. Clinging to her mother, shaking and afraid, Jess glanced down at her dream-self and saw silver fur and flippers tipped with long, curved claws.

Jess came awake with a wail, her arms wrapped tight around herself as she sat bolt upright. Her mind reeled and spun as she tried to come to terms with what she'd dreamed, knowing somehow that it had been more a memory than a real dream. It was a memory long buried and forgotten. One where the details had been distorted because the child she had been hadn't understood what had happened that day. It was the day she'd transformed, and the seals who had come to her that day hadn't been seals at all. They had to have been selkies, and they had known who and what she was.

"Holy shit, my family tried to drown me!"

"What?" Rory was up first, his strong arms wrapping around her and drawing her up against his bare chest as he struggled to make sense of Jess's sudden outburst.

"Sweetheart, what's wrong? Did you have a nightmare?"

"More like a repressed memory," she answered and snuggled into Rory's embrace. It was so dark she could barely make out Evan's face, but there was enough moonlight to let her pick out their features.

"The last time we came here, when I was a little girl, I saw seals. I thought they wanted to play with me. Mom used to tell me stories about seals that played with children. I thought the stories were real, but these two didn't want to play with me, they pulled me out into deep water and dunked me under."

"Oh crap," Evan breathed. "They were selkies?"

"I never remembered much about it until all this stuff came up about Mom and the cottage, but I dreamed about it and this time…" Jess shivered and she reached up to hold into Rory's thick wrist as he held her close. "This time I turned into a seal. When my mom came and pulled me out of the water, I'd already transformed into a seal. It's all real. I remember now. The two seals that were there had coats just like my pelt looked. Silvery gray with dark bits."

Rory sighed. "Then they weren't trying to drown you, they were trying to force your transformation, and they succeeded."

"Why would they do that?"

"I'm betting because one of them was your grandfather. You said your mom came back here every summer and you stayed at this cabin?"

Jess nodded. "Every summer until the year the seals came to play with me. After that we never went to a beach again, not ever."

"Your mom was right here, every year and none of us knew about it. That's crazy." Evan chimed in.

"She used to dye her hair brown, and she kept it short until I was a teenager. She told me it was because she didn't like being prematurely gray. Do you think she did it so no one recognized her? You're right, it was risky for her to come back here when the cabin is so close to the colony."

"I can't imagine how hard it was for her to give up the ocean most of the year. It would kill me to be away from the sea," Rory said. "Maybe she came back because she was homesick, or because she wanted you to know at least a little bit about where you came from. We'll never know now. But obviously one day your family recognized her, and when they had the chance to test you, they took it. Once you changed they had all the confirmation they needed."

Evan broke in, "I bet it was Jack, your grandfather. If your grandmother or Michael had known, they would likely not have said anything, and Michael's pelt is jet black, not gray. If the seals you saw were grays, then you must have seen your grandfather and your uncle Martin that day."

"It makes sense. They're the only two who would have considered it acceptable to half-drown a child just because they suspected she might be a selkie," Rory agreed.

"Back up a bit. Who is Michael again?" Jess asked, confused.

"Michael is your grandmother's other mate. Your grandfather died a few years ago, but Alicia and Michael are still here. I know this is a lot to take in at once." Rory sighed. "And they are going to be heartbroken to know that your mother's gone. Alicia never stopped hoping she'd come home one day. We'll take you to see them as soon as my parents have let them know what's going on."

Jess closed her eyes as emotions welled up and threatened to swamp her sense of calm. "Let's not talk about my family right now, please? I'm not sure I'm ready to deal with all of that. It's either very late, or very early, and I think I need a few more hours of sleep first."

"Sorry, sweetheart." Evan settled back onto the bed and opened his arms to her. "If you want to share the love,

I could use a hug. Then we can all go back to sleep for a few hours and we can explain more about all this after we've had coffee."

"Sleep and then coffee sounds like a brilliant plan," Jess muttered under her breath. She gave Rory a soft kiss before untangling herself from his arms and nestling in beside Evan. "Will you two teach me to change? Later today, I mean. I think I'll understand it better if I have done it. At least now I remember how to do it, sort of."

"If that's what you want, then that's what we'll do," Rory stated and stretched out beside her. "We haven't got a charter booked until this weekend, so we have a few days to spend together. Why don't the three of us take the *Storm Lord* out and we'll give you the Introduction to Selkie Life crash course."

"Sounds good." Jess relaxed as the warmth and comfort of being cocooned between her two men settled her nerves. "Love you guys."

"Love you, too, sweetheart."

"Always." Rory added his sentiments to Evan's and Jess let herself drift back off to sleep.

CHAPTER TWENTY-ONE

"So this is what you guys do all day?" Jess asked, her voice raised so she could be heard over the boat's engine. "Drive around and point out amazing scenery and animals to city folk who have never seen the ocean before?"

"You make it sound so glamorous!" Evan laughed and spread his arms wide. "People pay us to know where to find the animals, get them there and back safely, feed them, and keep them entertained. Which is why I do most of the talking, of course. Rory would bore them all to tears."

"And Evan couldn't navigate his way out of a paper bag without a GPS to help him. The man can get lost in a mall, there's no way I'm letting him plot a course for a tour. We'd end up in Japan!"

"I only got lost in the mall once. Once! He's never let me forget it." Evan shrugged. "Truth was I wasn't lost, I was following these two women..." he trailed off as Jess arched a brow at him.

"Oh, do tell."

"Would you believe it was two really ugly women who I thought needed keeping an eye on in case they were actually men in drag and they were casing the place for a robbery?"

"You are so busted." Jess shook her head. "Did you spend all your spare time chasing women before I came along?"

"What spare time?" they both asked at the same moment and all three of them laughed.

"You're seeing us in the off-season, baby." Rory turned around so she could see his face. "Right now we're only handling a few charters a month because not many want to come out when it's this cold and stormy. Once spring arrives we'll be going non-stop. You haven't met the twins yet. They're down south surfing in Bali right now, but they'll be back by March. They run the coastal zodiac tours for us while Ev and I take out the whale watching tours. We'll be going out every day for most of the summer, and then the gray whale migration starts and that takes us up to October."

"So what you're saying is that I shouldn't be worried about getting enough quiet time to write my next book?"

"You'll have plenty of time for writing, and we'll be home every night to make sure you don't get lonely." Evan winked at her and then waggled his brows. "You're never going to go to bed alone again, sweetheart."

Rory groaned and both Jess and Evan looked over at him.

"What?" Evan asked.

"You and I are going to go out of our minds if we're both on the *Storm Lord* and she's back home, *alone*."

"Oh shit."

"What are you two talking about?" Jess demanded. "What's wrong with me being alone? I've managed pretty well at it up until now."

"Are you forgetting how we met? You know, when you went out on the rocks alone and ended up doing an impression of *The Little Mermaid*?" Evan held up a hand to fend off her rebuttal. "That's not really the problem, though. The problem will be us. Once bonded, selkie men get all twitchy if they leave their mate alone for very long. It's programmed into us to be very protective of you, since selkie females were often hunted by men looking for sexy, obedient wives. It almost never happens anymore, but the instincts are still there. If we both go out on an eight-hour tour and leave you home alone, neither of us will be in our right mind by the time we get back."

"Well, fuck. How do the others deal with this?" Rory looked at Evan and then his face softened into a smile as he glanced over at Jess. "And don't you even start thinking this is because we don't want to be with you."

Jess smiled back and was grateful Rory understood her well enough to know that was exactly the sort of comment her Negative Nelly voice would come up with. Not that she'd heard much from the self-doubting side of her personality lately. She'd been too happy to listen to those voices, and so they had faded away.

"Maybe it's time to buy that second boat like we've been talking about," Evan mused. "The twins are ready to step up. They've been dying for a chance to do more with the company. We could have them do the full-day tours on the bigger boat, and you and I can manage the half-day tours."

"And who's going to manage the zodiacs?" Rory asked, but he wasn't frowning and Jess took that as a good sign.

"We'll ask around. I bet some of the younger ones would be thrilled to do it. It's good pay, decent hours, and it beats working for your dad at the marina." Evan shuddered. "You think Darius is cranky at home? Try working for him. Rory and I couldn't wait to scrape together enough cash to start our own business and escape him."

"Do you guys have the money for a bigger boat?" Jess asked as she did a bit of quick mental arithmetic.

"Not yet, but we can get a loan. We've got about half of what we need, but another boat would really help get us more business so we could pay it off pretty quickly."

"How much do you need?"

Both men looked at her and Evan said, "About sixty thousand dollars, give or take a few grand."

"You don't need to take out a loan," Jess told them. "We're going to be together forever once this bonding is done, right? And I'm moving in with you guys, so I want to do this. Let me pay for the other half of the boat."

"How the hell do you have sixty thousand dollars lying around?" Rory demanded.

"Some of it's from the sale of Mom's house after she died, but…" Jess ducked her head as her cheeks heated. "I got a really nice advance on this book I'm working on, and I have royalties coming in on the others."

"Holy crap, we bagged a rich woman!" Evan stood up and high-fived Rory, who was looking at Jess with a dazed expression.

"So I'm not the only one who really likes your books, huh?"

"You're still my favorite fan, though, big guy."

"Damn skippy I am. Anyone else tries for that position and I'll tear their head off."

"You're really that loaded?" Evan asked as he came over to hug her.

Jess nodded and Evan grinned. "Well then, I guess you're going to be a partner in Pacifica Tours. Welcome aboard!"

"We'll need to have a lawyer draw up the paperwork and make sure everything is legal, but if this is what you want to do, then who am I to say no. You really are the perfect woman for us." Rory dropped the engine into neutral and came over to hug her, clapping Evan on the back at the same time.

"And speaking of perfect, this is the perfect spot for us to take a swim. Time to get naked, Jess."

"Wait, what?" Jess's head snapped up and she looked around them. "We're in the middle of nowhere!"

"Exactly the point, there's no one out here to see us change. We're out of the way of the usual fishing holes and the orcas were reported forty klicks north of here, so we know they're not going to be a problem." Rory waved his arms to indicate the wide-open stretch of gray sky and ocean that surrounded them. "It's perfect."

"Orcas? You mean killer whales? Why would they be a problem?" Jess suddenly felt a lot less eager to learn to transform. Why the hell hadn't anyone mentioned killer whales before now?

"Why? Because orcas *eat* seals. Welcome to the food chain, baby."

"Will you stop panicking her, Rory? Holy shit you're an ass sometimes." Evan took Jess by the shoulders and turned her around so she was looking up into his sky-blue eyes. "Don't worry. Orcas are not going to swim up and eat us. Rory's messing with you. We make a living knowing where the whales are so we can bring the tourists to them, so I promise you that they're nowhere around here. And even if they were, the odds are good they wouldn't bother us. If you ever see them while you're in seal form, you swim back to the boat and hop out of the water."

"Okay." Jess nodded and then turned around enough to be able to glare at Rory. "But to be sure, your ass is going into that water first, buster."

Evan howled with laughter and Rory nodded, grinning. "Okay, okay, I earned that. I'll go in first. If nothing eats me, then you'll know it's safe."

Jess crossed her arms over her chest and glowered. "I don't see you getting naked, either."

"She's really cute when she's mad...at you." Evan snickered. "Do you need some music to accompany this striptease?"

"Shut. The fuck. Up." Rory ground out each word and unzipped his jacket. "If I'm going in, you need to put up the dive flag and help Jess make the change."

"I know the routine. You go ahead and get naked."

"Bastard," Rory snarled and started to strip off his clothes, hissing in discomfort as the winter wind hit bare skin. "Glory fucking hell, it's cold. Why are we doing this again?"

"Because Jess needs to learn how to do this without half the colony watching."

"Right. I knew there was a reason I'm freezing my assets off."

"And they're really fine assets," Jess observed as Rory skinned off his jeans, revealing every inch of his sculpted body to her gaze, along with the fact he wasn't wearing underwear again. Jess felt a flood of heat spread out from her womb as she drank in the vision in front of her.

"Once you change, you should be able to hear me in your mind. It's not as strong as the bond between Evan and me, but we all have the ability when we're in the seal form. It's the only way we can communicate."

Rory walked over to her and planted a slow kiss on her mouth. "Don't be afraid of what you're going to see or what will happen when you change. It's as natural to us as breathing. Now your pelt is free of that binding box, you'll be able to do it no problem at all."

He kissed her again and let her see the love in his eyes before he turned and walked to the side of the boat and simply dove over the side. Jess gasped and ran to look down into the water, half expecting to see a cold, wet Rory staring up at her. Instead a seal was swimming calmly below her, his dark eyes so familiar Jess knew without a doubt this was Rory. His dark brown fur was mottled with black, and as she stared at him the seal winked and then lifted a flipper out of the water to splash her.

"Hey!" she yelped and wiped the saltwater out of her eyes. "Not funny!"

"Oh, he thinks he's hilarious," Evan informed her. "Better hurry up and get in there before he decides to use his hind flippers instead. They're much bigger."

"So, what do I do?" Jess flailed her arms at her sides,

mimicking Rory's flippers. "Imagine I'm a fuzzy marine mammal and dive overboard?"

"Pretty much, yes," Evan reached into a cubbyhole and pulled out a bright-red flag with a diagonal slash of white across the middle. "I need to go put this up, so you stay here and get naked." He stepped past her and out onto the deck so he could clip the flag to one of the various antennae and poles that seemed to stick out of the deck in numerous places.

"What is that thing, anyway?"

"It's a flag that tells any other boaters who come within sight of us that we have a diver in the water and to keep clear and be careful."

Jess started stripping off her clothes and she was shivering from cold before she even got her jeans off.

"But we don't have a diver on…oh!" She ended lamely as she realized the reason for the flag. "That's smart."

"Thanks, sweetheart, we do have our moments."

Evan grinned as he came back into the semi-sheltered portion of the boat. "Naked is a good look for you, by the way, but blue with cold isn't really your best color."

"Thanks for the fashion tip. So how do I get myself wrapped in fur?"

Evan handed her the silver-and-black pelt they had found at the bottom of the box. "Hold onto that and imagine yourself wrapped in that fur. It's enveloping you, protecting you and keeping you warm and safe. You don't need it to shift, but it usually helps with the visualization to hold it the first time you try and transform."

Jess closed her eyes and wrapped her fingers into the soft fur. She tried to relax and let Evan's voice guide her imagination, but the rocking of the boat kept her off-balance and the wind was so cold against her bare skin it was almost painful.

Suddenly Evan was there, holding her and cutting the worst of the wind as he stood at her back and curved his big body around hers. "Just relax. You're trying to force it."

"I am not."

"Really? Then why are you gripping that fur so tight your knuckles are white?" Evan rested a hand over hers and squeezed her fingers. "All right, we're going to try something else." He teased the pelt out of her grip gently and set it down on a nearby chair, safely out of the wind.

"Trust me," he whispered and began nuzzling his mouth over her ear and down the side her neck, dusting tender, butterfly kisses to her skin all the way down to her shoulder. "Think about being warm, and buoyant, and gliding through the water." Evan words slid into her mind and she tried to relax and focus on his voice and nothing else. "You've already done this once, your mind and body know what to do. You just need to let it happen."

"I'm trying," Jess grumbled. "It's not working."

"I noticed." Evan pressed one last kiss to her shoulder and then scooped her up into his arms. "Remember, you already know how to do this!" was all he said as he walked her over toward the side of the boat. Jess realized what he was planning and started to kick and flail, but he had her in an iron grip.

"Don't you fucking da—" He heaved her over the side and Jess hit the water before she could even get out the last word and the ice-cold Pacific closed over her head. The cold was so intense it was painful, but her fury ran hotter than even the frigid ocean could cool and by the time her head broke the surface Jess wasn't feeling the cold anymore. She sucked in a lungful of air and turned her head to curse at Evan, but all that came out of her mouth was a harsh bark. *What the hell?*

"Well, that wasn't quite the way I thought he'd do it, but it worked." Rory's voice sounded inside Jess's mind and she shook her head at the strange feeling.

"Rory?" she sent out the tentative mental query.

"Right here, J.J." Rory's sleek, fur-covered face popped up in her vision. *"You are gorgeous in this form. I've never seen a prettier seal."*

"I'm a seal?" Jess glanced down at herself and got a face full of water for her trouble.

Rory's laughter filled her skull. *"Yes, now stop flailing around and try swimming. You have about thirty seconds before Ev joins us, and if you want to get back at him for tossing you into the drink I suggest you figure out how to do more than bob up and down."*

"How?"

"Stop thinking and act. You already know how to swim, you just need to let the magic do its thing. This is all part of who you are, you only need to accept it."

"Easy for you to say...or uh...think. You've been doing this since you were a kid!"

Rory barked, and to Jess's ears it sounded a lot like laughter. *"Get moving!"* he told her telepathically and dove under the waves. A second later she felt him nudge her sharply in the side. Without thinking, Jess reacted, flicking her hind flippers and arcing up out of the water and racing off. Holy crap, I'm fast! she thought as she drove herself through the waves. Jess felt like she was flying, and her senses flooded her with a myriad of details. Her nose identified odors with ease, telling her there was a kelp bed nearby and that hidden deep in its golden-green depths rock cod swam, ready to be caught and eaten. Her stomach rumbled and she realized the thought of eating raw fish didn't bother her. Ew.

Again she heard Rory's laughter in the back of her mind. *"You eat sushi, don't you?"* he commented and Jess couldn't come up with a reasonable argument.

Her ears detected a splash and then she scented something new in the water, a hint of spice that she immediately knew belonged to Evan.

"Hi, sweetheart." His voice touched her mind. *"Forgive me?"*

"Not yet!" She sent the thought flying back at him and doubled back on herself with a mental yell of exaltation as she launched herself at Evan. His coat was a mottled golden gray that stood out in the water, making him much easier to see than Rory's dark coloring.

"Shit!" Evan's curse came through clearly and then he darted away from her, managing to stay just out of her reach no matter how hard she swam. Rory joined in and soon they were playing an aquatic game of tag, both men encouraging her and showing her how to use her new body to its fullest ability.

Finally she had had enough and sent a message to both of them announcing she was tired. Within seconds they were swimming up on each side of her, escorting her back to the boat they had left adrift during their short but intense period of play.

"Just push yourself up out of the water and onto the swim platform, and once you're out of the water, imagine yourself human again and that's it. Easy." Evan sent the thought, accompanied by a faint hint of laughter and then flicked

his body and launched himself up onto the platform at the stern of the boat.

Easy my ass, she thought as she recalled the way he'd tossed her overboard. She spotted one of Evan's flippers and lunged forward, nipping him sharply. She could hear his yelp of protest and it filled her with a sense of satisfaction as she followed his example and propelled herself up onto the platform. This time she was prepared for the transformation, but even though she was paying attention, it still came so quickly that she barely had time to register a slight tingle and then all she felt was the shock of being soaking wet and naked in the middle of December.

"Cold!" she exclaimed and scrambled to her feet before another wave could hit her in the ass with icy spray.

"You bit me."

The hairs on the back of Jess's neck rose at the odd tone in Evan's voice, but she was too busy climbing back on board to really pay attention to what her instincts were telling her. She barely got her feet back on the deck before Evan was standing in front of her. His blue eyes had turned stormy and a trickle of blood flowed between the fingers he had clamped around the hand she'd nipped.

"You deserved that after what you—"

Evan growled again and Jess's mouth went dry, while the saucy retort she had been planning withered from her brain.

"Mine." His voice was as rough as a gravel road and his blood-streaked hand shot out to snag her wrist, hauling her up against his naked body and curving an arm around her so that she was pinned in place. Evan dropped his head to her neck and inhaled, and she could feel his chest rise as he drew her scent deep into his lungs. His cock surged and thickened against the rounded softness of her stomach and Jess felt her body react. She forgot about the cold, about the wind, she forgot about everything but the low, rumbling sounds rising from Evan's chest.

When he brushed his lips over the top of Jess's shoulder she moaned and tipped her head to one side, offering him her throat. Instead his arms locked around her and he growled her name once and then bit down where her shoulder joined her neck. Jess cried out in shock and tried to twist free, but Evan gave her no room to move and she didn't have the strength to pull away.

"Mine, always," Evan said as he finally lifted his head and released her, only to place his injured hand over the bite he'd put on her shoulder. A strange heat pulsed from his touch and Jess jerked again, but this time in surprise. The pain was gone, and instead she was infused with a sense of warmth and security.

"Ours." Rory stepped behind her and Jess could feel his rigid cock press up against the small of her back.

Jess turned her head to ask Rory what was going on when she caught a flash of metal and then watched as Rory ran a knife across his hand, reopening a scar that was nearly identical to the one Torin had shown her when he'd explained about blood bonding.

They're claiming me. Here and now. This is the bonding ritual.

Evan lifted his hand away from her shoulder and Rory took his place, covering the bite with his still-bleeding palm. Again a pulse of heat entered her shoulder and again the sense of safety and comfort filled her. Her legs gave way and she sagged against Evan as the euphoria grew and swept her along with her.

She heard whispers and fragments of conversations, but it all seemed to be happening to someone else.

"Jess?" She heard Rory's voice calling but her mouth wouldn't work and her body felt so heavy she just wanted to lie down. "Jess, answer me."

"Too loud," she told him, and it took her a second to realize she hadn't said anything. At least not out loud.

"Well, that didn't take long." Evan was talking now, and Jess realized she wasn't hearing them with her ears. They were speaking to her inside her head, just like when they'd all been in their seal form.

"Evan? Rory?" She pushed the thought out carefully past the fog that still shrouded her thinking processes.

"Hey, sweetheart."

"Baby, how are you feeling?"

She could feel their presence inside her mind, both of them radiating love and affection. Jess realized that while she'd been in her fugue her men had carried her down to the forward cabin and she was snuggled between the two of them on the same bed where she'd woken up after being rescued the first time. The three of them had come full circle.

"I feel pretty funky," she spoke aloud this time and was pleased to find that her mouth worked again.

"It'll wear off soon," Evan promised.

Jess opened her eyes and turned toward Evan's voice. "You bit me!"

"You bit me first."

"You threw me overboard!"

Evan chuckled. "Okay, you got me there. In my

defense, though, you did turn into a seal the minute you hit the water."

"You didn't know that was going to happen. I could have drowned."

Evan sat up enough that she could see his face, his expression completely serious. "No, you couldn't have. I would never put you in danger. Never, Jess. You're far too precious to both of us."

"You still bit me." Jess reached up to rub the spot on her shoulder, and as her fingers brushed over the tender skin she frowned. It was tender, but it didn't *hurt*. She pressed harder and got nothing but a slight twinge. She tried to turn her head to look at her shoulder, but it was impossible. "What the hell happened? I know you bit me harder than that!"

Evan grinned at her, looking irritatingly smug. "Sit up, please. I want to take a look."

Jess sat up and Rory brushed her wet hair off of her shoulder, exposing the place where they'd both touched her, blending their blood with hers.

"She's healed up perfectly." Rory ran a confirming hand over the spot.

"And the first time any of the women see that, I'm going to get my head handed to me." Evan glanced down and sighed. "If my mother doesn't kill me, yours will."

"What are you guys talking about?" Jess demanded, still trying to crane her head to see whatever they were looking at.

"Evan bit you, but it's healed already. But, like our hands, it's left a bit of scar."

"I have a scar? Evan Sinclair I am going to bite you

again next time we change! What the hell were you thinking?"

"I wasn't thinking. You bit me and I…it…damn it Rory did you have to tell her about the scar?" Evan scrubbed a hand through his blond hair and gave Jess an apologetic half-smile. "Biting is serious foreplay, sweetheart, especially considering we weren't bonded yet. Once you drew blood, I may have lost my mind a little bit." Evan held his thumb and forefinger about an inch apart.

"You lost your mind a *lot* bit." Jess held her hands up three feet apart to make her point. "How bad is the scar?"

"It's barely visible. Just a little half-moon circle of paler skin, that's all." Rory pressed an open-mouthed kiss to her shoulder and Jess shivered as a shimmer of heat passed between them.

"I thought we had going to cut our hands to do the bonding thing?" Jess took one of Evan's hands in hers and leaned back into Rory's embrace.

"Well, that's the nice and tidy modern-day approach. What we did was the barbaric, old-fashioned way. That's why Evan's going to be in trouble with our mothers when they see that scar. Not only did we bond before they could plan the party, but Evan finally showed his true colors." Rory laughed. "My mom thinks *he's* the sweet one, and sweet boys don't bite their mates."

"Well, we could do the bonding, anyway. I mean, it won't hurt to do it again, right?"

Evan and Rory exchanged thoughtful glances. "You're suggesting we don't tell anyone? Let Evan off the hook?"

"No, I'm suggesting we don't tell *everyone*. There's a difference. Anyone close to me is going to spot that scar at some point, so there's no point in lying about what it is.

That doesn't mean we can't have the ceremony. It's as close to a wedding as we're going to get, right? So why not do it anyway?"

"You'll be our wife in every way, Jess. It just won't be government sanctioned."

"I don't need a federally certified document to know where I belong," Jess announced.

"I just need the two of you. And now I have that, forever."

"You're ours." Evan's voice sounded in Jess's mind again, along with a sense of love and wonder.

"All ours." Rory's mind joined with hers and Evans and for a moment Jess felt a sense of completeness and harmony that filled her entire being with light.

Evan leaned in and kissed her, his lips possessive as they slanted over hers. She nipped at his lower lip and he let her feel his need for her, the heat and yearning blazing with golden fire as he let it flow into her mind. He lifted his mouth from hers reluctantly and Jess felt his mental withdrawal, leaving an empty place inside her that she knew only Evan would be able to fill from now on.

"I need to get us to anchor somewhere, and then we can be together." He winked as he rose from the bed, his engorged cock evidence that he'd rather not be leaving her to Rory.

"I drove last time we had you out here, so this time it's his turn." Rory pulled her down beside him as he dropped to the mattress and planted a torrid kiss to her lips as he waved Evan off. "I got this, you make sure we don't run aground or drift into a shipping lane."

"Just don't wear her out, bro," Evan shot back as he

disappeared through the door and headed to the deck where they had all left their clothes.

"Yeah, don't wear me out, big guy. I still have lots of family to meet, packing to do, and somewhere in there we need to do this bonding ceremony over in front of witnesses or your mom will kill you and Evan both.

CHAPTER TWENTY-TWO

RORY GATHERED Jess up and rolled them both over so she was lying on top of him. Once she was settled, he dragged a handful of blankets over them both so the weight of them pressed her even more firmly against him. Her hair fell over her shoulder and lay like cool, wet silk across his chest. She smelled of the sea and her own rich scent, and Rory's dick was a shaft of pure iron where it lay pinned between their bodies.

Jess poured her feelings for him directly into his mind, filling his thoughts with a heady mix of love and lust. As Jess pushed further into his mind, Rory instinctively started to shield himself, but Jess was not backing down. Her soft hands framed his face and he found himself staring up into her pale blue eyes.

"I love you, Rory. Let me see you. All of you." Her thoughts were a silken whisper and there was nothing but love in her expression as Rory finally dropped his walls and let her in. He waited, expecting her to turn from him,

but instead she smiled and tears fell from her eyes to splash hotly against his neck and chin.

"How could you think I'd be afraid of this?" She said the words out loud, but in his head she was holding up images, fragments of his memories for him to see. He and Darius fighting, the two of them screaming and pushing at each other as their tempers got the better of them yet again. Another memory, this one of his younger self watching his grandfather berate his father, the old man's anger and disappointment clear as he called into question everything that Darius believed. Self-loathing filled Rory and he tried to push her out of his mind, away from the dark side of his nature but she held him off.

"I'm not a good man," he told her, ashamed.

Her mental voice grew louder and more insistent. "You are a good man, Rory. You just don't see it. I understand what Evan was talking about now. You think you're like your grandfather, but you're not." Jess held up more memories, ones Rory had forgotten. Memories of him and Evan rescuing a seal pup that had been orphaned when his mother had been shot by a fisherman and carrying it carefully back home wrapped in Rory's jacket. They'd visited it at the local wildlife rescue center every week until it had been returned to the wild. There were recollections of fishing with his father, the two of them enjoying peaceful companionship with never a harsh word spoken.

Just as he thought she was done, Jess shared one of her memories, and Rory nearly came off the bed as she let him experience the spanking he'd given to her that night in their hotel room. Her excitement, her lack of fear, and the pleasure he had given her struck him hard, destroying the last of the walls he'd built up.

She isn't afraid of me. She loves me.

Rory speared his hands into her hair and dragged her head down to his, kissing her wildly. The link between them stayed wide open and for the first time he shared everything he was, letting their minds and thoughts blend until he no longer knew whose thoughts were whose. He loosened one hand from her hair and slid it between them, homing in on the seam of her pussy that he could feel resting along the hard swell of his dick. He slipped a finger inside and found her already wet, and when he teased the delicate pearl of her clitoris with his fingertip a fresh flood of juice flowed over his hand and made her even slicker. Jess made a soft, impatient sound and wriggled herself over his cock and then arched her hips, taking him inside her with a slow, steady roll of her hips.

Her cunt was hot, slick, and so tight around his dick that he could feel every twitch of her inner muscles as they rippled up and down the length of his shaft. Her mouth was still on his and he plunged his tongue past her lips, needing to possess her body completely. Her mouth, her pussy, every part of her was his, now and always. Her thoughts were as wild as his and he caught echoes of needs that were not his own, along with flashes of pain and sadness that he knew came from Jess. As he loved her with his body he pushed into her mind just as she had pushed into his, finding the shadows where her self-doubts and loneliness were hidden.

He let her see herself the way he did, every lush curve and sensuous inch of her, ripe and soft and able to bring him to arousal with only a smile. When she cried and tried to retreat from the double assault of his mind and body he flipped them over so that she was beneath him, their tongues entwined and his dick slamming into her pussy again and again. With each thrust he shared his love for her, driving back the sadness and tearing away her insecurities. Salt flavored their kisses and he realized she was crying, but he couldn't feel fear or pain from her so he pushed again, until finally the two of them were of one mind as well as one body, racing together toward the shared oblivion of orgasm.

Rory reached down and coaxed her legs higher until her legs were wrapped around his waist and her body was open to him. Her juices coated his cock and her thighs, easing his passage as he plunged deep into her body, needing to possess her completely. He ended their kiss and lifted his head as he braced himself on his arms and pushed his upper body up above hers, increasing the angle so that he could hit her sweet spot, pushing her closer to release.

Beneath him Jess cried out and writhed in time to his thrusts, taking him into her body with a hunger that was as fierce as his own. Her fingers curled into claws and she raked her nails down his chest, the fiery sting adding another level of pleasure to their lovemaking. He felt her channel pulse and tighten around his cock as the first flutter of her orgasm bloomed and sent a rosy flush up her body and stained her breasts, then her throat, and finally her cheeks pink.

With her love and her need still echoing inside his mind, Rory let himself go, pounding into her with everything he had, all of his desire focused down to the point where their bodies met. "Come for me, Jess. Let it all go and come for me," he encouraged her and he knew the moment she was swept away. Her pussy locked around him so tight he bordered on pain and she arched up off the bed as she screamed his name. Her nails slashed down his chest again and the overwhelming force of her orgasm traveling from her mind to his shattered the last threads of his control and sent him spiraling into his own release.

Again and again he shot his seed deep into her womb, until his balls emptied themselves inside her and he lowered his head to brush a kiss to her lips, both of them panting and dazed as they stared into each other's eyes.

"I love you," she whispered and gave him a half smile that melted his heart. "All of you, even the parts you don't think are worth loving."

"And I love you, every part of you. You are beautiful and sexy and I am going to spend the rest of my life proving it to you." Rory was moving off of her and to one side when both of them heard footsteps coming down the stairs. Seconds later Evan appeared at the door, his expression one of frustrated lust. He tore his shirt over his head and hit the bed with a groan.

"Do you to have any idea how hard it was to concentrate when you were both broadcasting so *loud*? Holy fuck, porn has nothing on the two of you!"

He lay down on his side right beside Rory and leaned in to kiss Jess on the cheek.

"Please tell me it's my turn now? I was a good boy and got us anchored and secured, despite the fact that I had the two of you in my head doing the wild thing the whole time."

Jess was still reeling from the intense and emotional moment she had shared with Rory when Evan came back to bed. As he sprawled beside them she was amazed to realize that no matter how incredible what she and Rory had, she had missed Evan even for that short period of time.

"That's the bonding kicking in, sweetheart," Evan whispered inside her mind, his mental touch colored by lust and laughter. *"It's only going to get stronger as time goes by, so you better get used to it."*

Aloud she said, "Stop eavesdropping on my thoughts! I'm sorry about before. I didn't realize you could, um, hear us."

Evan grinned. "Well, you haven't learned how to shield your thoughts yet, but Rory knew exactly what he was doing." He reached out and poked Rory's naked chest right over one of the sets of scratches Jess had given him. "Bastard."

"I didn't want you to feel left out." Rory grinned back at him and Jess's mouth fell open.

"You looped him in on purpose? Rory Frazier that was *mean*!"

"Yeah, you tell him, sweetheart!" Evan gathered her into his arms and stuck out his tongue at Rory before dropping a kiss on her already kiss-swollen lips. "I can think of a few ways you can make it up to me."

Jess reached between them and wrapped her fingers around Evan's cock, gliding up and down its length. The silk-covered steel of his shaft jerked in her fingers and she couldn't help but laugh as a low, rumbling groan rose up from Evan's throat.

"That's a very good start." He was almost purring as

she pumped his cock again. "But I actually had something else in mind."

"What were you thinking?" she asked.

"This." Evan managed to scoop her into his arms and haul her off the bed as he stood up, carrying her back up into the main cabin and then out to the partially covered area beyond it.

"Evan! We're naked! Take me back inside before I freeze to death. I've already done my polar bear swim for the day!"

"Relax, we're not going swimming," Evan reassured her as he settled them both onto the bench that ran along one side of the covered part of the deck. Jess found herself straddling Evan's naked thighs, and then he reached down and produced a faded, patchwork quilt which he carefully wrapped around her, swaddling her body in its soft warmth. With the quilt shielding her from the elements and prying eyes, Jess relaxed and looked around. They were close enough to a beach she could make out individual trees, but far enough away no one would be able to see anything. "The island isn't inhabited. It's just a good spot for us to anchor. We're out of the wind and there's no one around to hear you scream."

"I'm going to be screaming?"

"I have every intention of making that happen." Evan gave her a lopsided grin. "I like making love outside, and I figure this is the best of both worlds. Fresh air and comfy seating."

"You're going to do her outside? I love you like a brother, but you have some very weird ideas about sex. First you go and bite our girl, and now you want to fuck her outside? Someone's been spending too much time watching Animal Planet." Rory appeared on deck, now dressed in a heavy sweater and a pair of jeans, though Jess noticed he hadn't bothered to do up the fly.

"Shut up, bro. You had your time with Jess, now it's my turn."

"Don't mind me, I'll be over here, waiting for J.J to come to her senses and tell you to get her cute ass back inside where it's warm."

"I'm warm enough." Jess grinned. "And I've never made love outside before. You never know, I may come to like it."

"Great, then we can all get frostbite together."

"Don't listen to him. He's been bitter about the great outdoors since an unfortunate incident back in high school involving a cute girl and an undetected patch of stinging nettles."

Jess burst into a fit of giggles as Rory cursed a blue streak and flipped Evan off with both hands.

"Now, if we are through being distracted, I believe I promised to make you scream."

"Yes, you did." Jess snuggled closer to him so that her breasts brushed over his bare chest. "Though I'm not sure how you're going to manage to do that when you keep talking to Rory."

"Brat!" He stopped her next words with a kiss that nearly melted her brain and emptied her head of every thought but him. Evan's mouth plundered hers, taking everything and giving no quarter. His tongue swept past her lips to tangle with hers, and his hands came around her hips to lift her a few inches off of his lap.

"Put your legs around my waist." His voice was in her head, giving her directions, and she followed them. As

soon as she got her feet behind him, Evan leaned back, pinning her legs so tightly she could barely move.

"*Gotcha.*" Jess heard Evan's single thought and then an outpouring of need and love hit her and she was lost to everything else. Along with the emotion, Evan sent her images of the two of them making love, some of them memories and some of them his fantasies. He whispered promises that they would try each and every one of them in their years together and Jess felt her pussy flood and her inner walls flutter as his words, thoughts, and vivid pictures sent her lust skyrocketing.

When Evan finally lowered her back down into his lap, his cock speared through her folds and the thick head pressed up into her pussy, sliding into her easily as Jess leaned her head back and moaned.

Evan's arms held her suspended there and she tried to wiggle herself further down but he stopped her. After chuckling aloud he told her, "Sweetheart, this time we are going to fuck on my schedule, not yours. I want this slow, so slow you are shaking and begging for it by the time I let you come."

Jess's moaned again, this time in protest and she lifted her head to give Evan a look of pure frustration. "You're doing it again."

"Doing what?" Evan was laughing as he lowered her another slow, sweet inch onto his cock before stopping again. His eyes were blazing with desire and it gave Jess a sense of satisfaction to know that this was nearly killing him as well.

"You're getting all bossy, like him." She inclined her head toward Rory and then whimpered as she saw that

Rory was fisting his dick, playing with himself as he watched the two of them.

"No one's as bossy as me, baby." He winked at her. "You better get on with it, Ev, or I'm going to come over there and join you two."

"Not until she's screamed for me, you're not." Evan let her slide another few inches down his cock and she clamped her body tight around him as he finally went deep enough to feel good instead of merely teasing her.

Evan let his head fall back with a groan and relented, lowering her rest of the way so that he was buried balls deep inside her, his thick cock filling her so completely that even the smallest movement sent ripples of pleasure flowing outward from her womb. His hands moved from her hips to her ass, kneading the soft flesh there and rocking her body into his.

"You are so wet and tight. God, I love fucking you. Being inside you is like being home." He lifted his head to kiss her then, his tongue flicking over her lips until she parted them. He kept kneading her ass, moving her into him and then away again in a slow, hypnotic dance that made her heart pound and her cunt pulse around his cock in eager patterns.

"Slowly," he whispered into her mind and lifted her up a bare few inches before thrusting upward, filling her up and then retreating. Again and again he did that, fucking her while he held her high enough that she could not gain any leverage and was completely at his mercy. When she realized he was not going to let her have her way she finally relaxed and let him take complete control, and soon she was shuddering with the force of the orgasm that was building up inside her.

Evan and Rory were both in her mind, stoking her passion with words of love and sexually charged visions that had her nearly wild with need, but still Evan controlled the pace, keeping her on a slow, steady upward spiral toward some impossibly high peak. His cock filled and stretched her, rubbing against her G-spot with every gentle lift and glide of his hips and her entire body was slowly kindling into a single blazing flame of pure need.

Just as Jess felt as though she couldn't take another second of waiting, the quilt was torn from her shoulders and Rory's strong arms were encircling her ribs and drawing her back against his chest. His hands cupped her breasts and she heard him utter a single word.

"Now."

Jess felt herself being lifted higher and then Evan was slamming into her hard, his cock tunneling deep into her pussy and back out again at a wild pace that sent her flying headlong into the most powerful orgasm of her life. She screamed as her world scattered into white-hot fragments of sound and light and pleasure. Her entire body arched and shook as she came and came again. Somewhere on the distant edge of her perception she heard Evan groan as her cunt gripped his cock tight and he let himself go, coming hard and filling her womb with his essence as he ground himself against her with a cry of raw satisfaction.

As her wits slowly returned to her Jess found herself being gently draped over Evan's chest and his arms came around her to hold her close.

Evan's breath fanned her ear as he whispered, "I told you I was going to make you scream."

"I think you broke me," Jess whispered back, barely able to form the words.

"I hope not, because we're planning on staying out here a few more hours. We're not done making you scream yet."

"I'm not done with you two, either, but for the next round, I do have one request."

"Anything," Evan promised.

"Take me back inside. The great outdoors is beautiful, but it's also damned *cold*!"

From somewhere behind her Rory laughed. "I knew you'd come to your senses, baby. I promise the next time we do this outdoors, it'll be warmer."

EPILOGUE

THE DAYS HAD FLOWN by in a glorious flood of laughter, love, and some emotional highs and lows that had brought Jess to the verge of exhaustion more than once. Meeting her family for the first time had been an incredible experience, and Jess had found herself accepted with open arms by the grandparents she had never known.

"You look so much like my Mara." Alicia had been crying as she had folded Jess into her embrace and hugged her. "It's like she's come back to us, as young and beautiful as the day she left. Isn't she beautiful, Michael?"

"Just like her grandmother," Michael had agreed, his arms circling around them both in a bear hug.

Even her uncle Martin had been welcoming, if a little distant, and since that initial visit Jess had spent countless hours with her newly discovered kin, sharing everything she could about her mother's life. At the same time Alicia and Michael had made her a part of their family, teaching Jess about her heritage and what it meant to belong to the colony. She was home.

∾

Today was a special day, and Jess knew they needed to get back to shore soon. She hadn't expected it, but now the moment had come she was finding it hard to let go. Their bonding ceremony was set to happen that evening, but before she celebrated her new life with Rory and Evan and the family she had never known she had, there was one thing she needed to do first. She needed to say good-bye to her mom.

The three of them were out on the *Storm Lord*, and Evan had them idling so that they were hovering near the spot where they had pulled her out of the ocean the day they had met. Rory was beside her, his hand on her shoulder, offering her his silent support as she stood at the stern of the boat with the urn hugged tight to her chest.

The weather was almost balmy for the time of year, and the wind was only a chill breeze that ruffled Jess's hair. She looked over to the rocky headland that marked the line between her land and Kismet Cove, and her heart filled as she saw all the people standing there in silent vigil, waiting for her to scatter her mother's ashes. Vivian was easy to spot with her red hair and brilliant yellow scarf. Evan's parents had cut short their stay in Scotland and were standing beside Rory's family, including Rory's sister, Kaitlyn, who had ended her self-imposed exile to attend her brother's bonding ceremony. Evan's brother Cameron hadn't arrived yet, but he would be up in time for the festivities tonight.

Jess spotted two other faces and had to bite back a fresh wave of tears as she recognized her grandmother and Michael standing with the others. The only person missing from the day's events was her father. She had invited him, but when he'd learned that she was committing her life to not one man, but two, he had told her that he would not be attending. Jess hadn't been surprised, but she hoped that one day they would be able to work through their issues and have some sort of relationship again. They'd been close once, but his choices and now hers had put a lot of distance between them.

"If you're not ready, you don't have to do this today," Rory told her, squeezing her shoulder.

"No, I think I'm ready now. I just realized that this is why Mom sent me here. She knew what I needed more than I did. I needed a family." Jess pointed to the headland and then waved. "I needed you and Evan and all of them. You're what's been missing from my life, and Mom sent me to find it, for both of us."

Tears sprang to Jess's eyes and she had to swallow down the lump in her throat. "She wanted us both to come home."

"Ev, it's time." Rory called and Evan turned off the engine before coming out to join them, putting his hand on Jess's other shoulder. She leaned out over the stern, trusting in her men to keep her steady as she opened the lid off the top of the urn and turned it upside down, letting the pale-gray ash fall into the ocean.

"I miss you, but I made it, Mom. I got us both home," Jess whispered as her tears flowed down her cheeks and dripped off her chin to land in the ocean to mix with her mom's remains. As the urn emptied she leaned back and her mates closed in around her, holding her between them as they kissed away her tears. Jess let herself cry for a little while longer, but her grief faded quickly, to be replaced with a feeling of contentment and peace.

VIVIAN SETTLED the crown of flowers on Jess's hair and pinned it into place. "There, you're all set." She stepped back and gave Jess a head-to-toe check. "You are the most gorgeous non-bride at a non-wedding I have ever seen. Your men are going to fall all over themselves when they get a look at you."

Jess took a deep breath and tried to fight down the mutant-sized butterflies that were currently bouncing around her stomach. "I really shouldn't be nervous, after all this is only a formality, right?" Jess brushed a hand over her gown and was surprised to see her fingers were trembling.

"Jess, you're getting married, or as close to it as you're ever going to get. If you weren't nervous, I'd be worried about you. You're supposed to be nervous on your wedding day, or at least that's what I've always been told." Viv shrugged. "I am still jealous you managed to find not one man, but two, and they're both gorgeous. Not to mention they are both nauseatingly, completely, and utterly smitten with you."

She put her hands on Jess's shoulders and turned her around so that Jess could see her reflection in the mirror that had been brought in to her makeshift dressing room, and Jess gasped in surprise.

"Is that really me?"

"One hundred percent." Viv smirked. "I told you that dress was perfect."

Jess's wedding dress was a rich amethyst purple with shots of silver running through the fabric here and there. The sleeves and hem were trimmed in lace, and they'd picked white roses for her bouquet and to form the crown of flowers that she wore instead of a veil. Her pearl earrings were a gift from her grandmother, and the only other jewelry she wore was the necklace that marked her as Rory and Evan's mate to the other members of the colony. Vivian had spent an hour curling and styling Jess's hair so that it hung in ringlets all the way down her back. She'd also touched up the purple streaks, so they were an exact match to her dress.

"You are positively glowing. I think that being in love suits you." Viv brushed a quick kiss to Jess's cheek and then hugged her. "Let me grab your bouquet and we are good to go."

"You have the rings?" Jess asked for the fifth time. Or maybe it was the sixth. She was getting so nervous she couldn't remember anything.

"Yes, I have the rings. No, we haven't forgotten anything. If you ask me one more time, I swear I'm going to get you to knock back a shot of tequila before you go out there!"

"I can't, no booze until afterward or the cut will bleed too much, remember?"

Vivian wrinkled her nose. "Yeah, I remember. I still don't get the whole thing about cutting and bleeding on each other. It seems weird to me, but if that's the local tradition, who am I to question it. I'm not the one getting cut."

Jess didn't like lying to Vivian, but there were some things she knew her friend wouldn't be able to accept, and

307

even if she could, Jess was now bound by the laws of the colony, and that meant she had to keep the existence of selkies a secret, at least for now.

"It's just a scratch, and then the hand-fasting and it's all over."

"Not quite. After that, we party!" Viv crowed and spun Jess around, laughing. "And I am going to dance with every single hottie here. Did you see some of the eye candy? Holy crap, I may never go back to Toronto!"

"You're welcome to stay in the cabin as long as you like. I've missed you so much." Jess hugged Viv one last time and then someone was knocking on the door.

"It's time, Jess."

Vivian shot Jess a wink and then handed her the bouquet of roses. "It's show time. Let's go get you hitched to your stud muffins."

Viv went first, leading the way down the short hallway and into the small communal hall that made up part of the Kismet Cove colony. The utilitarian space had been filled with flowers and lit up with fairy lights, transforming it into something resembling a garden at twilight. As Jess stepped into the hall all eyes were on her, but she didn't see anyone save for her two men, waiting for her under an arch of evergreen boughs.

"Holy crap, they're wearing kilts!" Vivian whispered. "You could have warned me!"

"I didn't know!" Jess hissed back.

Both Rory and Evan were wearing formal tuxedo-style jackets that were fitted to go with their kilts. Their tartan patterns were predominantly green and blue, but Evan's had a border of white that Rory's lacked. As Jess got closer she saw the look of approval in their eyes and she smiled, pleased at their reactions. When she got to the arch, Viv took her bouquet from her and stood to one side, waiting for the moment she'd hand over the rings to Jess.

As Rory and Evan stepped forward and took her hands, Darius appeared, nearly overflowing with pride as he began the ceremony. Jess knew that words were being said, but none of it really sank in. Her mind was already linked to Rory's and Evan's and they were whispering wicked promises that had her distracted from the solemn vows they were each speaking in turn.

When it came time for Jess to speak, both men managed to stay quiet long enough for her to get out her vows without distracting her, for which she was extremely thankful. They exchanged rings, and Jess was stunned by the white gold band with a diamond that was set between two smaller sapphires that they slipped onto her finger. She had picked out simple bands gold for both her men, and as she placed the matching white gold bands on each of them she let her love for them flow from her mind to theirs.

Darius then produced a small but well-honed dagger, and both men offered up one hand, while Jess presented both, palm up so that Darius could make the cuts that would bond them for life. At least that is what would have happened if Evan and Rory hadn't claimed her that day several weeks ago. Darius was well aware of that fact, and as he carefully made the identical slices along Jess's lifelines he winked at her.

"I'll make these shallow, since they are only for show. Just remember to look woozy," he whispered so softly no one else could have heard him. But it was enough to make Jess blush and distract her from the temporary pain in both her hands. The moment it was done all three of them joined hands, and Darius bound each of their joined hands together with a piece of knotted silk cord. Three knots, three cords, and then they were bound together, physically as well as spiritually.

A cheer went up as Darius declared them bonded, and then Jess was in Rory's arms as he claimed the first kiss. She didn't have to pretend to feel overwhelmed. Her love and the love of her two men was enough to make her head spin as Rory kissed her. His lips were gentle and his kiss was as tender and sweet as she had ever known from him and as he lifted his head he grinned. "You're mine now, baby."

"Ours, bro. She's *ours* now." Evan laughed and tugged her out of Rory's arms and into his to give her a passionate kiss that curled her toes and made her pulse race.

"I think you both have it wrong," Jess declared when she finally got her breath back. "You two belong to me, now and forever."

Both of their voices sounded in her mind at the same time, making her heart swell. *"You have us both, always."*